The Not so Golden Oldies

LIZ DAVIES

PROLOGUE

'We can take it in turns to sleep at each other's houses,' Caroline said, glancing around at the other girls for approval. 'It'll be fun,' she insisted.

Meena wasn't so sure.

She'd never spent the night at anyone else's house before (apart from her Granny's), and she wasn't entirely certain what you were supposed to do. She checked that their teacher wasn't in earshot, and saw Miss Pendry was over the far end of the classroom. As usual she was dealing with Andrew Machen who had been pulling Melanie Williams's hair. Melanie liked the attention, especially when she squealed loudly and the whole class turned to see what all the fuss was about.

'You can come to mine first,' Caroline declared, 'because it was my idea.' She seemed extremely proud of the fact that she'd come up with the suggestion.

The other two girls in their friendship group nodded enthusiastically; Meena just gave a small, uncertain smile.

She didn't want to agree to something she wasn't sure of, but neither did she want to appear reluctant.

'We can have midnight feasts and read ghost stories in the dark,' Karen cried, her face shining.

'How about I bring my *Tiger Feet* single, and we can have a dance?' Wendy suggested.

Caroline wrinkled her nose. 'Don't like 'em. Have you got that new Three Degrees record?'

Wendy shook her head, her expression crestfallen.

'I was thinking we could have a facial and a manicure,' Caroline said. Her mother was a beautician, and Caroline often came to school with her nails painted.

Meena had never painted her nails in her life. She wouldn't know where to start. Her mum didn't own a bottle of nail polish, and neither did she own any other make-up, apart from one single orange lipstick. Meena had wanted to try it once, but when she'd taken the top off and twisted the bottom like she'd seen girls do when they were trawling the make-up counter in Woolworths, there hadn't been much of it left, and what there was had been tacky and gloopy. She'd hastily dropped it back in the drawer, not wanting to have it anywhere near her mouth.

'Ooh, would your mum do our make-up?' Wendy asked. 'My mum won't let me try hers. She says I'm too young, but I think she's just being mean.'

'I expect she will. I'll ask her. She's got a big box with it in, like my dad's toolbox.' Caroline sent Meena a look.

Meena smiled to show she wasn't bothered about anyone mentioning their dads. Just because she didn't have one, she didn't expect everyone to never talk about theirs.

But they gave her that look anyway – as though they felt they shouldn't talk about their dads in front of her.

'Girls, why are you talking? If you haven't learnt your spellings by tomorrow because you've been too busy nattering…' Miss Pendry's warning was clear. Meena didn't fancy a rap across the knuckles with a ruler because she spelt one of the words wrong.

'Ignore her,' Caroline instructed as Meena bent her head to the piece of paper on her desk and began copying the words on it. 'Are you going to sleep at mine or not?' Caroline demanded.

Meena was saved from having to say anything by the bell signalling the end of the school day, and she carefully folded the paper with the spellings on and put it in her bag.

'Ask your mum, yeah?' Caroline called over her shoulder as everyone headed for the door.

Meena hung back a little, not wanting to get caught up in the inevitable shoving and pushing as the boys tried to go through it first, eager for freedom and the chance to kick a ball around in the yard for a few minutes.

Caroline's mother was waiting for her, as was Wendy's.

'We're going to my granny's house for tea,' Caroline announced, by way of explanation. Wendy pulled a face and scowled at her mother.

Not many kids in their class had their mothers pick them up from school. At eight years old, most of them were considered old enough to walk home by themselves, and Meena had been making her own way home from school since she was six. But Wendy's mum insisted on waiting outside the school every day, thoroughly embarrassing

Wendy, who was teased unmercifully because of it, especially by Caroline. Which was why Caroline felt the need to explain the reason her mother was waiting in the yard today.

Karen waved to her friends and skipped off with her brother, going in the opposite direction to Meena, who usually walked home by herself. Wendy lived a couple of streets away and sometimes the two girls would walk together, but Meena didn't like Wendy's mum very much, so she often dawdled until they were out of sight.

Today though, Wendy's mum and Caroline's mum were busy gossiping, walking slowly towards the side gate, their daughters racing on ahead.

Meena trailed behind, scuffing her feet and dragging the bag containing her PE kit with its smelly black plimsols and navy knickers, her attention on Caroline and Wendy. They had their heads together and she wondered if they were talking about this sleeping-at-each-other's-house thing.

She was so busy fretting about spending the night at Caroline's house that she almost bumped into the two mothers. They had halted just outside the little wooden gate, their backs to her, and Meena was forced to stop too, not wanting to say 'excuse me', or to try to squeeze past. She didn't like drawing attention to herself, especially when it came to grown-ups because she had a feeling they could see right through to the heart of her.

It was while she was waiting for them to resume walking that she heard them say something that froze the blood in her veins and made her feel more wretched than she'd ever felt before.

'I'm happy for Wendy to stay overnight at your house and at Karen's, but…' Wendy's mother lowered her voice, '…not at that Meena girl's house. Have you seen the state of it? You know Mrs Wright who lives two doors up from me? Well, her sister lives next door to Meena's mother and she said she's ashamed to have that woman as a neighbour. The outside is bad enough.' Wendy's mother made a noise of disgust. 'Dirty windows, curtains practically hanging off the rails, her step hasn't seen a scrubbing brush in years, and the garden looks like a jungle. But if you think that's bad, she says the inside is much, much worse. I wouldn't allow my Wendy within a mile of Anita Blake's house, let alone stay the night. Goodness knows what she'll catch – nits definitely, or fleas, or even food poisoning. It's a wonder that child of hers isn't ill.'

'I didn't realise,' Caroline's mum said, and Meena wanted Mr Spock off the telly to beam her up into the spaceship, because she thought she was going to die of embarrassment.

'Soap and water doesn't cost anything,' Wendy's mum continued. 'I don't think Anita Blake can be bothered, the dirty so-and-so. She might be happy to live like a pig in muck, but I'm not letting my Wendy anywhere near that house. It's filthy and there are piles of rubbish all over the place.'

'It's the child I feel sorry for,' Caroline's mum said.

They began to move off, Wendy's mother calling for her daughter to wait up and not to run too far ahead.

Meena felt sick.

She waited until they were out of sight, tears gathering in the corners of her eyes and spilling over. Then she made her slow and reluctant way home. Is that what people thought, that her house wasn't as neat and as tidy as theirs? She was aware that her mum was messy and didn't put things away, and she knew that sometimes Miss Pendry would look at her with a mixture of disgust and sympathy on her face when Meena was sent off to school wearing a grubby blouse or mismatched socks, but she didn't realise other mums felt the same.

As she crept home, her face aflame and her heart heavy, she couldn't help peeping in through the windows of the houses she passed. She also couldn't help noticing how much nicer all of them looked compared to her own.

Her mum did her best, she knew, but Meena also felt a burning resentment that her mum's best wasn't good enough. There was no way she could invite any friends to sleep at hers – the shame would be awful.

But there *was* one thing she could do: she made a vow to herself that when she had a house of her own she'd never, ever let it get into the state her mum's house was in.

CHAPTER 1

'Your dinner is in the microwave,' Meena Fisher said, giving her husband a swift kiss on the cheek as she passed him in the hall. 'Did you have a good day?'

She was surprised to see him as she hadn't expected him home so soon; he usually played golf after work if the weather allowed. Today had been lovely, so she would have bet her last penny that he would have played a round, before coming home.

'Pretty good.'

He dropped his briefcase on the floor next to the hall table and flung his keys into the bowl on top, then headed towards the kitchen.

Meena checked her appearance in the hall mirror and gently moved his briefcase with her foot so that it sat *under* the table and not next to it. He left his case there every single evening, and every evening she moved it. She'd tried putting it in the cupboard under the stairs where she kept her handbag, but he'd made such a fuss about not being able to find it despite it being right there in front of his nose when he'd opened the door, that she'd given up trying to tidy it away.

Meena swiped lipstick across her lips and pressed them together, then bared her teeth at her reflection to check she hadn't got any colour on them.

'I won't be late,' she called, patting her jacket pocket to make sure she had her keys.

'What is it tonight?' Oscar asked, leaning against the kitchen door with a bottle of beer in his hand.

She knew she'd find it empty and abandoned on the side table next to his favourite chair when she came home.

'Governors' meeting,' she replied.

He nodded once, in acknowledgement. 'Enjoy.'

'I should be back around eight o'clock,' Meena said, hurrying out of the door. She prided herself on her timekeeping and hated being late, especially for something as important as this. The school was having a restructure of the senior leadership team and none of them were aware of it except for the headteacher, and it was imperative that it was kept hush-hush until the details had been ironed out.

Apart from Clive Baker, the Headteacher, and the Chair of Governors, Veronica Stanley, Meena was the first to arrive. Some years ago, she'd been asked if she would stand for the role of Chair, but she'd had too much on her plate already – mainly her job in the doctor's surgery – so she'd reluctantly refused. Much of the work of the Chair of Governors took place during the school day, and she wouldn't have been able to commit to the role as much as she would have liked or as much as it deserved. She'd been a part of the school ever since Anton started in the first year, and she was coming up to her twentieth anniversary of being on the board, so although she had loads of experience to draw on it wouldn't have been practical.

She hadn't intended to stay on after her son had left the school for university, but she'd become so invested that she had remained, and she now felt part of the fixtures and fittings. She'd also seen several headteachers come and go, and she'd sat on the selection panel which had appointed the current one.

The other members of the board began trickling in and Meena took on her self-appointed role as tea and coffee maker, and once everyone had a drink and had taken their seats, she sat down, got out her notepad and pen, and tried to give the meeting her full attention.

If a job was worth doing, it was worth doing well, was her mantra, but for some reason she was unable to fully concentrate on the matter at hand today. Her mind kept drifting to her mum and the issue with her health. At eighty-four she wasn't *old* old – but her mum had suddenly become frail and unsteady over the course of this year, and she'd had a couple of falls. Thankfully, none of them had been serious but it had frightened both of them, and Meena was slowly coming to the conclusion that the stairs and a cluttered house was becoming too much for her mum to cope with. What she thought her mum needed was a small bungalow or a granny flat. There was a new build specifically for elderly people not far from here, which would be ideal. The problem was, Meena had to persuade her mum that it was for the best if she moved, and that wasn't going to be easy.

Meena visited as often as she could, and she paid for a cleaner to go in three times a week to keep on top of things (she dreaded the thought of her mum's house descending into the state it had been in when Meena was a child) but her mum could create chaos in a matter of hours, and Meena couldn't be there all the time to clear up after her.

'What do you think, Meena? You've been part of this school longer than any of us. Do you think it will work?' Clive Barker was looking at her expectantly, as were the rest of the people on the board.

'Let me see…' she said slowly, trying to buy herself some time as she quickly scanned the PowerPoint on the whiteboard and compared the new structure to the old one. 'My only concern is whether this is future-proofed. From what I can gather,' she said, getting into her stride, 'the number of pupils in years three and four in the feeder primaries are greater than we've seen for several years. Will the new structure be able to cope with the increased numbers of pupils on our role?'

'Um… we've just talked about that,' the Chair said.

Meena felt silly and her cheeks reddened with embarrassment. It wasn't like her to miss anything significant. It didn't help that she could also feel a hot flush begin to surge through her, and she willed herself to ride it out. Damned menopause.

Veronica carried on, thankfully oblivious to Meena's hormonal discomfort. 'Clive said he could create an additional Assistant Head if the two in the new structure found they were overloaded. Of course, it would have to be a seconded post, which would mean a minimal impact on the budget if the salary was at the lowest point of the leadership scale.'

Budgets, that's what most things came down to these days and schools were no exception. Headteachers and Chairs had to be mindful of the finances, and with the Deputy Headteacher (who was rather expensive in terms of salary) having obtained a headship of his own, this was a perfect opportunity to cut costs and possibly get rid of some dead wood. Meena understood that, but she was also mindful that people's futures were affected.

However, there was no room for sentiment, so she said, 'I think it will work.'

'That's settled,' Veronica said. 'We'll take a vote. All in favour raise your hands.'

Meena's hand crept up, but even as she lifted it, her thoughts had once again turned to the problem of her mother.

***

Oscar was half-asleep in the armchair with the TV blaring when Meena's return jolted him awake.

'Gosh, is it that time already?' He turned the volume down then yawned and stretched, wincing at the ache in his right hip from sitting awkwardly. He got stiffly out of his chair, feeling more like eighty than his actual age of sixty-one. Once he got moving, he'd be fine, but these days it took his joints and muscles a bit of time to warm up.

'Did you eat your dinner?' Meena asked.

He heard her put her bag away. When she poked her head into the living room, she had her shoes in one hand and her jacket in the other.

'Yes, thanks, it was lovely.' It *had* been tasty, but Oscar had the feeling it would have been even tastier if he had been able to eat it as soon as she'd cooked it. Reheating wasn't the same.

He waited for her to go upstairs to change into one of the lounge suits she liked to wear in the evenings when she was at home, and he yawned again. Tired didn't begin to describe how he felt today. It had been manic in work, with the Managing Director wanting to push on with the opening of the new part of the factory, even though it wasn't ready yet. Oscar kept telling Nat that the deadline was unrealistic, but the man was adamant. Sometimes Oscar wondered why these companies bothered to employ experts for their expertise, and then refuse to listen to the advice they were paying for. These days Oscar felt like he was banging his head against a brick wall – although, if he was truthful, what he actually wanted to do was to bang *Nat's* head against one, to make the man see sense.

Oscar was more than happy to work hard, but the number of hours Nat expected him to put in to get this project up and running was ridiculous, especially when it impacted on his golf. Oscar loved the game, and although he wouldn't go as far as to say he lived for it, it did feature heavily in his life, and not just for pleasure, either. It was on the green or in the clubhouse that deals were often made, and alliances were forged. And there was also a very strong sense of 'you scratch my back and I'll scratch yours'.

If only he could persuade Nat to take up golf, Oscar was convinced that the Managing Director would see things from his point of view. It was far easier to get the measure of a man when you both had a wedge in your hand. That was Oscar's theory, and it had served him well over the years.

'Can I make you a cup of tea?' Meena asked, coming downstairs.

This evening's lounge suit was pale grey, and he gazed at his wife appreciatively. She was still a fine-looking woman, her figure trim, her hair nicely cut, and she always took pride in her appearance. Oscar thought her as beautiful today as she had been on their wedding day. He was lucky to have her, and he didn't know what he'd do without her.

He followed her out to the kitchen to see if she needed any help, but she'd got it all in hand, as usual. Not only was she making the tea, but she'd rinsed off the plate he'd used and had popped it into the dishwasher, and she was also quickly wiping the inside of the microwave.

Meena was incredibly houseproud, often to the extreme, and years ago it used to irritate him that he'd not be able to put a mug down without her swiping it away to be washed up, but now he simply accepted it. He was never going to change her, and he honestly didn't want to. He loved her just the way she was.

'Good meeting?' he asked.

'Hmm. A difficult one. The governors had to make some hard decisions.'

'You look tired,' Oscar said. She'd been looking tired a lot lately and although she hadn't said anything, he'd noticed she was having trouble sleeping. 'Do you think it might be time you stepped down?'

'It's got nothing to do with that,' she snapped, and he blinked in surprise.

Meena was rarely cross; she could be irritable at times, but then so could he, and he wondered what was bothering her.

'What is it?' he asked.

'Mum.' Meena's expression was troubled.

'Has she had another fall?'

'No, thank goodness. But it's only a matter of time. I think she should move into one of those flats near the school. It'll be perfect for her.'

Oscar guessed what was coming. 'She's not going to want to go,' he warned.

'I know. That's the problem. But it'll be more of a problem if she breaks a hip. She'll have to go then.'

'Have you thought about putting a stairlift in?'

'I have, but that's only part of the issue.' Meena poured boiling water into the mugs and gave them a stir before fishing the tea bags out. 'I'm not so much worried about the stairs, although they are a concern. I'm more worried about her tripping over her own feet.'

'She can always move in here, if you think that's for the best,' Oscar said. 'That way, you could keep an eye on her.'

Meena looked horrified. 'She'd hate that even more. I can't see us living together, can you?'

Oscar shrugged. His mother-in-law had always been a bit of an odd-bod. Meena wasn't at all like her. In many ways Meena and her mother were polar opposites. Meena was a neatness freak – her mother not so much. Saying that, no one was as fanatical as his wife when it came to cleaning. So maybe Meena was right, and her mum wouldn't want to move in with them. Besides, with both him and Meena out at work all day, and with his golf and all Meena's various committees, clubs and activities, her mum wouldn't benefit from living with them because she probably wouldn't see much more of Meena than she already did.

'I'll have a chat with her,' Meena said. 'Broach the subject.' But she didn't sound hopeful.

And neither was Oscar.

CHAPTER 2

Meena smiled with satisfaction as she regarded her pristine kitchen. It looked exactly the same when she'd arrived home this evening as it had when she'd left for work this morning. That was the advantage of Oscar having such a demanding job – she knew she wouldn't come home to a mess, not during the week anyway. Occasionally on the weekends, when she was out and Oscar wasn't, she had to grit her teeth to stop herself from saying something when she saw that yet again he'd failed to put his rubbish in the bin; instead he left it on the worktop *above* the bin. Was it so hard to put your foot on the peddle, wait for the lid to pop up, then drop the rubbish into it?

However, she didn't like to complain or to nag, and right from the start of their married life she'd taken it upon herself to do all the household chores. And everything else too, from making sure the bills were paid, to booking Oscar's dental appointments for him. She did the gardening, bought Oscar his clothes, sourced thoughtful birthday and

Christmas gifts for the family, arranged evenings out with friends... *everything*. And she enjoyed it.

Most of the time.

Relieved that she didn't have to cook this evening, she sent Oscar a quick text to remind him that they were going to dinner with Janet and Dean, then she went upstairs to pick out what she intended to wear.

After she did that, she gave her mum a quick call.

'Meena? Where are you?' Her mother's voice was querulous and Meena sighed.

'At home, Mum.'

'You didn't call in.'

'I told you we are going out to dinner with Janet and Dean.'

'Is it Friday?'

'It most certainly is.'

'It can't be – Nora didn't come.'

'She didn't?'

'No.'

'Are you sure?'

'I'm old, not stupid.'

'Sorry, Mum. What I meant to say was, she usually lets me know if she can't make it. I'll send her a text. I hope there's nothing wrong.'

Nora cleaned Meena's mum's house three times a week – Mondays, Wednesdays and Fridays. It didn't need cleaning as often as that, but it did need tidying, and Meena simply couldn't manage it by herself. So she paid Nora to do it. Between them they kept on top of Anita's tendency to create little piles of mess all over the house. Meena used to do it herself, and it had been a strain even when Anton was little and she was a stay-at-home mum, but when she'd gone back to work when Anton was old enough to start school, she'd found it impossible to look after two households, so she'd employed someone to clean her mum's.

At first it had only been once a week, with Meena popping in between cleans, but as time went on she had come to realise that once a week wasn't enough and had upped the number of times the cleaner came to two, and then to three. Obviously, even with all that help, Meena couldn't keep her mum's house to the same standard as she kept her own, but it was in a far, far better state nowadays than it had been when Meena was a child. At least she hadn't been ashamed when she'd had to call the paramedics after her mum's first fall; and although she knew they wouldn't judge her or her mother, a little voice in her head (which sounded remarkably like the one belonging to Wendy's mum all those years ago) kept whispering to her that they might. Meena didn't want her mum to be in a position like that again and she hated the thought of anyone saying anything horrid about Anita, or even thinking it, not while Meena was in a position to prevent it.

It wasn't her mum's fault she was messy; it was just the way she was, and over the years Meena had lost count of the number of times she'd hated herself for feeling embarrassed because of her mum's poor housekeeping. So, as soon as she was old enough to take on the cleaning and the laundry herself that's what she did, and she'd been doing it ever since.

No one ever realised how Meena had worked herself to the bone to keep their house clean and tidy, and Meena had always been too embarrassed to tell anyone. Not even Oscar knew. He was aware that her standards were higher than her mum's (and his mum's too, God rest her soul) but not the reason why she was so obsessive. Meena knew from bitter experience how fast the cleanliness of a house could deteriorate, and she was determined to keep on top of it.

'I'll call in tomorrow, as usual,' she told her mother. 'And in the meantime, I'll see if I can find out what's happened to Nora.' Meena hoped to goodness the woman was OK.

Nora had been cleaning Anita's house for the past seven years, and was diligent, honest and reliable, as well as friendly. Meena would struggle to manage without her unless she gave up some of her hobbies or interests, and she didn't want to do that.

She sent a message to Nora, asking if she was OK, then she began to get ready for the evening. She was looking forward to it – Janet and Dean were good fun and good friends. Meena and Janet had met first when their children were small, and over the course of many birthday parties, play dates and babysitting for each other, the two men had also gradually got to know each other and were now firm friends.

Oscar had even introduced Dean to golf, although Dean had yet to manage to persuade Oscar to join *The First Act*, the amateur dramatics society that Meena, Janet and Dean were all enthusiastic members of.

Pushing her worry about her mum to one side, Meena was determined to enjoy herself tonight. If her beloved husband wasn't late, that is.

***

Oscar pulled Janet into a hug and kissed her on the cheek, then shook hands with Dean.

'Haven't seen you on the fairway for a while,' he said, patting Dean on the stomach. 'You've got to make sure you get enough exercise at your age or you'll start to pile on the pounds.'

Dean chuckled, knowing Oscar was teasing. Dean's stomach was washboard flat and he had the physique of a man half his age. Oscar was rather envious, if he was honest, even though he would hardly class himself as podgy. He didn't think he had much of a paunch either – if he held his breath and sucked his tummy in.

'I love your dress,' Meena enthused, and the women were soon engrossed in a conversation about clothes and shops, and Oscar turned to Dean and made a face.

'How are things?' Dean asked as they were shown to their table.

'Great, thanks.' Oscar pulled Meena's chair out for her.

'See, Dean, that's what gentlemen do for their wives,' Janet observed.

'Would you prefer a gentleman? Or a bloke who knows how to load the dishwasher?' Dean joked. It was well-known that Oscar couldn't tell the dishwasher from the tumble dryer, and Dean was a whizz in the kitchen.

'Both?' Janet said, waggling her eyebrows.

Dean turned to Oscar. 'She's greedy. And she knows I don't have a romantic bone in my body.'

'Neither do I,' Oscar confessed. 'How goes it in the world of corporate tax?'

'Ugh, let's not talk about it. I'm counting down the months until I can retire.'

'How many is that?'

'Fifteen.'

'You'll be sixty?' Oscar asked.

'That's right. Janet and I have made a pact that we'll both finish work when we're sixty.'

'There are only a couple of months between you, aren't there?'

Dean nodded. 'I'm surprised you're not making retirement noises,' he said.

Oscar barked out a laugh. 'Not me – I'm too young to hang up my boots.'

'You're the oldest out of the lot of us!' Dean exclaimed.

'Ah, but the secret is, I don't feel it.'

'How about Meena? Wouldn't she like the two of you to spend more time together?'

'Hardly.' Oscar snorted. 'She's got so much going on that if I retired I'd only be sitting at home twiddling my thumbs while she was off to the WI, or her amateur dramatics group,' he nodded at Dean, who was the group's director, 'or God knows what else she's got going on. And she still works, don't forget.'

'She could retire, too?'

'She loves her job,' Oscar declared. 'So no, there won't be any retirement for her just yet. It might be the right thing for you two, but we're perfectly happy with our lives just the way they are!'

And he meant it.

CHAPTER 3

Oscar wasn't looking forward to his meeting with Nat this morning. He knew exactly what the man would say, and he knew exactly what he himself would say in response. This whole "get the new wing ready by the end of July" directive was beginning to sound like a stuck record. It simply wasn't going to happen. Not unless Nat was prepared to throw more money and resources at it. Which he wasn't. These director types were all the same – they wanted everything done yesterday, to the highest of standards, and on the lowest of budgets.

Oscar was getting fed up of repeating himself but he nevertheless printed off the most recent data and figures he had, which was up to and including the Friday just gone, and he prepared for battle. There was no way on earth he could make the reports and spreadsheets tell a different story. He felt like saying 'watch my lips, the wing *will not be ready*', but of course, he couldn't. All he could do was present Nat with the information – *again* – and hope that this time the truth would sink in.

He could do without this extra hassle today. Mondays were always busy, because although he didn't work weekends apart from the occasional Saturday morning, the factory was a twenty-four/seven operation, so he always had to play catch-up on Monday mornings.

And now Nat had called a meeting. As if Oscar didn't have enough to do.

'Ah, Oscar, come in,' Nat said when the MD's secretary showed him through. 'Take a seat.'

Nat shuffled some papers on his desk, but he didn't glance down at them, and all of a sudden Oscar felt unaccountably nervous. Something was going on, he could sense it, but he didn't have the foggiest idea what it might be.

'How are you?' Nat asked earnestly, and Oscar's "something was going on" antennae bristled. Nat had never asked him anything like that before, probably because he didn't care and wasn't interested. Yet he was asking now…

'Good, thanks,' Oscar replied cautiously.

'Good… good…' Nat cleared his throat.

Here we go, Oscar thought, he's going to ask me to do the impossible.

'We're, er, having a reshuffle,' Nat said, then paused.

Oscar looked at him expectantly. 'Go on.'

'A *management* reshuffle.'

'OK…?' Oscar wasn't sure how he was meant to respond to this announcement, or what it had to do with him.

'There will be fewer managers at a senior level,' Nat continued.

'Directors, you mean?'

'No…' He looked over Oscar's shoulder, then he seemed to shake himself and his focus came back to Oscar's face. 'There's no easy way to say this, but your layer of management will no longer exist.'

Oscar blinked. There were only *two* people in his layer of management.

'Sorry,' Nat added, but to Oscar he didn't sound sorry at all.

'I don't follow,' Oscar said, knowing he did but praying he didn't.

'We – when I say *we*, I mean our parent company in the US – have decided that the current structure is too management heavy.'

'But it's been like this for years.'

'Exactly. They feel it's time for a change, to ensure the business is fit for the future. As it currently stands, some managers don't have any people directly reporting into them and they should do. All your direct reports will be split amongst the production managers.'

Oscar didn't care about that. He didn't like having people reporting into him anyway, but what he *did* care about was the implication of having his man-management responsibilities taken away from him. 'Where does that leave me?' he asked, confused.

'We are offering you suitable alternative employment. If you want it.'

'Doing what?' Oscar shifted uncomfortably in his chair, wishing he had an antacid tablet for the encroaching heartburn.

Nat pushed one of the sheets of paper across the desk.

Oscar took his reading glasses out of the top pocket of his jacket and put them on.

By the time he'd finished reading, he wished he hadn't bothered. 'I'm far too over-qualified for this,' he objected. 'And the salary is considerably less. Of course I don't want it.' Oscar's chest was tight and there was a churning sourness in his stomach.

'You are rejecting the company's offer of suitable alternative employment?'

'I certainly am!' It was an insult to expect him to take it. He'd be a laughingstock, or worse – people would feel sorry for him. The position was an untenable one.

'You'll need to put your decision in writing,' Nat said.

Oscar narrowed his eyes at him. He couldn't be entirely certain, but he had a feeling Nat was enjoying this. He also had a feeling there was a catch. 'Are you making me redundant?'

'Whilst the position you hold in the company will no longer exist after the end of the month, we are, however, offering you suitable alternative employment.'

There was that phrase again. Nat kept saying it, as though he was reading from a script and not deviating from it.

'But I don't want it,' Oscar repeated.

'In that case, we have no option other than to give you notice of your termination of employment.'

Oscar sat there, stunned. He'd given this company the biggest part of three decades of his life and they were making him *redundant?* He couldn't believe it. He *refused* to believe it.

'This can't be happening,' he muttered.

'I'm sorry, I know it's a shock. Perhaps you should take some time to think about it?' Nat sat back, resting his clasped hands on the edge of his desk. Although he appeared to be making all the right noises, his expression was one of boredom.

Oscar's anger bubbled to the surface, unexpected and sharp. 'I don't need time to think about it, thank you very much. I've made my decision – I'm not taking that bloody job.' He shoved the offer letter at Nat, who raised an eyebrow.

'Well, then, I don't believe we have anything left to discuss, except for me to wish you well for the future.'

'Yeah, thanks.' Oscar's tone was sour and sarcastic. 'You haven't mentioned my redundancy pay.' It was going to be a decent amount, considering how long he'd worked there. Enough to give him some breathing space whilst he looked for another—

'The company isn't in a position to offer redundancy,' Nat said.

'*You what?*' Oscar couldn't have heard him properly.

'You are not entitled.'

'I am! I must be! I've worked here for nearly thirty years.'

'I'm sorry, perhaps I didn't make myself clear? Because the company has offered you suitable alternative employment and you have refused that offer, you are not entitled to any redundancy payment.'

Oscar froze, the blood turning cold in his veins. 'That can't be right,' he whispered.

'I'm afraid it is.' Nat smiled. It didn't reach his eyes. 'Are you sure you don't want to accept the alternative position we are offering?'

Numbly Oscar shook his head, then he nodded, before shaking it again. What choice did he have?

'Which is it to be?' Nat's smile was still in place and Oscar wanted to wipe it off his face with his fist.

Trembling, feeling sick, scared and angry, Oscar was unable to say another word.

'There is a third option,' Nat carried on. 'Given your age, and in light of this, you might want to consider early retirement?'

The bastard! It was suddenly very clear – the MD had planned this all along. Retirement? Oscar wasn't old enough. He had a few more years to go before he reached retirement age. He wasn't ready to join the OAP brigade, or even the smug early-retiree lot. He was too young, for God's sake!

'I get it,' Oscar snarled. 'This has been your plan all along, hasn't it?'

'I've no idea what you mean. This restructure has nothing to do with me, I assure you. It's come directly from the US. They intend to streamline this branch of their portfolio, starting with the top.'

'You've still got your job, I see,' Oscar said bitterly.

'The company will always need someone to steer the ship.' Nat was smug and he didn't even have the decency to hide it. 'But this meeting isn't about me, it's about you.' He leaned forward and steepled his fingers. 'Let's be realistic here, Oscar; you're not going to get another job at your age. Not one like this. So maybe it's better if you retire.'

'Better for whom?'

'You, of course. Think of all that free time you'll have to play golf.'

'I don't need more free time. What I need is my job.'

'But that's what I'm trying to tell you. Your job, as you put it, no longer exists. There *is* a job for you in the company, but you've told me you don't want it.'

'At half the salary and reporting to a man I trained? No thank you!'

'I think we're at an impasse. Why don't you take a few days to think about it? Go home and have a chat with your wife. Consider your options.' Nat got to his feet, signalling that the meeting was over.

Oscar remained in his seat for a few seconds longer, then he too, rose.

Nat shuffled the various papers on his desk until they were in a neat pile, then he slipped them into an A4 envelope and held them out. 'These are copies of everything we've discussed. Let me know by the end of the week, what you decide.'

Numb and close to tears, Oscar snatched the envelope and stalked out. The man knew how shocked and upset he was – Oscar hadn't been able to hide it – but there was no way on this earth that Nat would have the satisfaction of seeing Oscar cry.

Oscar held himself together long enough to inform HR that he was feeling unwell and long enough to get into his car and drive out of the car park.

Then he pulled into the side of the road and wept.

***

Meena braced herself as she put the key in the lock of her mother's front door and stepped inside. Nora hadn't been able to see to her mum since last Wednesday, and it was now Monday. Meena had done as she promised and had called in on Saturday, sharing the news with her mum that Nora hadn't been able to come on Friday because her daughter had broken her arm. Meena had done some cleaning then, as well as a few other bits and pieces such as nipping out to fetch her mum some shopping and renewing her TV licence for her. It had taken Meena all of Saturday morning.

But in less than forty-eight hours the living room looked like a bomb site, and the kitchen was even worse. Meena had no idea how her mum could make so much mess in such a small amount of time. There were dirty cups and plates dotted around the livingroom, some of them on the floor and which Meena almost stepped on, and there were more dirty dishes on the kitchen counters and piled up in the sink. There was also a vague smell of decay in the air, and Meena shuddered to think what was in the bin. It shouldn't need emptying after just two days, but that was the first thing Meena did, holding the bag which she had tied tightly at arm's length, before taking it outside and dropping it in the wheelie bin, then she went back into the kitchen, put on a pair of yellow rubber gloves and ran some hot water in the sink.

'Aren't you going to say anything?' her mother asked.

'Sorry mum, how are you?'

'Not so bad,' Anita said. She waved a hand crossly in the air. 'Why don't you leave all that and talk to me?'

There was no way Meena could leave "all that" and neither did she intend to. If she didn't sort it out now, it would be twice as bad the next time she came. She knew this from experience. It didn't take her long to clean up the kitchen, and it took her even less time to clean up the living room. Nora always did a good job of hoovering in corners and dusting skirting boards, which meant Meena only had to see to the superficial stuff.

Anita didn't like Nora doing her laundry for her, which Meena could understand. She didn't think she'd like anyone else handling her dirty underwear either, so she set about putting a load into the machine and switching it on.

She'd wait until the programme had run its course, then she'd take the laundry with her. If she left it up to her mum, it would still be in the machine the next time Meena paid her a visit, and would smell absolutely disgusting.

Meena would take it home with her, dry and iron it, then pop it in the airing cupboard where the boiler was to make sure it was thoroughly dry, before returning the clean laundry to her mum's house and putting it away where it belonged. She'd learnt not to just leave the clean clothes on her mum's bed for her mum to put away, because they would still be there six weeks later, in a crumpled mess with most of them kicked off onto the floor.

'What did you do yesterday?' her mum asked her, when Meena finally made the tea and sat down to drink it.

'Anton, Grace and the kids popped over for Sunday lunch,' she said. 'Did I tell you they're off on holiday as soon as the kids break up from school? Lucky things! I'm thinking of booking somewhere for Oscar and me – we could do with getting away for a week or two.'

'Abroad?' Anita asked.

'Probably. You can't guarantee the weather in Britain, can you?'

'Somewhere with a golf course?' her mother asked, knowingly.

Meena sighed. 'I expect. Oscar doesn't consider it a proper holiday unless a few games of golf are involved.'

'I don't know how you put up with him.' Anita scowled at her. 'You're like ships passing in the night. He's never at home.'

'He could say the same about me,' Meena retorted. 'I'm hardly ever in, either.'

'You don't *have* to come and see me you know,' her mother said, and Meena rolled her eyes.

'That's not what I meant, and you know it.'

'I can manage perfectly well on my own,' her mother continued.

Meena wondered how far into its cycle the machine was, and she hoped it didn't have much longer to go. Sometimes her mum could be in an argumentative mood, and it looked like today was one of those times. Besides, Meena was tired. She'd been out of the house since seven-thirty a.m. and she wanted to go home. Thankfully she didn't have anywhere to be this evening, which was rare, and she was looking forward to sharing an evening meal with Oscar for once, then settling down in front of the TV with her knitting.

She considered knitting to be incredibly soothing. From a young age Meena found it very difficult to sit still. It probably had something to do with the fact that she hadn't been able to sit still for long when she lived at home with her mum, because there was always something that needed doing.

So she'd gotten into the habit of being perpetually busy, and it suited her. It was who she was, and she tended to get a little angsty if she had too much time on her hands. Knitting allowed her to feel as though she was doing something useful whilst she was sitting there staring at the TV.

Finally, to her relief, she heard the washing machine's door mechanism click to let her know that the load was ready, and she retrieved one of the big bags from the cupboard under the stairs and preceded to fill it full of clean damp washing. She'd pop it into her tumble dryer as soon as she got home.

She kissed her mum goodbye, after telling her she'd call in again on Wednesday if Nora couldn't make it and she hurried out of the door.

Why did her mother always make her feel so guilty? She felt she should have invited her over last Sunday, but with Anton, his wife and the two children for lunch it just seemed a little much somehow to have her mum there as well. She would invite her mum over this Sunday if she wanted to come.

Meena could tell that her mum didn't feel very comfortable in her house. Meena couldn't help whisking mugs away immediately they were finished with or plumping up cushions as soon as somebody got up from a chair, and she knew it made her mum feel uncomfortable. Meena tried not to be so obsessive, but it was ingrained, and Oscar didn't seem to mind. He had complained a little when they'd first got married, but now he just accepted her as she was. Meena had the feeling that he was quite proud of how she kept the house, and the way she did it so effortlessly.

If only he knew that it wasn't effortless at all. A great deal of time and energy went into it, but it was second nature to her now, and she did most of it on autopilot and without thinking: like when she cleaned around the wash hand basin in the bathroom at the same time as she brushed her teeth. Or when she gave the shower screen a quick wipe over while she was in the shower. Cleaning as she went along and tidying up as she went along, saved doing it in one big session every few days.

Meena was well aware that she was obsessive, but she wasn't harming anyone, and it was nobody's business but her own.

As she pulled onto the drive she noticed Oscar's car in its usual spot, and she was surprised. He didn't normally arrive home until about seven if he wasn't playing golf, later than that if he had a game.

She could guarantee he wouldn't have started preparing dinner, though; he never did. He probably had no idea what they were going to eat this evening, but he didn't blame him for that. He didn't do the shopping, he didn't plan the meals, and neither did he do the cooking, so she could hardly expect him to do so now just because he happened to be home earlier than usual.

She struggled in the front door with the bag of washing and went straight through the kitchen and into the utility room, where she loaded the laundry into the tumble dryer. Then she turned around and went in search of her husband.

Oscar was upstairs, sitting on the end of the bed, staring at the floor.

He was still wearing his work shirt, but he had taken his trousers off, displaying his rather pale and slightly hairy legs which ended in a pair of black socks. He didn't look up when she came in.

'Just give me a chance to change and I'll start dinner,' she said.

Oscar didn't move, he didn't say anything, and he didn't look at her.

She began undoing the buttons on the blouse, but something made her stop and she stared at him.

He didn't look well: his skin was wan and slightly grey, and his shoulders were slumped.

'Are you OK? she asked. 'Are you not feeling well?'

She waited a second for a response, but when she didn't receive one she walked over to him, knelt down at his feet and looked up into his face.

'What's wrong?' she asked, worry making her feel suddenly sick. Was he ill? Please God, she prayed, don't let him be ill.

'I'm all right,' he said, his voice hoarse. He cleared his throat.

He continued to stare at the carpet, and she peered up at him, trying to see his expression. And when he finally looked at her, she gasped. His eyes were moist and there were deep lines underneath them that hadn't been there this morning.

'Oh God,' she said 'What's the matter? What's happened?' Her thoughts immediately flew to Anton and the grandchildren. 'Is it Anton—?' she began, her heart thudding madly as her stomach knotted and twisted.

'They've sacked me,' he said.

'*What?*' It took her a moment to collect her racing thoughts, and she felt shaky as the adrenalin whizzed around her body when she realised that her husband's distress thankfully had nothing to do with their son or his family. 'Why?'

'They said my job doesn't exist anymore.'

'They can't do that.' She paused. 'Can they?'

He nodded again. 'Apparently, they can. They offered me suitable alternative employment.' He sounded bitter.

'What kind of employment?' she asked slowly, sensing there was more to this.

'The kind I couldn't possibly accept,' he replied. He jerked his head towards the dressing table, and she turned to see a white envelope sitting on it.

'It's all in there,' he said.

'What are you going to do?'

'There's nothing I *can* do.'

'Are you going to look for another job?'

He smiled sadly. 'We both know I'm not likely to get one, not at my age. I could probably be a school crossing patrol person if they still have them. But that's about it.'

She sat back on her heels, not knowing what to say or how to comfort him. He was in shock and hurting, but what he said was true; he *was* unlikely to get another job at his age, and if he did it wouldn't be the sort of job he was used to, and neither would it pay the sort of salary he was on now.

'How much have they offered you?' she asked. When he looked at her blankly, she added. 'Redundancy payment?'

He barked out a laugh and she jumped. 'Nothing!' he spat.

'What do you mean, *nothing*? They *are* making you redundant, *aren't they*?'

'Yes, they are. But because they offered me suitable alternative employment and I've refused to take it, apparently they don't have to pay me anything.'

Meena gasped. 'That's not fair!'

'No. It isn't.'

'Can you fight it?'

'What's the point? Nat was in his element: he loved every second of humiliating me, sitting there and watching me squirm. I hate him. I wouldn't go back there now if they paid me in golden unicorns.'

'When do you finish?' she asked carefully.

'They've given me a month's notice, enough time to sort my pension out.'

Meena blinked. 'You're going to *retire*?'

'I haven't got any choice. Nat, the bastard, engineered it that way. I either take a job that is so far beneath me I might as well be doing the filing, and for considerably less money than I'm on now, or I can leave without any redundancy pay and try to get another job, and we both know that's not going to happen. Nat intended for me to take early retirement all along. The bastard,' he repeated.

Meena was stunned, unable to think through the fog in her brain. She simply couldn't envisage her husband not working. He loved his job; at least, she hoped he loved it, because he spent enough time at work, and if he wasn't at work then he was on the golf course, playing against people *from* work and talking *about* work.

What was he going to do with himself all day?

What about *them*? She and Oscar were fine as they were. How were they going to cope with this? Meena liked her life just the way it was and the thought of anything changing made her feel cold all over.

CHAPTER 4

Four Weeks Later

It was the little things that would break her, Meena decided: not the great big unforgivable issues like finding out that your spouse or partner was having an affair or had a secret love child. And not just break her – those little things would break *them*.

Not that Oscar had ever had an affair (as far as she knew) or was in possession of a secret son or daughter (again, as far as she knew), so she couldn't honestly say how she'd react. However, she hoped – she prayed – that if anything so astronomical did happen, that she and Oscar would be able to work through such a seismic shift in their marriage and put it all behind them. She would hope, if such a thing were ever to be revealed, that they'd be able to keep their thirty-six-year-old marriage alive.

But that wasn't what was troubling her today. It was nothing so drastic or marriage-shattering. It was something quite small. But small things, which were tolerable on their own, gained more significance when they were accompanied by more, equally small things. Many more small things.

Dear God, she thought, if Oscar left a trail of crumbs scattered across the kitchen worktop one more time, like a grey-haired, craggy-faced Hansel, she was going to do a wicked witch impersonation on his backside and shove him headfirst into the oven.

She snatched a dishcloth from the sink – stained with tea from the bag he couldn't be bothered to put in the bin – and swiped furiously at the crumbs. Half of them landed on the floor.

Scowling, she swiped some more, muttering to herself. Look what Oscar was turning her into: someone who swiped furiously. A furious swiper.

If she had her way, she'd be a furious *sniper*, and put an end to his crumby exploits once and for all.

See, she said to herself, it was the little things that sent thoughts of doing away with her husband scurrying through her mind.

To be fair it wasn't just this one thing, because if it had been it would mean she was borderline psychotic. There were *lots* of little things, too numerous to list. And although she had tried not to let them get to her, in the dark depths of the night, when her fury kept her awake (as well as his sodding snoring) she'd counted her grievances.

They were legion.

'I was just about to clean that up,' Oscar said, strolling into the kitchen without a care in the world, scratching his nether regions with one absent-minded hand. In his other he held a half-eaten piece of toast, which dripped a trail of melted butter down his arm to fall onto her once-pristine flagstone floor.

"Once" was the operative word and resentment rose up in her chest like a half-digested meal sitting uneasily in her stomach, before she realised it wasn't just resentment she was feeling and that she really did have heartburn.

She'd been suffering from it a lot recently. She'd never suffered from indigestion prior to Oscar getting a golden handshake. Or should she say a 'happy retirement' card and £135 in Tesco vouchers. Whoop-de-do.

'You do know what plates are for, don't you?' She stared pointedly at his toast, and hoped he'd slip on the blob of melted butter that was slowly congealing next to his right foot. Although, knowing her luck, she'd be the one to slip on it as she was rushing around getting ready for work *and* still doing most of the damned housework.

'Wipe that up,' she instructed, throwing the dishcloth in the sink and pushing past him.

'Wipe what up? You've just done it.'

'That!' She jabbed a finger at the blob on the floor.

Oscar bent slightly to peer at it. 'What is it?' he asked, as another drip of butter plopped onto the tiles.

'Melting butter. From your toast,' she explained, in case he wasn't able to put the two things together and come up with the right conclusion. 'Because you couldn't be bothered to use a plate,' she added, for good measure.

'Oh, I see. I'll do it in a minute.' He took another bite of his toast and crumbs rained to the floor. 'I was trying to save on washing up.'

Meena rolled her eyes and gritted her teeth as she grabbed the mop from the utility room, viciously scrubbed it over the floor, then shoved it into her husband's hand, ignoring the astonished expression on his face as she stomped into the hall and up the stairs. It was strange how he should only be concerned about the amount of washing up now that it was his job to do it. Supposedly. She hadn't noticed much of a decrease in her washing up duties since he'd finished work. She was still doing the lion's share of it.

And the tidying up, she saw, as she reached down to pick up a pair of boxer shorts (M&S, naturally) and an odd sock which had been lying on the floor next to the laundry basket in the bathroom.

Yes, well, he'd never had that good an aim, she grumbled silently to herself, eyeing the floor around the loo with a curling lip. It was dry, to her relief, and she ungritted her teeth for long enough to brush them.

Until she saw the state of the bath, that is, and her jaw went into a full lock again; she was so tense that the muscles in the back of her neck hurt.

Meena stood there for long seconds, her stockinged toes clenching as she surveyed the grubby ring around the bath and the tiny flecks of shaved hairs coating the sides and the bottom.

He'd had a shave in the bath and failed to clean it afterwards. Yet another job she'd have to add to her list.

It would have to wait, however, because if she didn't get a move on she'd be late for work. And that would never do. People were grumpy enough at having to go to the doctor's surgery in the first place, without being forced to wait outside in the cold and the drizzle for the practice manager to arrive. The staff probably wouldn't be too pleased, either.

Meena lifted her ID badge from where it was hanging by its lanyard on the edge of her dressing table mirror and slipped it over her head. With a final check to make sure she didn't have lipstick on her teeth or that her skirt wasn't tucked into her knickers, she was ready.

As she shoved her feet into her navy court shoes and shrugged on her jacket she shouted, 'I'm off. Can you remember to take the steak out of the freezer?'

Oscar appeared in the hall. The toast was gone, replaced by a mug of tea. It was nice to see he had the time to make one and drink it. She'd taken one sip of her morning cuppa and had popped it on the side, where it undoubtedly still sat, cold and undrunk because she'd run out of time this morning, having been too busy wiping counter tops and mopping up butter splats to finish her drink.

As she reversed the car off the drive, she was silently seething.

She was still silently seething as she negotiated the rush hour traffic. And the seething continued as she parked her car and dashed across the terrace to the main door of the surgery.

'About time,' an elderly gentleman muttered when he saw her. He was leaning on his walking stick and had a dripper on the end of his nose.

Meena resisted the impulse to whip out a hanky and give it a good wipe.

'It's only seven forty-five, Mr Jenkins,' she pointed out. 'The surgery doesn't open until eight and the first appointments aren't until half-past.'

She unlocked the main door and hurried inside to disable the alarm, and Mr Jenkins shuffled in behind her before she could stop him. Hastily, she closed the door and twisted the key in the lock in case anyone else thought to come in.

'I'm here to see Dr Khan,' the old gent said, standing by the desk and peering at the computer's blank screen. 'It'll say on there that I've got an appointment. It's about my bowels.'

'I haven't had a chance to turn it on yet,' she pointed out. 'Give me a minute to take my coat off.' The door rattled and she glanced at it, seeing two of the admin staff waiting outside. One of the doctors was behind them, and she let them all in.

'Have you turned it on yet?' Mr Jenkins asked, his voice hopeful. 'I'm worried that if you don't tell it I'm here, it'll think I'm late.'

Meena took pity on him. It wasn't his fault if technology was passing him by. Heck, it was moving so fast these days that she often felt bewildered by it herself. Only last year, a new database had been installed and she still didn't think she'd fully got to grips with it.

'I know you're here,' she said to him, 'and that's what counts. Take a seat, Doctor will call you through when he's ready.' Which might be a while, because the GP that Mr

Jenkins was due to see hadn't arrived yet and was notorious for being late.

The morning passed swiftly, as it always did, filled with appointments, clinics, the collection of blood and other bodily fluids, repeat prescriptions and the general day-to-day management of a busy practice, so it was gone midday before Meena could draw breath, and have her second cuppa of the day. Not that she'd actually managed to drink her first…

There was a lull between the morning appointments and the start of the afternoon ones, during which the doctors caught up on paperwork and phone calls, and where everyone took a lunch break. Meena took her sandwich into the staffroom, made a cup of tea and sank into one of the low-slung chairs with a deep sigh.

'Busy morning?' Dana asked. She was one of the GPs and was heavily pregnant with her first child. She was sitting with her feet up and rubbing her stomach.

'No more than usual,' Meena said. 'How are you feeling?'

'Knackered. Hormonal. Stressed. The usual.'

'You should be taking it easy. Is there anything I can do to help?'

'Have this baby for me?'

'No chance. I had enough of being pregnant when I was carrying Anton, and as for the birth…?' Meena shuddered. 'Seriously, if there's anything *else* I can do…'

'Thanks, but no. I've just got to get through the next three weeks with my sanity intact, then I can start my maternity leave. Anyway, you've got enough on your plate.

What is it tonight – the WI? Amateur dramatics? Knit and Natter?'

'Governors' meeting at the school,' Meena replied.

'Do you ever sleep? I don't know where you get your energy from. Do you think you'll slow down now that Oscar is retired?'

'I don't see why I should. We've always had separate interests. His was work and golf. If he wasn't in the office, he was on the golf course, or in the clubhouse.'

'Will he find it strange, do you think? Suddenly having all this free time?' Dana shifted uncomfortably and winced. 'This baby has more feet than a centipede. If you opened me up you'd find me black and blue from all the kicking. If she isn't a professional footballer when she's older I'm going to ask for a refund based on the trade description act.'

'Can I get you anything?' Meena asked.

'An early Caesarean?' Dana paused. 'Joking,' she added swiftly, but Meena wondered if she was serious. 'Will Oscar find it strange?' Dana asked again.

'I honestly don't know. *I* will, though.'

'In what way?'

'He's always going to be there.'

'It's his house, as well as yours,' Dana pointed out with a chuckle.

Meena rolled her eyes. 'I know that, daftie. What I meant was, that I'm not used to him being there all the time. He's already getting under my feet, making a mess, moving things, and this is only day one. I'm not used to it,' she repeated.

'What do you think he'll find to do all day? I'm interested because my dad is retiring at the end of the year, and he's worried he's going to be at a loose end.'

'Oscar has said he'll take care of the house: do all the chores, be responsible for the upkeep. And the cooking.' Meena pulled a face.

'Isn't that a good thing?'

Meena said flatly. 'I know he only finished work on Friday, but he was a nightmare this morning.' She thought back to the list of things that had needed doing at home and wondered whether he'd done any of them. Or if he'd even noticed they needed doing at all…

Probably not. She'd simply have to do them herself later.

Meena wrestled herself out of the low chair and straightened up, just in time to hear Mr Jenkins's quavering voice call, for the second time that day, 'Shop?' from the waiting area, followed by, 'I've got an appointment. It's about my bowels.'

Some things never changed.

CHAPTER 5

Was it wrong to breathe a sigh of relief when your wife walked out of the door, Oscar wondered, doing precisely that, his shoulders relaxing as he heard her slam the car door and start the engine.

Until he'd been forced to retire, he hadn't realised what a fusspot she was in the mornings, or how anxious she could get before work.

Of course, he'd never witnessed it until recently, because he'd always left for work before Meena got up. He'd creep out of bed, and get ready as quietly as possible, only making any kind of noise when he took a cup of tea up to her just before he left.

It was strange to think he had *retired* – and he didn't know what he was supposed to do with all this free time he suddenly had. This was the first day of the rest of his life and he wasn't sure he liked it.

He'd worked since he'd left school, and at first it was because he'd wanted the money and the independence that having a regular wage brought, but gradually, as he'd worked his way up through the ranks of the company and he'd been promoted to positions with more responsibility, he'd come to love it. The cut and thrust, the in-house jockeying, the corporate politics… he revelled in all of it.

As well as working hard over the years, he'd played hard, too. Golf, mostly, and towards the end it was golf exclusively because that was where much of the networking took place and where many of the deals were done.

Meena understood that and initially, in the early part of their marriage, she'd had their son to occupy her. Her role had been to raise Anton and to see to the house, Oscar's role had been to put a roof over their heads and food on the table. When he hadn't been working, he'd played golf and she'd… well… Meena had so many interests and hobbies he didn't know where to start.

He remembered that she'd been a very active member of the PTA at Anton's primary school, and that she'd always been involved in the Women's Institute. And by the time Anton was in secondary school, Meena had taken a part-time job as a medical receptionist, to go alongside her seat on the school's board of governors and all the other things she was involved in.

Nowadays, even though she was the practice's office manager, she was still a school governor, and was just as involved in the WI, plus she'd now added amateur dramatics and a new-found love of knitting to her many and varied interests. And don't forget babysitting the grandchildren once in a while, although how she managed to fit them into her hectic life was beyond him. But she did.

He'd never had to lift a finger when it came to the house or childcare. Meena had taken care of it all, leaving him free to concentrate on what he did best, and that was making money.

Now that he was in receipt of a pension and didn't have to go out to work, it meant he had much more time to devote to his beloved golf. So he and Meena had agreed that as from today it was going to be up to him to take care of the house.

The problem was, he didn't know where to start.

Why wasn't the sink filling up? Oscar was running the tap but the water, instead of filling the sink up with hot soapy suds, was draining straight back out of it. Why wasn't there a plug?

Now that he came to think about it, there weren't any plugs in the bathroom either, or the wash hand basin in the downstairs loo. But those had a sort of a pop-up cap-thing over the hole, that you pressed down to seal then pressed again to release. However, the sink in the kitchen had a kind of drainer. There was no cap, so he turned off the tap, frowning in annoyance.

Oscar wanted to wash the breakfast things, but instead of using the dishwasher he'd decided to wash up the old-fashioned way. His mother never had a dishwasher. She used to use a washing up bowl and Fairy Liquid. If it worked for her, then it would work for him. He only had a few things to wash, and he didn't see the point in turning the dishwasher on for a couple of mugs, two glasses from last night, two teaspoons and a buttery knife. Besides, he'd examined the dishwasher and concluded that its operation required a degree in engineering or computer science.

Ditto the washing machine, so he planned on rinsing out the contents of the laundry basket by hand, too. *If* he could find where Meena kept the washing powder, that is.

The utility room was her domain. Oscar couldn't remember the last time he'd been in there until this morning when he'd put the mop back that Meena had shoved into his hands.

She'd been cross, and he guessed it was because he was at home and she had to go out to work. He wished with all his might that it was the other way around, because he'd *liked* working, and she was far better at the domestic stuff than he.

She'd had loads more practice, for a start. And she must enjoy it, because she did enough of it. Take earlier, for instance; she'd given the kitchen floor a quick going over with the mop before she'd dashed off, although he didn't think it needed it. It had looked clean enough to him, but obviously not to Meena. And because she'd done that, she'd almost made herself late for work. She'd whirled around the house, irritation following in her wake like the perfume she always wore, and (if he was honest) he'd been glad to see the back of her.

He hoped she wasn't going to carry on being like this in the mornings, because he found it quite unsettling. He was a firm believer in not making work for oneself, but Meena seemed to enjoy doing that very thing, and then she got cross with him when he either didn't do it, or didn't do it to her satisfaction. Which was going to be a problem, because what was once Meena's responsibility was now his.

That's what they'd agreed. It was up to him to do the housework, the cooking, the laundry, the shopping, and whatever else she did. It was only fair, considering his time was now his own and hers most definitely wasn't.

He hadn't been expected to wash up so much as a cup when he'd been working, and neither would Meena be expected to now that their roles were reversed. It wasn't a total reversal because she didn't work all hours God sent and neither was her job particularly onerous from what he could tell, but she *was* out of the house for eight hours a day, so it was up to him to keep the house running until she too retired.

And his first task was to get to grips with this damned sink. How was he supposed to wash up like this?

He knew it was possible because he'd seen Meena do it, so maybe there was a proper plug somewhere. In the cupboard underneath, perhaps?

He opened the door and peered inside, frowning. Good grief, how many bottles of assorted cleaning products did one house need? Bleach, glass cleaner, hob shine, disinfectant, antibacterial spray, oven cleaner… the list was impressive. There were also several pairs of yellow rubber gloves still in their packaging, sponges, wire soap pads, wet wipes, antibacterial wipes, kitchen roll, and air freshers. But no plug.

Drat.

Oscar had a thought. Maybe it was kept in the utility room along with the mop, but after a quick rummage about during which he'd found the vacuum cleaner – a delight he had yet to experience – he hadn't found it, and neither had he found a washing up bowl in there, which he'd hoped would negate the need for a plug. But he had found a black bucket. If push came to shove, he'd use that.

Push *did* come to shove, he discovered, because his quest for both a plug and a washing up bowl proved fruitless, and after ten minutes he gave up and used the bucket.

Afterwards, feeling as though he'd finally accomplished something this morning, Oscar located the tea towels and dried the breakfast things. He even put them away. He'd managed to splash some water on the floor though, so he used the sponge on the drainer to mop up the droplets, and as he was doing so he noticed a scattering of crumbs on the flagstones and wondered whether it was time to have a go with the vacuum cleaner.

Maybe not just yet though. He'd have a cup of coffee first and a biscuit.

Aside from the plug issue, which he'd sort out when Meena came home, he had a feeling housekeeping was going to be a piece of cake. No wonder Meena found so many other things to do with her time, because running a house wasn't exactly arduous, was it? Apart from cooking dinner, just a few minutes a day was all it would take to keep on top of things. Which meant he could spend the rest of the time on the golf course.

Result!

***

Meena expected to see at least some hint that a meal was being cooked when she returned home that evening, but there wasn't a sniff of anything.

'Hello? Oscar?' she called, taking her coat off and hanging it up in the closet under the stairs. She removed her shoes, shoved her feet into her slippers and went into the kitchen.

What the hell? The black bucket, the one she used for swilling the patio down, was sitting in the sink and her rather expensive multi-directional Dyson vacuum was propped up against the fridge. What had Oscar been doing? And where was he now? And why was there no sign of an evening meal when he'd expressly told her that he'd be responsible for all the household chores, including the cooking.

'Oscar!' she called again, but her shout echoed faintly back to her, and she knew that the house was empty.

With an irritated sigh she put her bag on the island which separated the kitchen from the dining area and went over to the vacuum cleaner with the express intention of putting it back where it belonged before it got knocked over. Anyway, she always kept it on charge, so she could whip it out if anything dropped on the floor.

But on feeling a certain grittiness under the soles of her slippers, she realised that Oscar might well have got the vacuum out, but he hadn't *used* it, because the crumbs from this morning were still on the floor.

Eyes narrowed and wondering what else her husband had, or *hadn't*, done, Meena performed a quick tour of the house, and discovered that he'd left a dirty mug on the coffee table in the lounge with yet more crumbs next to it indicating he'd eaten some kind of a snack (biscuits, she suspected), that the loo seat was up (her pet hate) and that he'd not bothered to clean the bathroom.

He'd also left his tracksuit bottoms and the T-shirt he'd been wearing before she'd left this morning draped over the chest of drawers, and she almost tripped over the slippers he'd left on the floor just inside the door.

Not only that, she usually gave the house a good clean on a Sunday morning, not having the time to give it much more than a lick and a promise during the week, but he'd insisted she leave it to him and that he'd do the cleaning today.

He hadn't. Her husband, it seemed, had fallen at the first hurdle.

Crossly, she kicked his slippers across the room, turned on her heel and stomped downstairs. It looked like she'd have to cook dinner after all. And to add insult to injury, he hadn't even bothered to take the steak out of the freezer.

Marvellous. Simply damned marvellous.

***

'What are you doing?' The smell of frying onions and garlic wafted up Oscar's nose as soon as he opened the front door and his mouth watered.

'What does it look like?' Meena was standing at the stove. She had her back to him, stirring the contents of a pan with a wooden spoon, and she didn't turn around.

'I thought I was supposed to be cooking dinner?' he said, puzzled. That *was* the new arrangement, wasn't it? Or had he got it wrong?

'So did I.'

She still hadn't looked at him and Oscar got the impression he was in the doghouse.

'Why are you cooking it?' he asked.

She finally glanced around and he blinked, startled at the annoyance on her face.

'Because *you* aren't,' she said, distinctly.

'I would have done if you'd waited for me to come home.'

She slid a plate across the countertop and rested the wooden spoon on it, then glared at him. 'You know what time I get home from work, and you know I'm going out this evening,' she said. 'I had no idea where you were or how long you were going to be. Oh, wait a minute, forget I said that; I knew *exactly* where you were – playing golf – and I knew how long you were going to be – as long as it takes. So I decided that if I wanted to eat before I went out, I had better cook it myself.'

'But I've come home to do it so you don't have to,' Oscar argued. She'd probably only arrived home ten minutes earlier than him. There was no need for her to make such a song and dance about it.

'I've got to be at the school for six-thirty,' she said.

'Have you? I thought your meeting was later?'

'Is that why you didn't get the steak out of the freezer? You didn't want to risk it defrosting too early?'

Sarcasm dripped from his wife's every word and he winced.

'Is that what we're having, steak?' He craned his neck to see into the pan, but its bubbling red contents didn't look in the least bit like steak. Besides, he liked his grilled not fried, and preferably without a tomato sauce.

'No, we're not having steak.' She turned back to the hob and prodded a fork into another pan. Steam rose from it in billowing clouds. 'Just as a matter of interest, what *were* you planning on cooking for dinner?'

'I… erm… Hell.' *That's* why she was cross – he'd forgotten to take the steak out of the freezer.

'Yes, we were.'

'What's that?'

He pointed to the frying pan. No harm done; they could have the steak tomorrow.

'Spaghetti bolognese – a mushroom version, because there wasn't time to defrost any mince, either.'

Ah. Oh dear, he really was in the doghouse, wasn't he?

Still, he'd had a darned good game of golf, and coming home to find her cooking was just like the old days, when he had a job.

'Sounds good,' he said brightly. 'Shall I lay the table?'

'What makes you think I've cooked enough for two?'

'Oh.' Oscar pressed his lips together.

Damn and blast – his first day on the job and he'd cheesed Meena off already. But it wasn't like her to be so petty.

He started to walk out of the room when he heard her say, 'Lay the table. It'll be ready in fifteen minutes,' and he sighed, realising she'd forgiven him. Vowing to try to do better tomorrow, he got the cutlery out of the drawer, pleased that Meena was making dinner – at least he knew it would be edible!

'What was the bucket doing in the sink?' Meena asked a little later as they were sitting down to eat.

Damn, he'd forgotten to put it back where he'd found it after he'd washed up. 'I couldn't find the plug or a washing up bowl, so I had to use a bucket.'

'What plug? And we don't have a washing up bowl.'

'The plug for the sink.'

Meena frowned. 'We don't have a plug.'

'How do you wash up?' He could have sworn he'd seen her run a sink full of water.

'That's what the dishwasher is for.'

Not wanting to admit that he didn't know how to use it, he said, 'There were only a couple of things, so I thought I'd do them by hand.'

Meena shrugged. 'You don't have to run the wash cycle every time you put something in it. I wait until it's full. But that doesn't explain the bucket.'

'Yes, it does – we've not got a plug.'

'We have.'

'Where is it?'

Meena looked at him as though he were an imbecile. 'It's in the sink.'

'It's not. I checked.'

'Have you moved it?' she asked. 'It was there last night.'

'I haven't touched it,' Oscar protested.

Meena finished her last mouthful, and with an exaggerated sigh she got to her feet and checked for herself, peering into the sink. When she turned to him, she was holding the silver thing with holes in it. 'Here it is. See?' she said. 'Did you push it in all the way? Because if you didn't, the water will seep out.'

He wanted to tell her that the water would seep out anyway because the thing she was holding had *holes* in it, but he had a feeling he might make a prat of himself.

Meena put it back. 'I need to get changed. Please can you clear up and put the dishwasher on? But don't put my best pan in there, you can wash that by hand.'

I could if I knew how to work the dishwasher, he thought.

He waited for Meena to leave the room then he slowly clambered to his feet and peered into the sink. Push the drainer down and it acted like a plug. Pull it up and it allowed the water to drain away. Why hadn't he known about that? And why hadn't he been able to work it out for himself?

Feeling slightly foolish, he sighed deeply.

He'd obviously not been much use around the house in the past if he didn't know how a drainer like this worked. But that was going to change. It might take him a while to do things to the standard that Meena demanded and expected, but he'd get there. He'd have to – because how else could he prove he could still be useful, when the company who had employed him for all those years thought he wasn't?

CHAPTER 6

Meena was in a right grump when she arrived, out-of-sorts and slightly breathless, at the rehearsal for her amateur dramatics society's new production a few days later.

'Hello, you,' Janet said, spying her hurrying in. 'I was beginning to think you weren't coming.'

'So was I. I couldn't find my lines because *someone* had moved them and couldn't remember where he'd moved them to.'

'How *is* Oscar enjoying his retirement?'

'Don't ask. *He* might be enjoying it, but *I'm* not,' Meena stately flatly, taking her lines out of her bag and shuffling them. Her usual method of trying to learn them off by heart had also been scuppered because Oscar had kept interrupting her or asking who she was talking to, so she was feeling woefully underprepared.

'It's only been a week,' Janet said. 'Give it time. It's a big adjustment for you both. I must admit, I'm really looking forward to having Dean at home all day. I can't wait to do all those things we want to do together, but don't have the time.'

She glanced over her shoulder and Meena followed her gaze.

Dean was the director of their amateur dramatics society and was in the middle of setting up the impromptu stage area by the simple act of arranging some chairs into a semi-circle.

Neither Meena nor Janet would be needed for the first scene they were rehearsing this evening, so Meena jerked her head towards the door. 'Shall we grab a cup of tea?'

'Good idea.'

They slipped out of the main hall and made their way along a corridor to the kitchen. *The First Act* rehearsed in the local community hall twice a week. It was only when they were in the final stages of a show did the rehearsals become more frequent and move to the theatre, so they kept a stash of tea, coffee and sugar in one of the cupboards. Thankfully someone had remembered to bring milk.

'It probably doesn't help that you're still working,' Janet observed, getting the mugs out as Meena filled the kettle.

'Oh, believe me, it *does*. If I was at home all day I think I might have dug the patio up by now.'

'Why would you want to dig the patio up?'

'So I can re-lay it, with him under it,' Meena muttered.

Janet laughed. 'It's not that bad, is it?'

'Yes.' Meena was emphatic.

'Do you want to talk about it?'

Meena didn't usually like moaning about her husband – she wasn't the type of person to talk about another behind their back, especially when it was her husband who she wanted to grizzle about – but she felt that if she didn't talk to someone, she might blow a gasket. And Janet had been a dear friend for many years. Meena and Janet had supported each other throughout their children's fraught teenage years, and Meena had been there for her when Janet had unexpectedly become a grandma when her daughter was only seventeen. They'd been through thick and thin together, but the one thing they tried not to do was to slag their husbands off to each other. But Meena was at her wit's end and she simply had to get things off her chest.

'You might want to sit down, as this could take a while,' she warned. 'To be honest, I'm not sure whether it's me, or him. Or both of us.' Burning heat abruptly burgeoned in her chest, rising up her neck and into her face, and she tugged at the collar of her jumper, flapping it to get some air. She knew her face was puce, and she could feel a sheen of sweat spreading across her upper body. Even her scalp felt damp.

'Hot flush?' Janet asked, sympathetically.

Meena nodded, waiting for the sensation to subside before she carried on. 'Damned menopause. I'm fifty-six, for God's sake. You would think it would all be over by now, but no. Anyway, where was I? Oh, yes, Oscar. He's driving me insane.'

'How so?'

Meena rolled her eyes. 'It's nothing major, and that's the problem. It's lots of little things that never mattered when he was out at work all day. Let's face it, we hardly saw each other during the week. He did his own thing and I did mine, and even on Saturdays we didn't always see a great deal of each other.'

'Little things? What kind of little things?'

Meena hardly knew where to begin. 'For starters, he puts the rubbish *next* to the kitchen bin, rather than *in* it because he can't work out the recycling system. I mean, this is a man who used to oversee over a hundred staff and controlled a multi-million-pound budget. Yet he can't figure out whether the newspaper goes in the recycling bin or in the general waste. If he's asked me once, he's asked me twenty times.' She pressed her lips together and shook her head. 'He has always put the rubbish on the counter next to the bin so I suppose I shouldn't be surprised he is still doing it. But although it bugged me before, it's driving me insane now that he's at home all day. Why can't he just put the bloody rubbish in the bloody bin?'

'That's not so bad,' Janet soothed as the kettle came to the boil. She picked it up and poured the water into the mugs.

'There's more,' Meena said, grimly. 'If it was just that, I could cope, but...' She shook her head again. Eye-rolling, head-shaking and deep, heartfelt sighs were becoming an increasingly large part of her daily life, and she'd recently added tutting too.

'If he *remembers* to check the laundry basket, he'll put a load in the machine, I'll give him that. *However*, he either forgets to switch the washing machine on or he forgets to peg the washing out, and I find it still in there a couple of days later smelling all musty and horrid. Or if he *does* remember to peg it out, he forgets to bring it in. Remember the torrential rain we had the other night? I was out the garden in it, in my slippers and dressing gown at two in the morning, fetching the washing in because he'd forgotten to do it. I only noticed it because I got up for a wee and heard the rain lashing against the window, and I looked out to see how bad it was. Imagine my reaction when I saw my smalls flapping about on the line. I had to re-wash everything. I nearly blew my top when Oscar said I should have left it on the line because the forecast was fine for the next day, and it would have dried eventually.' Meena paused for breath, aware that she was ranting.

'Oh, dear…' Janet was chewing at her bottom lip.

'Don't you dare laugh,' Meena warned. 'And as for the ironing – he has no idea how to put the ironing board up, let alone how to use the iron itself. I've taken to waiting until he's in the shower, then quickly ironing a few bits.'

'Why don't you show him what to do?' Janet asked.

'I have,' Meena said through gritted teeth. 'It doesn't seem to sink in. I *told* him not to turn the dial all the way to hot, but he did, and he ruined one of my blouses for work. I swear to God he did it on purpose just to wriggle out of doing any more, but when I said *I'd* do the ironing in future, he got all defensive and cross. So I've taken to doing it behind his back; I've become a secret ironer. This is what I'm having to resort to.' She threw her hands up in the air.

By now Janet was openly laughing and Meena felt her own lips twitch. Before she knew it she was bent over, clutching her sides and wheezing with laughter.

She knew that letting off steam was a good idea, and now she'd managed to verbalise some of her irritation she felt a little better. As she'd listened to herself moaning, she'd realised how petty she sounded.

But after she'd calmed down, she suspected that the little things would be her undoing and, despite the hilarity of the moment, she still couldn't shake off her vexation.

Oscar had better pull his socks up pretty soon because she was getting mighty fed up of pulling them up for him.

***

There was only so much golf one could play, even for him, Oscar thought as he looked at the clock yet again and wondered what time Meena would be home.

Tuesdays and Thursdays were her amateur dramatics evenings. He was well aware that she didn't come home until after ten on those nights. But it had never bothered him in the past.

It bothered him now, though.

Before he'd been forced to retire, on a late spring evening like this one he'd have stayed in work until six, then he would have headed to the golf course to enjoy a couple of hours teeing off, before a quick pint at the *19th Hole* and sometimes a bite to eat if Meena had one of her clubs or meetings.

On other days, when the weather wasn't nice enough or it was too dark to play a game after work and Meena wasn't off out, he would have gone home and eaten dinner with her.

The arrangement had suited them both.

But not now.

He didn't know how Meena felt about it, but he didn't like this new normal one little bit. She was out, more often than not, and he was in. On his own. Alone.

Previously he would have been too tired from a day at the office, with or without the golf afterwards, to do anything more than slump in front of the TV with a G&T or a beer, so if Meena wasn't at home he hadn't minded all that much.

Anyway, even if Meena did stay in, she could never just sit there and watch a programme with him; she had to be *doing* something. Lately that something was knitting for that group she was in. Knit and Natter it was called, and it provided knitted garments for a whole variety of good causes, from tiny hats for premature babies to thick jumpers to send abroad. If Meena was at home in the evening, she'd sit there clicking and clacking away, long steel needles in her hands and a ball of wool in a wicker basket at her feet.

Lately, the noise had begun to irritate him. He hadn't minded it so much before, but he minded it now. Click clack, clack click, on and on it went, and out of the corner of his eye he could see her hands constantly moving, never still.

More often than not her attention was on whatever it was that she was making, and not on the programme. So much for them watching something together. He watched, she listened – *if* she could hear above the sound of those needles clicking together.

But Meena wasn't here tonight. She was out. Again.

He missed having another person in the house. He missed *her*. He even missed the blasted knitting.

Oscar barked out a laugh. Perhaps he should take up knitting himself, so they had something in common? They could discuss patterns and colours, and whatever it was that knitters talked about.

He eyed her knitting basket with dislike and felt like giving it a kick but thought better of it. She'd know if he did; she'd be able to tell. She always did have eyes in the back of her head. It used to come in handy when Anton was little, but now it was just another irritation. At the risk of being crude, Oscar couldn't fart in the house without her knowing about it, even if she was out at the time.

Her eagle eyes were everywhere. As soon as she stepped through the front door, he felt like a soldier when the barracks was being inspected. He almost stood to attention and saluted as her critical gaze took in every tiny detail, from the squashed cushions on the sofa where he'd sat to enjoy a mid-morning cup of tea, to the stray crumbs that had somehow migrated under the microwave when he'd taken his toast out of the toaster, and that he'd forgotten to wipe up.

But still he missed her.

Oscar could never remember feeling as alone as he did now. He'd gone from being so busy he didn't know what to do first, to being so unbusy (if that was a word) that he eked out the chore of folding the clean laundry in order to fill half an hour.

And even then, Meena went behind his back and refolded it.

He knew she did because he'd seen her do it when she'd thought he was otherwise occupied. Towels were her favourite thing to refold. They lived in an alcove in the bathroom where three deep shelves had been installed, and all of them were folded to within an inch of their lives and looking as though they belonged in a posh hotel or in a magazine. Clearly he didn't fold them to her satisfaction so, after the first couple of attempts when he was quite put out that she felt the need to redo them, he'd folded them any old way just to annoy her.

What *had* his life come to? He was obsessing about the way towels were folded? *Really?*

Feeling rebellious, he grabbed a packet of crisps from the cupboard, returned to the living room, ate them noisily, then cast the empty packet to one side. It could stay there. And so could the mug that had contained the cocoa he'd just drank. He was going up to bed: he'd clear it away in the morning.

If it was still there.

Which it wouldn't be.

He'd bet his last penny on that.

***

Meena wasn't late; it was only ten-past ten, so she was surprised to find the living room empty and no lights on apart from the little table lamp in the corner of the living room.

Oscar must have gone to bed already.

It was most unlike him. He usually waited up for her, sprawled across the sofa, watching the match or some other sport, a glass in his hand, his feet propped annoyingly on the coffee table.

His feet were absent, as was he, but he'd left a dirty mug and an empty crisp packet in their stead, and she took her ire out by aggressively plumping up the cushions in the living room.

Tutting loudly, when she was done plumping she grabbed the mug and the empty packet and carried them into the kitchen. Was it so much trouble to put a mug in the dishwasher and the rubbish in the bin?

Clearly it was, because she found a used plate on the countertop next to the sink and an apple core on the counter next to the bin.

Her tutting became louder.

Before Oscar had retired he'd do things like this all the time. But it hadn't bothered her then. She'd taken it in her stride, accepted it as her lot. She also bore in mind that he didn't use to make half the amount of mess that he made now, because he simply hadn't been at home for much of the time. She could leave the house in the morning as neat and as tidy as a new pin and know it would be in exactly the same state when she arrived home. Meena rarely made a mess. Any messes were down to Oscar. Whilst he had been at work all day, she could cope with the odd bit of mess from him in the evening and on the weekend, but now that he was at home and especially since he was the one who should be doing the clearing up, it got on her nerves.

She tutted for a third time and added a shake of her head for good measure.

After a quick scan of the ground floor of the house, where she noted the lack of spare loo roll in the downstairs bathroom, the dirty footprints on the mat by the back door, and sundry other things that Oscar needed to do tomorrow, she made her way up the stairs, her feet dragging, her heart heavy.

Meena had anticipated retiring at the same time as Oscar. She hadn't expected him to retire early and for her to carry on working. And neither had she thought about what their lives might be like when they had to spend all day together. In the back of her mind, if she'd thought about it at all, she'd assumed she'd carry on much as she did now when it came to her hobbies and interests. And she'd assumed Oscar would spend most of his time on the golf course.

Having him in the house all the time, and under her feet when she was home, was seriously getting on her nerves. She wasn't used to it. She wasn't used to *him!*

Oh, my, God. Meena paused halfway up the stairs. Had they become strangers living in the same house? Surely not…

Meena knew Oscar inside out, and he knew her. They mightn't live in each other's pockets, unlike some couples, and they had their own busy lives outside their marriage, but that didn't mean they were strangers.

Did it?

Of course not, she decided. They might not have the passion they once had, but they *had* been married for over thirty years, and she realised that relationships could and did change over time. They had a good marriage, didn't they?

She shook her head, to free it of those silly thoughts. Of course, they did. Their marriage was fine. Nothing wrong with it.

Every couple had their blips, and this was one of theirs. As Janet had said, Meena had to give it time. This was new for both her and Oscar, and it would take a while to get into a new way of living together.

Her problem was that she'd had sole dominion over the house ever since they were married. She had taken charge of everything from the cooking and cleaning, the laundry and the gardening, the DIY (she usually got a man in to do anything more than changing a lightbulb), and the admin. Oscar had never had to even think about whether the car needed to go in for an MOT, let alone book it into the garage or drop it off. He'd never needed to – she'd done it all.

She'd also reared Anton, more or less single-handedly. It was she who had got up in the night with their son when he was poorly, she who had taken him to after-school clubs, and she who had attended parents' evenings. She'd been the disciplinarian, too. Oscar had had the nice parts – reading him a story at bedtime, taking him to the park for a kick around, teaching him how to play golf. He'd spent time with Anton, quality time. He hadn't had to try to persuade the boy to eat his greens, or ground him, or wrestle his Gameboy out of his grip because it was late and he should be asleep.

But neither had she begrudged Oscar the role he played, either in their son's upbringing or in the house in general.

They had their separate responsibilities, and they each knew where they stood and what was expected of them.

The way she and Oscar did things mightn't be to everyone's taste, but it worked for them.

Until now…

Meena crept across the landing, not wanting to disturb Oscar if he was asleep, and slipped into the bathroom. As she pulled the dangling cord, bright, white light bounced back off the large mirror above the sink and the stark white tiles, and it took her a moment for her eyes to adjust. But when they did, she had an urge to scream.

Oscar had shaved in the bath, leaving a dirty rim around its sides which were coated in tiny hairs. More of them lay in the bottom of the bath, mocking her.

She'd been planning on having a quick soak with a cupful of her favourite bubbles and a scented candle, but she'd now have to clean the bath first. And the wash hand basin, she saw, as she noticed several blobs of toothpaste on its porcelain surface.

And he'd left the toilet seat up again, which meant that when he'd flushed, thousands of tiny droplets had been released into the air and had probably settled on every surface, including her toothbrush.

Ugh!

Hastily, she rooted around in the cupboard and found a new one. The old one was relegated to the pedal bin in the corner. As she was brushing her teeth, she made a note to look for a case for hers, and to make doubly sure, she'd keep it in the cupboard and not leave it in the stainless-steel holder.

That holder was far too near the toilet for her liking – she'd read somewhere that aerosols from a flush could travel as much as six feet.

Double ugh!

Oscar was on his back, snoring, when she was finally ready for bed a half an hour later. She hadn't been able to leave the bathroom in that state, she simply hadn't, so she'd given it a good clean, and by the time she'd done that she no longer felt like having a bath. She'd had her fill of water for tonight, what with all the scrubbing and swilling she'd done to force those stubborn little hairs down the plughole, so all she did was wash her hands and face, change into her nightie and get into bed. Where she lay for quite some time, praying that things would get better, but worrying that maybe they wouldn't.

CHAPTER 7

'Mow the lawn and cut the bushes back,' Meena had said to Oscar before she'd left for work that morning. Over the course of the previous two weeks since he'd officially been in charge of the house, Oscar had taken to asking her each day if there was anything in particular she wanted him to do, because he was fed up trying to guess.

Aside from the obvious, such as clearing up after meals and emptying the laundry basket on a regular basis (although he'd had a couple of washing-related disasters that he didn't want to dwell on) he honestly didn't see a great deal else that needed doing.

And that was where the problem lay, he'd begun to realise – he simply didn't see what Meena saw. Or if he did see it, it didn't register. Which was hardly surprising since she'd had decades to perfect this housekeeping lark. Besides, old habits were hard to break, and he wasn't used to having to check whether the oven needed cleaning, for instance – that had been yesterday's job, and it had taken him most of the morning by the time he'd figured out how to remove the glass plates in the door. Getting them back in had been fraught, as he'd been terrified of dropping them. Meena had had to tell him it needed doing, otherwise he wouldn't have noticed.

Even the garden had been Meena's domain, although he would mow the lawn if she asked him. But he used to have to be reminded several times before he would get around to doing it and more often than not, Meena would have become fed up with waiting and would have gone ahead and mowed it herself. He felt guilty about that as she wasn't getting any younger, but he'd always been so busy. And she had always been perfectly capable of mowing. Their electric mower was a breeze to use, and the lawn wasn't that big.

Oscar stepped into the garden and put his hands on his hips as he studied the bushes. Immediately outside the patio doors was a paved area with a table and six chairs. A large umbrella stood to the side, folded neatly into its plastic cover. Beyond the patio was the lawn, edged on three sides by an assortment of bushes and shrubs.

As he examined them, he tilted his head and narrowed his eyes.

Surely they hadn't been this overgrown the last time he'd sat out in the garden which, if he remembered rightly, was only two days ago. He'd taken his elevenses out there and basked in the early summer warmth. But he could have sworn the greenery had been less exuberant.

The fence that enclosed the garden was completely obscured by luscious growth and it was encroaching outwards into the lawn. Every shrub and bush probably needed a good four foot lobbed off it to open up the garden, and he'd better take some off the height too, to let more light in.

He'd do that first, clear away the fallen branches and stems, then get the mower out.

At least this was something he was confident of not messing up, so with a spring in his step and a whistle on his puckered lips, he set to it.

***

Oscar had just had a shower and was about to get changed for golf, when he stopped dead in the bedroom doorway.

Meena had re-made the bed.

He could tell because the pillows had been straightened and so had the cushions, although why any bed *needed* cushions on it was a mystery. Cushions were for sofas and armchairs, weren't they? He could understand them being on the bed if they were used, but these weren't. They were purely for show and were religiously removed every night before going to bed. And who were they on show for, he wondered? Only he and Meena saw their bedroom and he couldn't care less about them. But Meena did, and she'd found his bed-making to be not good enough.

Now that he came to think about it, he suspected she'd been remaking the bed every morning.

Crossly, he rubbed his wet hair and dropped the towel on the duvet. If his bed-making wasn't up to scratch, then she could darned well do it herself tomorrow. See how she liked that.

He dragged a pair of golfing slacks up his legs and fastened them, but as he did so he noticed that they were snugger than usual, so he walked over to the full-length mirror and turned sideways.

He sucked his gut in, then let it out. In, then out.

Yep, as he thought, he'd only been retired for two weeks and he was already starting to put on weight.

Oscar narrowed his eyes at his reflection. He'd have to do something about that, but what…? Golf obviously wasn't enough.

Swimming? He wasn't too keen on chlorine – he smelled enough of the stuff at home. Meena was the queen of bleach; she used it everywhere. He was surprised she didn't douse *him* in it.

Hiking? No fun on your own. He could always suggest that Meena go with him, but when was she going to fit it into her busy schedule?

Squash? Badminton? Tennis? Too energetic. He fancied a less frantic form of exercise, especially when starting out. Golf had always been enough to keep the pounds off, but he'd been working as well, hurrying here and there, attending stand-up meetings (at least by standing up it ensured that the meetings were kept short), walking around the factory to make sure everything was running smoothly, dashing off to deal with a crisis or two… He'd been at it non-stop.

The only thing he was doing non-stop these days was staring at daytime TV once he'd done his chores, or wandering around the supermarket with a list in his hand. Meena wrote the lists, of course, and she decided what meals they ate. But now that he was doing the lion's share of the cooking (under supervision), surely he should make the decision about what he was going to cook each night? To his surprise and delight, he was turning into a decent cook, although his repertoire was so far limited to anything out of a jar, usually with pasta. And grilling stuff – he was fairly good at that, which he put down to being in charge of the barbeque throughout the course of many summers.

Oscar sucked his stomach in one last time and held it there while he pulled a clean polo shirt over his head, followed by a jumper. It could be a bit drafty on the course and he hated being cold because it affected his swing if he was tense.

Realising the time and knowing that if he didn't get a move on he was going to be late, he shoved his feet into a pair of trainers, grabbed his golf shoes and went downstairs. He'd have a quick drink of water because he was thirsty after all that gardening, and then he'd dash off.

It was as he was filling his glass that he spotted several clumps of dirt near the patio doors and a trail of footprints leading into the kitchen and coming to an end when they reached the old shoes he'd used for gardening. The area directly underneath the overgrown bushes had been more soil than grass and as he'd trimmed and pruned, he'd churned it up a little.

Damn it! He didn't have time to clean it up now. He'd do it when he got home later. He'd have plenty of time.

***

As Meena pulled onto their drive she noticed that Oscar's car wasn't there, and she breathed a sigh of relief. He was almost certainly out playing golf, which meant she'd be on her own in the house for a few precious hours.

The first thing she'd do would be to change into her scruffy clothes, make a cup of tea, then do some baking for the WI's stall at the church's bring-and-buy sale tomorrow. She usually worked on Friday afternoons, but she'd stayed until the surgery closed at six-thirty yesterday because a member of staff had been off sick, so she'd decided to take the hours she was owed today, hoping that Oscar would be where he usually was in the afternoon – on the golf course.

It looked as though her gamble had paid off, and the house was blissfully silent when she stepped into the hall. It was awful of her, but sometimes she resented not having the house to herself.

Only sometimes?

It was more like all the time, but she had been so used to Oscar not being there, that having him continually at home was starting to grate on her. The weekends were different to a certain extent because she was more geared up for his presence, and she was also out a fair bit herself what with Saturday being the only day she could go shopping, have her hair cut, have a manicure, or simply have a coffee and a chat with friends. And occasionally she and Oscar would do something together, like visit a country house, or take a walk along the canal and have lunch out in a quaint pub.

Sundays were for Anton and his family, although she hadn't seen her son for a couple of weeks because they'd been on holiday in Majorca. Lovely at this time of year. Not too hot for the kids, although her daughter-in-law might have appreciated it being a little hotter. Grace was a sun-lover and she enjoyed nothing more than lying on a lounger with a good book, whilst Anton entertained the kiddies in the pool.

Hopefully, Meena would see them this Sunday, and she was already planning a roast with all the trimmings, which she would cook. Oscar was starting to find his way around the kitchen but there was no way she was going to entrust him with a joint of beef. It would either be burnt to a crisp or so rare a good vet could get it going again.

'For goodness' sake,' she muttered, spotting a pile of dirty clothes on the bathroom floor.

For someone who was supposed to be in charge of the house, he was doing a pretty poor job if he couldn't even pick up his own clothes and put them in the laundry basket. Although why he hadn't taken them off in the utility room and put them straight into the washing machine was beyond her. He'd worn them when he was cutting the shrubs back, she guessed, because there was mud on the hem of the trousers, and when she nudged them with her foot, she noticed a sprinkling of leaves and twigs on the floor underneath which must have become caught up in his clothing and had subsequently fallen out when he'd stripped off.

She left the mess there for the moment, intending to change out of her work clothes first. But when she saw a wet towel dumped on the bed and noticed the damp patch it had left on the duvet cover, she was hard pushed not to phone him and give him a piece of her mind.

Far from enjoying an afternoon of baking, she was now going to have to strip the duvet cover off and dry it, plus dry the duvet itself, because the dampness had soaked through. As well as that, she'd have to vacuum the bathroom floor and brush the mud off his gardening clothes before she put them in the washing machine.

Which reminded her…Meena glanced out of the window to see how he'd got on in the garden. If he hadn't finished yet, he might as well wear the same clothes tomorrow to save dirtying another set. What she saw made her feel like crying. Oscar had cut the bushes back all right. There was little left of them except for some bare twigs.

Putting a hand to her mouth, she felt like crying. They'd only needed topping and about half a metre of pruning. Instead, they looked as though they'd been attacked by a maniac with a chainsaw. All her beautiful plants, carefully chosen for their summer blooms and sweet scent, were nothing more than pathetic stumps and the odd bare branch. Had he missed them, she wondered, or had he left them there deliberately to taunt her?

Would they grow back?

She bloody hoped so, otherwise she'd be paying the garden centre a visit soon, and she'd also be paying a man to put them in for her – because there was no way she'd trust Oscar to plant even so much as a dandelion after this.

Her once-lovely garden, the fence hidden by lush green bushes, had been decimated. The ugly fence was visible, the edge of the lawn had been churned into a muddy mush, and he'd left branches, twigs and leaves all over the place. The patio was covered in debris, and she'd only brushed it last week. It needed doing again, or it would get trodden into the house.

Meena quickly changed into old clothes, muttering darkly as she did so. Then she removed the damp duvet cover and shoved it into the laundry basket. Now she'd started, she may as well go the whole hog, strip the bed off and put fresh linen on. It would be one less task for Oscar to cock up.

Quickly she re-made the bed, inhaling the delicious scent of freshly laundered sheets, and scooped up the used bed linen from the floor and went downstairs. She'd stuff this lot into the washing machine, then she'd sort out Oscar's gardening clothes and the mess he'd left for her in the bathroom.

But when she entered the open-plan kitchen-diner and saw the mess he'd left for her in there, she really did feel like crying.

Instead of going into the garden via the utility, Oscar had only gone and used the patio doors, and he'd left clumps of mud and earth on the floor, along with a trail of dirty footprints leading from the door, across the dining area, through the kitchen and into the utility – where she discovered his shoes, which were placed neatly side-by-side in front of the very door he should have used.

'Dear God, give me strength,' she whispered, feeling like crying once more. Didn't she have enough to do without coming home to this? She was spending more time cleaning up after Oscar now than she'd ever done, and she was supposed to have been relieved of all household chores.

If this was how it was going to be from now on, Meena wasn't sure she could cope with it.

And when a hot flush swept through her, burning her from the inside out and leaving her feeling sick and slick with sweat, she burst into tears.

***

Friday afternoons on the golf course were traditionally when Oscar and his colleagues got together to strengthen bonds, hash out deals and iron out problems. Unfortunately, he no longer had colleagues whose bonds he needed to strengthen and the only ironing he was able to do was with the aid of an ironing board (although why Meena insisted that fitted sheets needed to be ironed was a mystery). So it wasn't long before he began to feel out of the loop.

Last Friday, the first since he'd left the company, hadn't been so bad because many of his former colleagues had walked up to him for a chat and to congratulate him on his retirement; he hadn't let on that retirement hadn't been his choice and that it had been thrust upon him. Some of them were aware of the circumstances, but even those people pretended that it had been his decision to leave, and they joked that he must be loving life now that he had all day every day in which to play golf and do whatever he liked.

Little did they know that his wife was a female version of Attila the Hun and that her exacting standards were higher than the chief housekeeper at Buckingham Palace, and that if he didn't do things the way she wanted them done, woe betide him.

As he waited to tee-off, he picked at the long scratch on his forearm that had been dealt him by a sharp branch, and listened in dismay to snippets of conversation between the men he was playing with today, and abruptly he felt excluded and surplus to requirements. It shocked him to think how fast things had moved on in the world of work.

Only two weeks away from it and his former colleagues were already discussing new projects and new procedures. Whereas in the past he might have been deferred to, or his opinion sought at the very least, now it was as though he were a ghost.

He might as well not be there for all the notice they were taking of him, and whenever he tried to join in or ask a question, he was brushed off with 'it's a new thing they've brought in – you wouldn't understand' or 'it's a bit hush-hush'.

Anyone would think they were trading international secrets or information of national security, Oscar thought sullenly, taking his frustration out with a particularly aggressive swing that saw his ball go flying into the rough.

'Oh, bad luck,' someone said.

Oscar ignored the comment and stomped off to try to retrieve it, along with his composure. He found it particularly galling because he'd been looking forward to this all week. He'd seen it as a way of staying in touch and involved in his pre-retirement life, but the only thing he felt now was humiliated and inconsequential. And as he located his ball and selected the correct club, he darkly marvelled at how swiftly he'd become irrelevant. For these people, from the moment he'd left the building for the final time it was as though he'd never worked there at all.

As he shuffled into position, making half-hearted practice swings, he felt like crying. All those years he'd given to the company, all the sacrifices he'd made, all the enthusiasm and dedication he'd poured into his job and all the pride he'd taken in it, had been for nothing. At the end of the day and when push came to shove, he had been nothing more than a payroll number. And now look at him…

Maybe he'd forgo the regular Friday afternoon round of golf in the future. He had nothing to contribute, and from the way they'd wandered off and left him on his own to dibble around in the long grass, they didn't want him there.

Oscar straightened up and watched them go. Quietly and without any fuss, he returned the club he was holding to the caddy and picked up his ball.

Maybe it was time he took up a different hobby.

***

Oscar's heart sank when he saw Meena's car on the drive and he slapped a palm to his forehead. Darn it, he'd forgotten she'd told him she'd be home early today. He'd been hoping for an hour or so alone to lick his wounds. He felt like an old sheepdog who'd been left behind in the barn whilst the younger dogs had gone out to round up the ewes. Useless, good for nothing and a burden. He wasn't in the best frame of mind to deal with his wife right now, so he sat in the car for a while until he noticed the woman from three doors up on the opposite side of the road peering at him through her living room window.

With a sigh he clambered out, taking his golfing equipment into the garage where he looked at it sadly.

He enjoyed a game of golf, but he wasn't sure he would return to the green any time soon. The men who he had once sat in meetings with, who he had downed pints with, had shaken hands with, seemed to have turned their backs on him and had effectively cut him out of their lives.

With a heavy heart, he locked the garage and went inside the house, to find Meena with the mop out.

Damn! He'd forgotten about that. 'I was going to do it when I came home,' he began, then stopped when he saw her face.

'Don't. Just… *don't.*' She continued mopping, squeezing mud-coloured water out of the sponge until most of it was gone.

He watched her pick the bucket up and walk into the utility room and heard the sound of running water. When she returned to the kitchen-diner, she still had the bucket in her hand, but this time it was full of clean, hot soapy water.

'Let me,' he offered, holding out his hand.

Meena ignored him.

Oscar tried again. 'I was going to do it, honest,' he said. 'But I was running late for golf.'

His wife stopped what she was doing and leant on the mop, both hands resting on the end of the pole. Her knuckles were white.

'There's one thing I don't understand,' she said, her voice deceptively quiet, and he cringed, guessing she was seriously annoyed with him. But, good grief, it was only a bit of dirt. It would have taken him two minutes to wipe it up, yet Meena insisted on making a song and dance about it.

'What?' he asked, against his better judgement.

'Why didn't you use the door to the utility room?'

'The door—? *Ah*. I... um... didn't think.'

'Unbelievable,' she muttered.

'I'm sorry, OK?'

'No, it's not OK! I come home from work hoping to do some baking, and I find this.' She swept her arm around the almost pristine floor. 'And that!' She flung the same arm out in the direction of the utility room.

Oscar tried to think what she might be referring to, but he honestly couldn't think of anything. The washing machine was chundering in the background, but she couldn't possibly be referring to him failing to do any laundry because he knew for a fact there was no washing to be done because he'd done it all yesterday. *And* he'd remembered to peg it out and bring it in when it was dry. The only thing he hadn't done yet was to iron it, and he was waiting until he'd plucked up the courage to get the blasted iron out. Out of all the jobs he'd done around the house these past two weeks, ironing had to be his least favourite, swiftly followed by almost everything else. Although strangely enough, he didn't mind cleaning out the fridge...

'What do you mean?' he asked, puzzled.

'I've had to change the sheets on our bed.'

'Why?'

'Because you left a wet towel on it. The duvet was damp, and the cover was wet,' she said.

'It would have dried. There was no need to change the sheets,' he pointed out.

As if speaking to a child, she said slowly, 'I don't want to sleep under a damp duvet or a wet cover, so I thought I'd better change them.'

'That's your choice to put fresh sheets on,' he said bluntly. 'Not my fault.'

'If you hadn't left a wet towel on the bed, I wouldn't have had to make a choice. And I certainly didn't have a choice when I cleaned up the mess you left on the bathroom floor.'

'What mess?' Oscar was genuinely perplexed.

'You left your gardening clothes on the floor and there were leaves and twigs everywhere. And as for the garden...' She pursed her lips.

Clearly he hadn't done that right, either. 'You *asked* me to cut them back,' he protested. What the hell had he done wrong this time?

'Cut them, not decimate them. Have you seen the state of them? You hacked them off almost down to ground level.'

He might have been a bit over-enthusiastic, he admitted, but they didn't look too bad. And they'd grow back. Eventually. He'd got a bit carried away, that was all. There was no need for Meena to get so annoyed.

'They'll grow back,' he said.

'Are you doing this on purpose?' his wife demanded. 'If you don't want to do the housework, just say so. I'm perfectly capable of doing it myself and I'm getting fed up of having to go behind you and do it properly.'

Oscar snapped. It was all right for her, she still had a job to go to and all those groups and societies she was a member of. Her life hadn't changed in the slightest, unlike his. His world had been turned upside down, and he felt as though he had no purpose any more.

'Do it yourself then,' he retorted. 'If I'm so bloody useless, you can do everything yourself. Nothing is ever good enough for you, is it? I've been trying my best but it's not enough. I quit. You make me feel like a lodger in my own home, always getting under your feet, always having to obey one stupid rule or another. And by the way,' he said, as his parting shot. 'I didn't iron the fitted sheet. So there!'

And with that, he turned on his heel and stormed out.

He would go back to the golf course, but he had no intention of playing a round. He was going to park himself in the 19th Hole and have a pint. Several, in fact. He'd get a taxi home, and if he got blotto and was sick on her rhododendrons, then so be it.

He'd had enough!

***

Meena stared at the door in disbelief. What had just happened? One minute they'd been arguing over the state of the garden – the next minute he'd stormed out. What on earth had got into him?

Oscar had never had a temper. He'd never walked out on her before. They'd their fair share of arguments, but not once had her husband walked out in the middle of one.

And what was all that nonsense about feeling like a lodger?

Tears prickling at the back of her eyes, Meena put the mop away and went upstairs to tackle the bathroom floor.

But as she vacuumed, all she could think about was how could their previously serene and ordered lives have deteriorated so suddenly.

Abruptly, she propped the vacuum against the bath and hurried downstairs to find her phone.

'Are you free for a chat?' she asked, as soon as Janet answered.

'Are you all right? You sound upset.'

'Oscar and I have just had the most horrendous row. He's walked out, and I've no idea where he's gone.'

'I'm sure he'll be back soon,' Janet said. 'In the meantime, do you want me to pop round?'

'Would you? I'd be ever so grateful.'

'Grateful enough to provide tea and cake?'

'It's the least I can do.'

Meena kept herself busy while she waited for Janet to arrive by finishing the cleaning and whipping up a couple of cakes, and she'd just put them in the oven when the doorbell rang.

'Come here,' Janet said when Meena opened the door, and she swept her into a hug.

Meena bit her lip, willing herself not to cry. This was ridiculous – she wasn't a crier, but over the last couple of weeks there had been more than one occasion where tears had been perilously close to the surface, and she'd already broken down once today. It was most unlike her.

Janet pulled back, held her at arm's length and studied her face. 'Now, are you going to tell me what all this is about?'

'I'm not coping with him being at home all the time,' Meena confessed. 'He says he wants to do all the housework so I don't have to because I'm still working, but he's making such a hash of it…' She paused. 'I swear to God he's doing it on purpose.'

'What's he done, or not done, now?'

'Come with me and I'll show you.' Meena led Janet into the kitchen and took her over to the patio doors and pointed. 'Take a look at what he's done to my lovely shrubs.'

Janet pulled a face. 'Oh dear, they don't look very happy, do they?'

'They most certainly do not, and neither am I. And that's not all – you ought to have seen the mess he made all over the floor in here, and in the bathroom. And he left a wet towel on the bed, so I had to put fresh sheets on and turn the heating on to air the duvet because it's too big to fit in the tumble dryer.'

Janet blew out her cheeks. 'Have you got the heating on now?'

'I've just turned it off.'

'I thought it was warm in here, but I assumed I was having a hot flush.' Janet fanned her face with her hands.

'Getting older is a bummer, isn't it?' Meena said, flicking the switch on the coffee machine. 'Don't get me wrong, I'm grateful to have made it this far, but I could do without the menopause.'

'Me, too.' Janet's reply was heartfelt, then she returned to the subject under discussion. 'Why didn't he clean it up? Or didn't he realise he'd made a mess? Dean can be a bit like that sometimes. If he puts a curtain pole up, or hangs a picture, he doesn't think to vacuum after he drills a hole in the wall. I'm not sure whether he simply doesn't notice the plaster dust all over the floor, or whether he thinks the cleaning fairy – aka, me – will magically do it for him.'

'He knew he'd left the house in a state,' Meena said, 'but he said that if he'd cleaned it up, he'd have been late for golf. I swear that's the only thing he's interested in these days.'

'At least he's interested in *something*,' Janet said. 'It's good that he has a hobby.'

Meena sighed. 'I suppose you're right, and I can hardly begrudge him that considering I have so many that I don't know where to start. Did I tell you I was making a quilt?'

'No?'

'Remind me to show you later. Instead of hanging on to all of Anton's baby clothes, I got the idea off the internet to cut them up and make a keepsake quilt out of them. It's better than letting them rot away in the attic and I'll get to see all those lovely fabrics every day.'

'Do you ever sit down and just *be*?'

'Not really.'

Meena had tried, but she couldn't seem to manage it. It seemed such a waste of precious time, when she could be doing something useful with it.

Janet sniffed the air. 'Something smells good.'

'I've got a couple of cakes in the oven for the WI tomorrow. Let's have that cuppa I promised you, and I'll cut you a slice of the lemon drizzle I made the other day.'

Once they were seated at the dining table with plates of deliciously aromatic cake and a mug of coffee in front of them, Meena took a deep breath.

'Do you think I'm overreacting?' she asked.

'It's hard to say. I'm not in your shoes. What winds you up, I'm not bothered about; but similarly, you might let slide the things that get my goat.'

'I'm so used to doing everything myself that it's been a bit of a shock. I don't expect him to do things the way I do them, but…'

'Don't you?'

Meena had been tempted to bristle at her friend's insinuation, but Janet's voice was kind and Meena knew she was coming from a good place. Besides, if Meena was being honest, Janet might have a point.

'Maybe just a little,' she conceded.

Janet raised her eyebrows.

'OK, maybe more than a little. But is it too much to ask?'

'I think it might be,' Janet said gently. 'You can be a bit of a perfectionist.'

'Is that such a bad thing?'

'Not if you do it yourself,' Janet said, 'but if someone else is doing it and they're not doing it to your satisfaction, then it could be a problem.'

'I've been a bit harsh, haven't I?' Meena acknowledged.

Janet held up her thumb and forefinger a centimetre apart. 'Just a smidge.'

'Blast. I'd better apologise.'

'I think you should.'

'But he needs to apologise to me too,' Meena said. 'He did leave the house in a state, for me to come home to.'

'Maybe you need to be a little more patient with each other?' Janet suggested. 'Oscar is probably finding it just as difficult.'

Meena shrugged. 'I suppose. He does seem to be at somewhat of a loose end. He needs to take up another hobby besides golf. I don't think he's got enough to do during the day. Or in the evenings for that matter,' she added. 'It doesn't help that I'm often out in the evening, or that when I am at home I have things to do, like baking or knitting.' She picked up her fork and teased a portion of cake off and put it in her mouth. 'Even if I do say so myself, this cake is delicious.'

'It certainly is,' Janet agreed, her own mouth full.

'I get the feeling Oscar doesn't like me knitting,' Meena confided. 'I've caught him giving me a couple of sideways glances, every so often. And he gets rather cross when he says 'did you just see that?' about something on the telly and I wasn't looking because I was concentrating on a tricky bit in the pattern. But I can't just sit there,' she said. 'I need to be doing something.'

'Why don't you get away for a few days?' Janet suggested. 'A break would do you both good and might help you reconnect.'

'I had thought of booking a holiday, but then Oscar told me he was having to take early retirement and until his pension was sorted out I didn't think spending that amount of money would be a good idea.'

'It doesn't have to be a fortnight's all-inclusive abroad jobbie. You could have a break in this country.'

Meena let out a breath. 'I hadn't thought of that. What a good idea!'

'I have my moments,' Janet smirked, dabbing her fork onto her plate to catch the last few crumbs of cake. 'Where will you go?'

'I'm not sure,' Meena said. 'But there's one thing I do know – there won't be a golf course within a hundred miles. How about you stay for dinner and you can help me choose somewhere? Unless Dean expects you home?'

'Dean can sort himself out,' Janet said. 'I don't intend to miss up the offer of a free meal, especially one I don't have to cook.'

Meena beamed at her. 'Great! I'll open a bottle of wine, shall I?'

Maybe a few days away was what she and Oscar needed, she thought, and she felt more optimistic than she'd done since he'd given her the bad news.

***

Oscar wasn't blotto, but he'd definitely had too much to drink. He felt a little woozy and his tummy wasn't the best. He was having trouble fitting his key in the front door, and for a panicked second he worried that Meena had changed the locks.

Ah, there we are, he thought, relief flooding through him as the key turned and the door swung open.

He staggered into the hall, shushing himself with a finger to his lips. The last thing he wanted to do was to wake his wife.

'Let shleeping dragons lie,' he slurred, heading towards the kitchen and banging against the wall. 'Shhhh.'

After downing a glass of water, which made his tummy feel worse, he went upstairs, pausing halfway up to sit down and take his shoes off, remembering at the last minute that Meena didn't like outdoor shoes on her carpets. Although walking on the rugs downstairs was fine, apparently – go figure.

There were so many rules in this house it was like being in prison.

Grumpily, he peeled his clothes off in the bathroom, folded them carefully and balanced the pile on the edge of the bath. Then promptly knocked them off again when he turned around to clean his teeth.

Oscar stared at the heap of discarded clothing. Knickers to picking them up, he thought as he recalled what he'd said to his wife earlier – Meena could do it. If she liked cleaning and tidying so much, then let her pick them up.

He bet none of his friends' wives or partners gave their other halves as much grief as Meena gave him. It was coming to the point where he was beginning to feel like a nuisance in his own home – unwelcome, useless and surplus to requirements.

Without making any further effort to be quiet, he careened into the bedroom, hitting both sides of the door frame with his shoulders as he did so, and launched himself onto the bed, feeling it bounce underneath him as his full body weight landed on it.

Only then did he realise that Meena wasn't in it.

He reached across the mattress, patting her side as though he expected her to be hiding under an invisibility cloak.

Her side of the bed was pristine, cold and empty. It looked as though she hadn't got in it at all this evening, and he wondered where she could be. He was pretty certain she wasn't downstairs, so maybe she was in the spare room.

Oscar sat up, bewildered and more than a little worried.

In all the years he and Meena had been married, she'd never once slept in the spare room, no matter how vigorously they'd argued.

Things must be really bad between them for her to not want to share a bed with him.

His heart heavy, Oscar heaved himself out of bed and stood beside it for a moment to get his balance. He was aware he was starkers, having forgotten to put on his pyjamas, but he didn't care, although he wished he'd thought to find his slippers when he stubbed his toe on the corner of the dressing table.

Cursing under his breath, he tottered across the landing, intending to have it out with her, and yanked at the door handle of the spare room.

The door flew open and as it did so he slapped a hand on the light switch.

Light flooded the room and he saw his wife, who was bundled up under the covers, begin to stir.

Except… it wasn't his wife, he realised in horror.

Oscar shielded his privates from view at the exact same moment their good friend Janet sat up in their spare bed and began to shriek.

Oh, hell…!!

CHAPTER 8

Meena took a carrot out of the paper bag and snorted crossly as she began to peel it. She'd been cross since she'd got up this morning, although she'd tried not to show her annoyance in front of Janet. Oscar had remained upstairs thankfully, so at least Janet had been spared the embarrassment of having to make small talk with him across the breakfast table.

He still hadn't emerged when Meena said goodbye to her, so Meena was now taking her irritation out on a carrot. Several actually, because she was about to make a moist and fragrant carrot cake.

Poor Janet, Meena thought as she peeled another. She would never forget the look on her friend's face. Or the expression on Oscar's, for that matter.

Janet had looked appalled. Oscar had looked mortified. And both of them had been embarrassed. Meena didn't think she'd seen anyone sober up as quickly as Oscar had. He'd gone from bumbling about downstairs, mumbling to himself and saying 'shush' every now and again, to shouting heartfelt apologies through the wall after he'd scuttled into their bedroom to frantically don some clothes. Luckily Janet had seen the funny side – although that wasn't the only thing she'd seen last night – and she'd hopefully chuckled herself back to sleep after a restorative mug of cocoa and more sincere and abject apologies from Oscar.

Oscar had slunk off back to bed, unable to bear the shame of Janet seeing him in his altogether, leaving Meena to tidy her sewing away and check that the house was secure.

Aside from the incident being extremely embarrassing, it was also rather troubling. Never once had Meena slept in the spare room, not even when Anton was little. If he'd been poorly, she'd snuggled in with him, in his bed, but that had been a rare occurrence, as he had been a healthy and robust child. So why did Oscar think she'd taken herself off to the spare room last night?

None if it would have happened if Oscar hadn't spent the evening propping up the bar at the golf course. Janet had asked Dean to keep an eye out for him, and he'd reported back that Oscar was drowning his sorrows and would most likely be the worse for wear by the time he returned home.

By that point, Meena had cooked her and Janet a meal and had opened the bottle of wine. And because Janet had drunk a couple of glasses, Meena had suggested she stay the night.

But when Janet had retired to bed, Meena hadn't felt at all tired and she hadn't drunk much of the wine either, so with worry about her marriage filling her mind, she'd occupied her hands with sewing, and had been in her workroom when she'd heard Oscar arrive home.

'Will Janet tell Dean, do you think?' Oscar asked, walking gingerly into the kitchen. He looked awful, green around the gills, unshaven, and rumpled. He had a crease down the side of his face where his cheek had been pressed against a pillow and he was walking like an old man.

'I expect so,' she replied shortly, before taking pity on him.

She put the knife down and poured her husband a glass of orange juice. Then she popped a couple of painkillers out of their blister packaging and handed them to him.

'Thanks,' Oscar croaked. He placed the tablets in his mouth, took a swig of the juice and swallowed with a grimace. 'I am never, ever drinking again.'

'I've heard that before.'

'Many moons ago,' Oscar retorted. 'When was the last time you saw me drunk?'

Meena had to think. 'Dean's fiftieth?' she guessed.

'Exactly! Eight years ago.' He pulled a face. 'I'm never going to live this down,' he groaned.

'Live what down, Dad?' Anton asked, walking into the kitchen.

Meena's heart swelled with love. 'Hello, darling, I didn't hear you come in.' She stepped forward to give their son a hug, then looked over his shoulder. 'Where are Grace and the children?'

'Right behind me.'

On cue, two children barrelled through the front door and thundered down the hall, bursting into the kitchen like a pair of excitable puppies, both of them speaking at once and yelling at the tops of their voices.

Meena bent down to give them a cuddle and hopefully a kiss if she could corner them for long enough, and she noticed Oscar wincing at the noise. That will teach him to drink too much, she thought.

'I wasn't expecting to see you until tomorrow,' she said, pecking Grace on the cheek. 'You look well. A tan suits you. Was the weather good?'

'Glorious, thanks. We were on our way to the supermarket and the kids wanted to call in to give you this. They couldn't wait until tomorrow, and I thought as it's Saturday you might fancy a tipple this evening.' She handed Meena a bottle of Spanish liqueur.

'I tried some, Grandma!' Robin cried. 'It makes your mouth and tummy go all burny.'

Grace rolled her eyes. 'He didn't really,' she said. 'But he's telling anyone who'll listen that he did because he heard me say it. I must say that stuff is rather moreish and if you're not careful it will give you a wicked hangover.'

Oscar let out a soft moan.

'Are you all right, Dad?' Anton asked. 'You don't look well.'

'It's a self-induced illness,' Meena said sharply. 'He deserves to feel unwell.'

'Oh, dear. Did you go to a party?' Grace asked.

'A party for one, and I wasn't invited,' Meena said. 'Shall I put the kettle on?'

'Not for us, thanks,' Grace said. 'We'd better be off. I've got loads of washing to do, as well as the shopping. Bye, Oscar.'

Oscar raised a hand and waved weakly.

The children shot out through the door, Anton hard on their heels, calling after them to mind the road, and Grace turned to leave.

'I'll see you out,' Meena said.

When they got to the front door, Grace hesitated. 'Is everything all right?'

'It's fine. Why do you ask?'

'Don't take this the wrong way, but I thought I sensed a bit of an atmosphere.'

Meena shrugged. 'It's nothing. We had a little quarrel yesterday and Oscar decided that getting drunk was a suitably grown-up way of dealing with it.'

'How is he enjoying his retirement?'

'I wish people would stop asking that,' Meena snapped, then immediately felt contrite. 'I'm sorry, I shouldn't take it out on you. It's just that retirement isn't all it's cracked up to be. Not for him and certainly not for me.'

'You've not retired as well, have you?'

'No, I'm still working. But that's the problem.'

'It's bound to take time to adjust,' Grace said.

'I was thinking that a few days away might do us good,' Meena said. 'Help us reconnect as a couple. Janet suggested it, and I looked at a few places online last night. What do you think?'

'Go for it, I say! Having just come back from a thoroughly enjoyable holiday, I can highly recommend it.

Although, I'd suggest not going to the places you usually go to, otherwise you'll be a golfing widow.'

'I keep myself amused,' Meena said.

'Going on trips on your own? Taking part in the hotel's activities on your own?'

'I see your point, and it did occur to me to avoid anywhere with a golf course,' Meena said.

'Come on, Gracie!' Anton called from the car. 'At this rate the supermarket will be closed by the time we get there.'

'He's exaggerating as usual,' Grace said. 'I'd better go. Give me a call if you need to talk.'

'I will. Sorry to sound off on you.'

'Go book something nice. Treat yourselves. A holiday will do you both good.'

That decided it. If both her daughter-in-law and her dear friend thought it was a good idea, then it must be.

Meena, despite her lingering irritation at the way Oscar had behaved last night, found she was very much looking forward to getting away for a few days.

***

Had Meena forgiven him for last night, Oscar wondered. It was difficult to tell. She had certainly still been annoyed with him when he'd crawled out of bed, considerably later than usual.

But she had supplied him with juice, paracetamol, coffee and toast, so maybe she was relenting a little.

Oscar was annoyed with himself too, and not just because he'd waved his tackle at Janet. The poor woman might be scarred for life after seeing him in his birthday suit. What he was cross about was losing the moral high ground. He'd made his point yesterday, then had waltzed out, leaving Meena to stew in her own juices – and then he'd gone and spoilt it by having one too many beers.

OK, more than one. But he'd got chatting to a couple of guys at the bar, Dean included, firstly about golf naturally, followed by a whole variety of sport, and by the time they'd got onto the subject of women and how they were a different species, one pint had become six, and that was the point where his world had grown a little hazy around the edges. But one good thing had come out of it – he'd been introduced to a new hobby.

Fishing.

It sounded idyllic and relaxing sitting beside a river with a rod dangling in the water waiting for a fish to bite, followed by a burst of excitement and activity when you caught a fish – and not to mention boasting about the size of it.

And the good thing about fishing was that he could do it on his own or with others, during the day or even at night. Plus, and this was another bonus – it wasn't overly strenuous like squash or going to the gym, and it didn't involve him having to wear Lycra. And neither was it an old man's game, like bowls. He wasn't old enough to play bowls. From what he'd seen of the bowls crowd, none of them were under seventy.

He might even have a go at fly fishing… He could set up a space in the garage. It would be his very own workroom. He could have a radio out there, and a kettle, and he'd happily sit there for a couple of hours, tying his own flies. How satisfying would that be – catching a fish with a fly he'd made himself.

There was a tackle shop just off the high street and since Meena had gone out this morning to do something with cakes and the WI, there was nothing stopping him from popping along and getting some advice.

Feeling better about life for the first time since he'd been given a golden handshake, Oscar headed out to the tackle shop, where a whole new fishy world awaited him.

***

Oscar seemed rather pleased with himself, Meena thought, when she returned from manning the WI's cake stall at the bring-and-buy sale in the church hall, and she wondered what he'd been up to. It hadn't been anything involving chores, because the bin in the kitchen was full and the dishwasher hadn't been emptied. The living room could do with being dusted and vacuumed, too.

Her husband didn't appear to understand that housework was never-ending. It wasn't like setting up a new factory – once it was done, it was done. On the contrary, no sooner had you cleaned the oven or defrosted the freezer, it needed doing again.

The same went for the laundry, the shopping, cleaning the windows… she could go on, but she didn't want to depress herself.

Of course, she could always do what her mother had done, which was very little housework at all. But that wasn't an option for Meena. She had grown up living in what she could only describe as a pigsty, because her mother had been the least houseproud person on the planet.

Meena's childhood home had been a far cry from the clean and tidy houses of her friends. None of them had piles of rubbish in the kitchen, or tumps of dirty clothes scattered all over the house. None of them had to pray they didn't catch anything wherever they had a bath or ran the risk of salmonella every time their mum cooked a meal. Even now, when Meena remembered the state the cooker used to be in (until she'd begun cleaning it herself), she felt sick.

It was no wonder she was a bit of a fanatic when it came to cleanliness and tidiness, and she wasn't ashamed to say she was rather anal about it. But at least no one would worry about food poisoning in her house, or would take one look at her bathroom and decide they didn't need a wee after all. Her house mightn't be as posh or as big as some, but it was as nice and as clean as she could possibly make it. She took pride in her home, and it bugged her no end that now Oscar was supposed to be the one who was running the house, he didn't take pride in it at all. He was more of a 'that'll do' person, which was why she'd found herself inspecting everything he'd done, then going behind his back and redoing it.

She wasn't going to apologise for it – after all, why should her standards slip? – but maybe she had been too harsh on him.

Oscar telling her that he felt like a lodger in his own home, had made her stop and think. Because, for years, that was exactly how *she* had felt about *him*, in a way. During the week and often on the weekend, they hadn't used to spend a great deal of time in each other's company. But, and this was important, when they did, she felt they were very much a married couple. They were friends and lovers as well as spouses.

Weren't they?

Meena allowed that maybe a holiday was overdue. Oscar had gone from working hard and playing hard, to wandering around the house like a boat that had been cast adrift, whereas she had gone from effortlessly doing everything that needed to be done without a second thought, to feeling like a sergeant in the housework police.

'Fancy a cup of tea?' Meena called.

Oscar was scrolling through his phone and making notes on a pad resting on the arm of his chair. He looked up. 'Hmm? Sorry, love, I'll make it.'

'You carry on doing what you're doing,' she replied. 'I'm perfectly capable of making a cup of tea.'

'That's not what I meant,' he began, and she saw him start to bristle.

'I know.' Her tone was conciliatory. 'I didn't mean it like that, either.'

Oscar subsided, and she realised just how prickly they had grown with each other over the past few weeks. It wasn't nice and it wasn't good for their relationship.

A holiday was definitely way overdue.

CHAPTER 9

The lake wasn't too big in that Oscar could walk around it in half an hour, but it was large enough so anglers weren't on top of one another. He quite liked the set-up. Jutting four or five feet into the water and nicely spaced apart were wooden pontoons, just large enough for a chair or two, and he noticed that some of them were occupied.

Oscar patted his pocket to check he had his fishing licence, then he headed to the far end of the lake, away from any other fishermen. He wasn't entirely sure what he was doing, so he didn't want any witnesses when he made a complete prat of himself.

He had all the gear, though – a decent rod for a first timer, a box containing an assortment of hooks, floats and various small things that the man in the tackle shop had assured him were essential, a folding chair, a net, Wellington boots and a pair of waterproof trousers. The only thing he hadn't had to buy was a sturdy coat as he already owned one of those, but he hadn't bought it with him today because the forecast had promised sun with the odd bit of cloud.

That little lot had cost him an eye-watering sum, but as he didn't usually spend much on himself apart from his golf club membership, he didn't feel too badly about it.

What he was more concerned about was being classed as the type of bloke others would describe as having "all the gear, no idea", but at present that's exactly what he was. He didn't have a clue what he was doing, despite having spent hours on the internet doing research. The man in the tackle shop off the high street had been a veritable font of knowledge and Oscar had picked his brains unmercifully. Saying that though, he wasn't much further forward when it came to knowing what he was doing so he surmised that he just had to get out there, put his rod in the water, and see how he got on.

All the theory in the world was never going to take the place of doing it yourself.

The day was set to be a nice one, the sun was already warm, and bees were gently droning from flower to flower. The banks of the lake were reedy with water-loving wildflower plants interspersed amongst the clumps of pointed fronds, and ducks and geese paddled up and down. Now and again he caught a glimpse of a moorhen or two pottering around at the water's edge. A dragonfly dipped and darted, its iridescent body a glorious greeny-blue, and he watched it for a while, transfixed.

Oscar liked the outdoors, but what he usually saw of it were sculpted greens, sand-filled bunkers and strategically placed patches of long, rough grass. Of course, there were trees and bushes for added interest, and the club which he was a member of had a small pond, but it was all very carefully constructed and maintained, whereas this lake was wilder and more natural. The golf course also had its fair share of wildlife, mainly rabbits and insects, but nothing like what he was seeing now.

Honking overhead and the sound of many wings made him look up and he saw a chevron of geese flying low, and he was mesmerised when they came into land in a flurry of wings and splashing water.

Why hadn't he been here before?

Come to think of it, he had, but it had been many years ago when Anton was little, and Oscar had been too concerned with trying to prevent his son from falling in the water to enjoy his surroundings. And no doubt Oscar had probably been thinking about work as well, so taking time out to sit and stare hadn't happened.

He could sit and stare to his heart's content now though, and after he'd set everything up and his rod was on its stand with the line dangling in the water, he sat in his chair, tilted his head back, feeling the sun's warm rays on his face, and closed his eyes.

Ah, this was the life. No startling thwack of a club on a ball, no shouts of "fore!", no waiting for someone to tee-off or finish a put. Just him, his rod and the great outdoors.

After a few minutes, Oscar couldn't resist opening his eyes and squinting at the two anglers in his eye line, curious to see if they had caught anything. But they were simply sitting there, too. One of them saw him looking and nodded. Oscar nodded back.

Of course, fishermen had to release anything they caught – the man in the tackle shop had been adamant about that

– so Oscar wouldn't have seen anything anyway. He'd have to wait for a flurry of activity from one of them, indicating he had a fish on the end of his line, in order to see what he'd caught.

Feeling slightly impatient, Oscar checked his rod.

It was in the same position it had been in when he'd set it up ten minutes ago. Nothing had moved and nothing had changed. No tugs on the line, no nibbles, nothing. He knew there were plenty of fish in the lake – the man in the tackle shop had assured him of that – and he could see the occasional bubble rise to the surface, or a ring of gently expanding water where one of the little blighters had gulped down an insect, so that wasn't the issue.

Maybe it was the type of bait he was using, or it was the wrong time of day. He knew from his research that fish were more active at sunrise and sunset, but he hadn't been able to get away yesterday because Anton and the family came to lunch (Meena had baked a carrot cake for the occasion), and he'd waited until she'd left for work this morning before he ventured out. He'd wanted to show her that he was trying to be a good househusband, so he'd had made her some breakfast and had put the used plates and cutlery in the dishwasher. He'd also wiped all the worktops down (trying his best not to sweep any debris onto the floor) and he'd even made the bed and sorted a load of laundry.

He could tell that she was trying not to be so critical about his attempts, so despite his threat when they'd had that little spat on Friday that she could do it all herself, if she was making an effort, he thought he should, too.

Which was why he'd not arrived at the lake until just gone nine o'clock this morning. But the fish had probably been up for several hours and had eaten their breakfasts by then, so they weren't hungry.

Oscar sat back in his chair and gazed around again. There was a young couple on the other side with their dog, strolling hand-in-hand. When was the last time he and Meena had held hands?

He couldn't remember; before Anton was born, he suspected. After Anton came along, their son was always in the middle, swinging off both their hands until Meena had complained that her arm was about to be pulled out of its socket.

Oscar smiled at the memory. As an only child, Anton had been the sole focus of his mother's attention. And of Oscar's too, of course. Look at him now – all grown up and with children of his own. Where had the time gone?

Oscar checked his watch and was surprised to see that it was lunchtime already. He'd been sitting on the pontoon for over two hours, and he'd yet to have a bite. He'd have a bite of his own now, though, and a coffee. He'd had the foresight to bring a flask and a foil-wrapped packet of sandwiches with him, and his stomach rumbled loudly as he opened them. This was the life, he said to himself. Retirement mightn't be too bad after all.

***

'I've booked a holiday,' Meena announced. She'd waited until they were tucking into their evening meal – pasta again, that was all Oscar seemed to know how to cook – before springing the news on him.

'Where to, and when?'

'New Quay in Wales. We leave next Saturday.'

'For how long?'

'Seven days.' She sipped at her water wondering if she'd done the right thing because Oscar didn't seem to be all that keen.

'We usually go abroad,' he pointed out.

'I know we do, but not this time.'

She'd deliberately not booked any of their usual foreign haunts, because golf courses tended to feature heavily. Besides, the forecast for next week was glorious, and when the weather was nice this country was as good as anywhere to have a holiday.

'You like going abroad,' Oscar said.

'No, *you* like going,' Meena replied. 'I'm not all that keen.'

'You never said!' He looked bewildered, but she couldn't keep pretending any more.

She'd gone because he'd wanted to. It hadn't been as much fun for her as it tended to be for him – a golfing widow was a golfing widow no matter which country you were in. At least at home she had loads of things to keep her occupied while he was off swinging a club. On holiday, she'd had to find things to do, and she'd often felt like a singleton.

She was determined this holiday would be different. She hadn't been able to find any part of the UK that *didn't* have a course within travelling distance, but at least they wouldn't be staying in a resort with a golf course on site. She'd booked them into a lovely hotel overlooking the sea. It had a spa, a wellness centre, and an à la carte restaurant as well as a normal one, and she was looking forward to long walks, pootling around the shops, several nice lunches in local eateries, and a boat trip around Cardigan Bay to try and spot some dolphins.

'You should have told me you weren't keen,' Oscar said. 'We could have gone somewhere in this country. Perth or Dundee…' His expression was thoughtful and Meena knew exactly what was going through his mind: both of those places weren't far from the famous golf course at St Andrews.

Oh, no, my dear, she thought – not on your nelly.

They were going to West Wales and they were going to spend some quality time together – whether her husband liked it or not.

***

Oscar pulled onto the drive behind Meena's car, got out of his and locked it, then went back to check that the boot was secure.

He had taken to keeping his rods in the car, partly because he had yet to mention to Meena that he had taken up a new hobby as he wanted to make sure he intended to carry on with it first, and partly so he could just hop in the car and go if the mood took him; which it had tended to do a lot over the past few days.

Ever since he'd lost a couple of hours by the lake the other day and hadn't caught a thing, he'd been hooked.

Excuse the pun, but he had. He was determined to catch a fish if it was the last thing he did.

He'd watched angler after angler scoop up fish after fish in their nets but he'd yet to have so much as a nibble, and he couldn't work out what he was doing wrong. Perhaps he'd go back to the tackle shop and have a chat with the fella who owned it.

He was quite enjoying himself though, despite his lack of success. It was soothing sitting on the edge of the lake with no need to rush to do anything or to go anywhere. And with the light evenings, he was able to nip back out once he'd fed and watered Meena, if she had one of her meetings. It was better than sitting on the sofa and watching the telly on his own.

Mind you, he was on his own when he was fishing and he sometimes missed the camaraderie of the golf club, especially the bar at the end of a round. A round at the end of a round? Ha, ha.

He was still chortling as he walked into the house. He was a little later than usual because the fish had been biting (although they'd ignored his hook and line) and he'd told himself just ten more minutes at least four times, so he was subsequently home about an hour later than he'd told Meena he would be.

She'd had a hair appointment this morning but maybe they could spend the rest of the day doing something together?

But when he saw what Meena was up to in the living room as he walked past the open door on the way to the kitchen, his good mood evaporated.

'What are you doing?' he demanded.

Meena was balancing on a stepladder, a feather duster in one hand (he didn't even know they owned a feather duster) and a lightbulb in the other.

If she wasn't careful, she was going to fall.

'Changing a bulb,' she said.

'I was going to do that,' Oscar said.

Meena jammed the feather duster under her armpit, clutched the top of the ladder with one hand and used the other to screw the lightbulb in place. 'When did you intend on doing it? I've said three times that this bulb needed changing.'

'I forgot,' he said. 'I would have remembered eventually.'

'When?'

Oscar shrugged. 'I don't know.'

'Exactly!'

He gave up trying to argue with her. If Meena wanted something done, then she wanted it done there and then – although to be fair, in the past she usually did it herself and hadn't had to wait around for him to do it for her.

'Sorry,' he said.

He watched her run the duster over the gold-coloured arms holding the bulbs and he debated whether he should ask her if she wanted any help, but he thought better of it. Meena was an independent soul, and if she could do a task herself she would, so he guessed she wouldn't take kindly to him interfering. He was suddenly aware that she was peering down at him, a frown on her face.

'Did you want something?' she asked, and he could tell he was getting on her nerves.

'Shall we go out for a couple of hours?' he suggested.

'Where did you have in mind?'

'I don't know. The garden centre?'

'You don't like gardening.'

Meena climbed down the ladder and Oscar rushed to hold it steady for her.

'I don't mind it,' he said.

She pointed out of the window at the decimated foliage. 'You could have fooled me.'

'You said you wanted them cut back,' he protested. Please don't start this again, he thought.

Meena narrowed her eyes at him. 'Do you do it on purpose? Do you enjoy annoying me?'

'I didn't do it on purpose,' he cried. 'You should have specified if you wanted a certain amount cut off. I used my judgement.'

'Your judgement is sadly lacking,' she retorted. 'Those bushes will take years to grow back.'

'Oh, give it a rest,' he sighed, sick to death of the petty squabbling. That's all they seemed to do these days, and he was tired of it.

'Do you think you can manage to put this away?' she demanded, slapping her palm down on the top rung of the ladder. 'I'm going out. I need some more yarn.'

'*More* yarn?'

'Why, is that a problem?'

Actually, he thought, it was. All she did these days was knit and nag. Knit and Natter should be renamed Knit and Nag.

'I've got an idea,' he said. 'Why don't you sort out your clothes and send them the ones you don't wear instead of making stuff? I'm sure you can find loads. Then you wouldn't have to spend so much—'

Meena gasped. Not letting him finish his sentence, she leapt in, saying, 'That's rich coming from the man who's just bought a shop's worth of fishing gear.'

'I was going to say *time – spend so much time knitting*. If you're not out, you're bloody knitting. You can't just sit and enjoy a film with me.'

Meena's face tightened, and Oscar saw the anger in her eyes and wanted to kick himself. Hang on— 'How do you know how much I spent on fishing gear?'

'You left the receipt in the pocket of your jeans.'

'Why were you going through my pockets?'

He was incredulous. How dare she! Anyone would think she didn't trust him. Did she think he was having an affair? A chance would be a fine thing – if he wasn't in work, earning enough to keep Meena in the style she'd become accustomed to, then he was schmoozing on the golf course.

Was.

Abruptly he remembered he didn't have a job any more and he'd given up golf.

'Because someone has to,' his wife replied. 'You leave all kinds of stuff in your pockets, and believe me I don't like having to pick bits of shredded tissue off my clothes because you couldn't be bothered to check your pockets before you put your jeans in the washing basket.'

'I thought *I* was supposed to be doing the laundry?' he said.

'So did I.'

'I give up! If you're that bothered, you do it.'

Meena thrust her hand up at the ceiling. 'That's why I changed the light bulb,' she retorted through gritted teeth.

There was silence for a moment. Oscar had no idea what she might be thinking, but he was seriously contemplating getting back in his car and returning to the lake. He'd pick up some supplies on the way and stay there for the rest of the day. Tonight, too. See how she liked that!

Although, when he thought about it, she probably wouldn't even notice he wasn't there, so he turned on his heel and headed towards the door.

'Where are you going?'

'Away from you. Enjoy your knitting.'

'It's not my fault you've not got a life now that you're retired,' she called after him. 'You didn't care what I did when you had your precious job. But now you haven't got a job any more you expect me to entertain you. How old are you? Three?'

Oscar halted, one foot in the living room the other in the hall, and looked over his shoulder. 'I'm old enough to expect to spend some quality time with my wife,' he said in a low voice. 'It's just a shame *she* doesn't want to spend any time with *me*.' And with that, he walked out of the house.

The way he was feeling right now, he didn't know if he'd ever want to go back.

CHAPTER 10

Meena bit back a sob as she heard the front door slam, and she sank onto the arm of the nearest chair wondering what had happened. One minute she was happily removing a bulb from the ceiling light, and the next she was having a ding-dong row with Oscar. How had it escalated so quickly?

And the things he'd said to her had astonished and upset her. He'd never before been bothered about her knitting, her sewing, her gardening, or any of the loads of other things she did to keep herself busy when he wasn't around, yet now that the tables were turned he'd become angry and resentful. Jealous, even, because she still had a job and her social life was as active as it had ever been, and he didn't and his… *wasn't*. If she thought about it, he didn't have a social life as such; he'd always maintained that golf, even though he enjoyed it, was a necessary evil, because it was on the golf course that deals were made, connections established and problems resolved.

Was that her fault that he now felt she didn't care?

Perhaps. Other women might well give up their activities to devote themselves to their husbands, but she didn't intend to. She'd worked too hard to make a life for herself outside of their marriage and their home, that she had no intention of giving it up.

He had no idea of the hours she'd spent when Anton was little, waiting for Oscar to come home from work and feeling lonely because their son had been in bed for hours. Or the weekends she'd spent on her own with their son because Oscar had been playing golf. Or the days when she'd been forced to amuse herself on holiday because he'd been playing golf yet again.

It had taken a great deal of energy and determination to get to the point where her free time was filled with activities which she loved doing and, more importantly, where she felt valued and respected. Which was more than she felt lately when it came to Oscar.

With a heavy heart she put the stepladders back in the shed, then lifted her bag from the hook under the stairs. She really did want to buy more yarn but all the enthusiasm she normally felt when a trip to the craft shop was imminent had disappeared.

Did Oscar really hate her knitting? She only did it in the evenings when they were sitting there watching TV, but from what he said he wasn't happy that she didn't give the screen her full attention.

She heaved a sigh and got in the car.

That's where he was wrong – she was a multi-tasker and was perfectly capable of knitting and watching a programme. She mostly knitted by touch and instinct: she didn't feel the need to stare at her needles or check the pattern every five minutes, so she was, in fact, watching TV. She just happened to be knitting at the same time. In future, she'd bugger off to her workroom where she *definitely* wouldn't be watching the telly, and let him see how he liked that.

And what was so wrong about her checking his pockets before she popped his clothes in the washing machine? She'd always done it. She'd had to – the amount of stuff she used to inadvertently wash before she'd got into the habit of checking was phenomenal: keys, coins, notes, his passport, even his wallet once, and no end of tissues which didn't half leave a mess when the fibres stuck to the clothes, especially anything black or dark-coloured. It was second nature to her to go through his pockets; if whatever he'd left in there was important she'd put it to one side, if not, she'd throw it in the bin. He'd never complained about it before...

To be fair, he probably didn't realise that's what she did. After noticing some white fluff stuck to her black jeans the other day, she'd made a point of riffling through the laundry before Oscar put it in the machine, and she'd noticed that there were enough dirty items to warrant putting a load on, so that's what she'd done. And that was when she'd spotted a receipt for an eye-watering amount.

She didn't for one second begrudge him spending the money; after all, he'd worked hard for it. She had wondered why he'd not informed her he had another hobby, but she hadn't dwelt on it, although she had been pleased that he had something other than golf and decimating the garden to keep him occupied.

To think that the simple act of changing a light bulb and sorting the washing could lead to him storming off. It was the second time he'd done that, and she was getting a bit fed up with his histrionics. If he continued, she might just ask him if he wanted to join *The First Act*, where he could put his penchant for the theatrical to good use. He'd better be in a more amenable mood when he came home, she thought, because if he wasn't she would take herself off to her workroom and he could stew in his own juices on the sofa.

***

For three and a half hours Oscar sat by the side of the lake before he got a nibble. But what a nibble it was!

Bubbling with excitement, he fought to bring the fish close enough to the pontoon for him to scoop it up in his net. A couple of times he thought he'd lost it when the line went slack, but each time the fish had merely been resting and gathering its energy for another attempt to fight him.

Oscar was dimly aware of a man standing behind him with a dog at his heels, but most of his attention was on the fish.

'Let the line out a little,' the man advised. 'Give him some slack and let him run with it, then reel him back in.'

'Why?' Oscar panted, surprised at how hard work it was to land a fish. The one on the end of his rod must be ginormous.

'It'll tire him out. Keep giving him some line, a little less each time, and keep reeling him in, bringing him closer each time.'

Oscar did as the man advised, seeing the rod bend with the strain whenever he reeled the fish in and watching as the tension eased when he let the line play out.

Finally, after numerous lettings out and reelings in, he could tell the fish was exhausted. So was Oscar. He'd never felt so knackered in all his life, but he was exhilarated too, and incredibly anxious that he didn't lose his fish at this late stage, especially since dusk was falling fast and he had to squint to see what he was doing.

'Bring him closer,' the man said, grabbing hold of Oscar's net and kneeling by his side. He dipped the net into the water, and Oscar held his breath, then… Voila!

It was a carp, and a decent sized one at that.

Exhausted, Oscar crouched down to examine it, delight flooding through him. He'd done it, he'd actually done it – he'd caught his first fish and it was glorious.

'Have you got any scales?' the man asked.

'In the box.'

Oscar heard the bloke lift the lid.

'Here you go,' he said, and Oscar took the digital scales from him and hooked it up to the net, working quickly so as not to distress the fish unduly.

The light was fading fast, so the man shone a torch at the display and read out, 'Five pounds, nine ounces.'

'Is that good?' Oscar asked.

'It's about average for this lake, although there are a few that are much bigger, but they're canny buggers and not easily hooked. Do you want me to take a photo before you put it back?'

'Yes, please.'

Oscar got his phone out of his pocket and handed it over, picked the fish up in his hands, and flinched when the flash went off.

Then Oscar gently lowered the fish back into the water, opening his hands so the creature could swim off. He'd read that the fish would head to the deepest part of the lake to rest and recuperate.

'Bye,' he whispered under his breath.

'Well done, mate,' the man said, and Oscar rose to his feet and looked at him for the first time.

The chap was in his mid- to late-forties, slim, with a bald head and a beard. Oscar thought he'd seen him before. He definitely recognised the bloke's dog.

'Thanks for the help,' he said, reaching out to stroke the spaniel's floppy ears.

'No worries. It's easier to land a fish when there are two of you, especially when you're starting out.'

Oscar grinned ruefully. 'Is it that obvious?'

The bloke smiled. 'I'm Ray, by the way. This is Sam.'

'Oscar.' He thrust his hand out and they briefly shook.

'I'll see you around,' Ray said, and Oscar was certain he would.

He'd been well and truly bitten by the fishing bug and couldn't wait for his next catch.

First, though, he wanted to get home to Meena, and tell her all about it.

Meena was half-asleep when she heard Oscar's key in the lock, and she let out a relieved sigh that he'd come home. She was beginning to wonder if he would.

Sitting up, she checked the time.

Nearly eleven-thirty.

What *had* he been doing until now?

She prayed he wasn't drunk again, but at least there was no Janet sleeping in their spare room for him to walk in on and flash his bits at this time.

He had reached the landing by the time she decided to pretend she was asleep. If he knew she was awake there was a chance the argument might continue, and she wasn't prepared for that. She hadn't wanted to row in the first place.

Snuggling down, she pulled the quilt up around her ears and turned on her side, facing away from both the door and his side of the bed, and waited.

He was trying to be quiet, but she nevertheless heard the shower running, then the sound of him brushing his teeth, and finally the creak of the floorboard on the landing as he crept towards their bedroom.

Meena drew in a long breath, then let it out slowly when he got into bed.

The mattress shifted under his weight, and she debated whether she should make a tiny noise. What would her sleeping self have done? Would she murmur? Move restlessly?

In the end she did nothing, just lay there rigid and unmoving, praying her husband would fall asleep before too long.

He didn't.

But what he did was unexpected and, in the end, very welcome indeed.

Oscar inched across to her side of the bed and curled his body around hers, then his arm came around her waist and he snuggled into her. She could feel his gentle breath on the back of her neck, and his chest pressing against her back.

It was familiar and comforting, and the tension she'd been carrying inside her ribcage loosened a little.

'I love you,' he whispered, his voice softer than summer mist, and with that the wall she had built up around herself over the past few weeks abruptly cracked and she felt a sob rising into her throat.

Twisting around, she faced him, and they lay there nose to nose. She could make out the shine of his eyes in the darkness as she said, 'I love you, too. I'm sorry.'

'Me, too. I didn't think you were awake.'

'I was pretending not to be,' she admitted.

'Turn over again and let me cuddle you,' he said, but Meena had something else in mind.

'I've got a better idea,' she said, and her hand slipped down between them. His gasp when she found what she was seeking told her that he thought it was a good idea, too.

CHAPTER 11

'Hi, Mum, it's only me,' Meena called as she turned the key in the lock, opened the front door and stepped into her mother's hall. 'I've brought you some bread and milk.'

She went into the kitchen and glanced around in satisfaction, noting that Nora had been in: she must have been, otherwise the room wouldn't be so clean and tidy. Meena put the bread in the cupboard and the milk in the fridge, then flicked the switch on the kettle.

Her mother was in the sitting room watching TV, and she didn't so much as glance up when Meena walked over to her and gave her a kiss on the cheek.

'What are you watching?' she asked, sinking into the sofa.

Anita shrugged. 'A stupid game show.'

'Shall I turn it off?' Meena stretched out her hand for the remote control, but her mother batted her away, her eyes glued to the screen.

Meena blew out her cheeks and sat back. For someone who thought the programme was stupid, her mother hadn't even turned to look at her, and Meena took a moment to examine her. Her mum was slumped in her chair, her chin almost on her chest, and although Meena could only see her in profile, from what she could see of her face, Meena thought she looked tired.

The kettle came to the boil and Meena returned to the kitchen. She fished a couple of tea bags out of the caddy, dropped them in some mugs and gave the bags a stir.

It was when she was spooning one of the teabags out, her foot on the pedal of the bin and holding the mug above its open lid, that Meena noticed several balled-up tissues in the bottom of the bin.

They were daubed with blood.

'Mum…?' she called. 'Did you cut yourself opening a tin?' It wouldn't be the first time. Her mother insisted on using a lethal contraption which looked more like a surgical instrument than a can opener. A couple of years ago, Meena had bought her an electric one, but as far as she knew her mum had never even taken it out of its box.

Meena carried the mugs into the living room and placed them on the table next to her mum's chair. 'Let me see? At your age you can't be too careful when you cut yourself.'

'I'm fine,' Anita said, waving her away.

Meena's attention was on her mum's hands, but she couldn't see an obvious injury so she couldn't have hurt herself too badly. Still, it had bled a bit and Meena wanted to make sure the cut wasn't too deep – her mum might need a stitch or two. Plus it might need a good rinse with antiseptic.

'Let me see,' Meena insisted and reached for her mum's hand.

Anita jerked her arm away but as she did so she knocked one of the mugs of tea over. Hot liquid spilled over the table and dripped onto the carpet.

'Now look what you made me do!' her mum cried, and Meena saw her mum's face clearly for the first time. Anita had a cut above her eyebrow and a bruise had formed, dark and ugly.

She let out a gasp. 'Mum! What happened?'

'It's nothing. Stop fussing.'

She turned her head away again so Meena couldn't see, but Meena scooted around to the far side of the chair to get a better look.

'Oh, dear, how did you do that?' She took her mum's face in the palms of her hands, and gently moved her head from side to side. 'It looks nasty.'

Meena could see that her mother was debating whether to tell her the truth or not, and she gave her a warning look.

'I tripped going up the stairs,' Anita admitted stiffly, 'and hit my head on the handrail.'

'Oh, Mum…' Meena felt close to tears. 'Come on—' she clambered to her feet '—we need to get that seen to.'

'*We* don't need to do anything,' her mum replied, not moving. 'I'm fine.'

'I think it needs stitches.'

'Nonsense. It's stopped bleeding, hasn't it?' '

'Yes, but—'

'There you go, then.'

'I still think you should get it checked out. Did you lose consciousness?'

'No.'

'Are you sure?'

'I'm sure.'

Meena pursed her lips. 'Please let me take you to the hospital, just to be on the safe side.'

'No.'

'Mum…?'

'Stop whining – you sound like a toddler.'

'If you won't let me take you to the hospital, I'll call an ambulance,' Meena threatened.

'Don't you dare. They've got more important things to worry about, than me.'

'I haven't,' Meena said quietly, sinking back down to sit on the floor at her mum's feet.

Her mother sent her a sharp look. 'I think you have. How *is* Oscar finding retirement?'

Meena blinked. 'What's that got to do with anything?'

Anita shook her head, then winced. She gingerly touched the cut and said, 'You think I don't notice, but you've been as miserable as sin since Oscar finished work.'

'I haven't!' Meena protested. 'In fact, I've just booked us a week away – and stop trying to change the subject. I'd like to take you to A and E: I'm serious when I say you might need stitches.'

'And I'm serious when I tell you I won't go. And I'll tell you something else too – I'm not moving out of my house, no matter how much you go on at me,' Anita said, her expression hard. 'I'm not moving, and you can't make me.

This is my home and I want to stay in it as long as I can. I'm not so decrepit that I can't look after myself.'

Meena thought that was debatable. 'We can't risk you having another fall,' she said.

'If I fall, I fall,' her mother said. 'I'm still not selling my house. I'd hate living in one of those pokey flats, or on an OAP complex.' Anita glared at her. 'You've never liked this house, have you?'

'Of course I do – it was my home,' Meena pointed out.

'And you left as soon as you could,' her mother argued.

Meena bit her lip. It was true: she *had* left as soon as she was able. She'd been desperate to get a place of her own, somewhere where she didn't have to clear up other people's mess. And by "other people" she'd meant her mother.

Which was ironic considering Meena had spent the next thirty plus years cleaning up after Oscar and Anton, until Anton had moved out. And occasionally she was still cleaning up Oscar's mess.

'Mum, I just want you to be safe, and I don't think you are, not in this house. I'm worried about you.'

Anita stared rigidly at the TV and narrowed her lips.

Meena rose with some difficulty, her knees protesting. 'Should I make us another cup of tea?' she asked, and made one anyway when her mum didn't answer. She also mopped up the spilt tea and washed the mug, and when she returned to the living room, the two of them sipped their drinks in silence.

It was Meena who eventually broke it. 'I wouldn't dream of forcing you to do something you didn't want to do,' she said quietly.

'So why do you keep going on at me about me leaving this house?' her mother snapped.

'You know why – because I worry about you.'

'Hmph. You'd be better off worrying about yourself. I'm perfectly happy with my life, but I don't think you're happy with yours, are you?'

Meena didn't know what to say; she couldn't deny it, because what her mum said was true. Meena *wasn't* happy, not since Oscar had retired. But she should expect to have a blip or two, because it had been a shock for both of them. Unlike most people, they'd had it thrust upon them. Janet and Dean were busy planning for the time when they no longer had work commitments, but Meena and Oscar hadn't given it any thought at all. No wonder they were both finding it hard to adjust.

They still loved each other though, and that's what mattered. The holiday would do them good. It better had, because she was now worrying about how she could possibly go away for a week and leave her mum all alone.

***

'Gimme, gimme, gimme!' Meena made grabby motions with her hands and held her arms out towards Dana and the gorgeous little baby she was holding. 'Let Auntie Meena have a cuddle,' she cooed. 'Oh, my God, Dana, she's gorgeous! How are you feeling?'

'Absolutely exhausted,' Dana said.

Bless her, Meena thought, she looked it too. Meena didn't envy her: she could distinctly remember how deeply tired she had been when Anton was a baby, what with all the middle of the night feeds and the constant crying, and he had been quite a good baby considering.

Dana handed her the cute pink bundle and Meena cuddled the baby into her chest, feeling the tiny girl's fragile solidity and the delicate little bones underneath her hands, and smelling that unique milky scent that all babies seem to have.

Her heart twisted and she felt acutely nostalgic for a time long past, as she carefully carried the baby towards the staff room, Dana following behind along with the rest of the admin team. At least the surgery was quiet on a Wednesday lunchtime, so there shouldn't be too many interruptions, because Meena wanted to spend as much time cuddling the baby as she was able before patients began demanding attention.

Everyone piled into the room all wanting a cuddle and a chat whilst they ate their lunch, but eventually they returned to work, leaving only Meena and Dana behind.

The baby started to grizzle and as Dana settled back to feed her, Meena remembered what that was like, so she made them both another cup of tea and retrieved a packet of biscuits from her desk drawer.

'I'm never going to lose the baby weight if everyone keeps feeding me,' Dana said, half joking.

'That's the last thing you should be worrying about,' Meena told her. 'You need to keep your strength up.'

'You've heard all my news, what about yours? What have you been getting up to since I've been on maternity leave?'

Meena smiled. 'The first couple of weeks with Oscar at home all day proved to be a little troublesome, but things are starting to get better.'

'You mean, he's stopped leaving a trail of breadcrumbs all over the kitchen?' Dana chuckled.

'He most certainly has,' Meena said, with a laugh. 'He's not so keen to make a mess now that he's got to clear it up himself.'

'Yes, funny that isn't it?' Dana said. 'I remember when I was a teenager, my mother was always going on at me for leaving stuff lying around the house, or she'd find dirty clothes shoved under the bed.' She shuddered. 'And all the plates and dirty glasses – I honestly don't know what I was thinking. But as soon as I moved into a place of my own, it was a whole different ball game. When you have to tidy up after yourself, you try not to make a mess in the first place, don't you?'

Meena didn't say anything. She was thinking that might be true for some people, but not for her. It had been the other way around in her house. Her mum had been the messy one, acting more like an irresponsible teenager, and Meena had been the grown-up. A memory of coming home from school one day after she'd made sure the house was tidy before she left, and discovering the absolute tip it had turned into in the space of a few hours, slipped into her mind. She could kind of understand why teenagers were so messy, because they were finding themselves, trying to work out who they wanted to be and how they wanted to be, and that included some kind of rebellion against their parents, which frequently translated into claiming their own space.

Why that had to involve making as much mess as possible Meena honestly couldn't say, but it had seemed to be a common trait amongst her friends' children and a source of much complaining and commiseration, although Anton hadn't been too bad.

She couldn't for the life of her think what her mother's excuse was. Had she been born with an "I don't give a damn" gene? Or maybe her own mother, Meena's grandma, had been excessively harsh on Anita as she was growing up, and Anita's rebellious side hadn't been able to manifest itself until she was in charge of her own house. Meena honestly didn't know. She had no explanation for her mother's slovenliness.

Dana lifted the baby onto her shoulder and began patting her back. When a burp was duly ejected, Dana exclaimed, 'There's a good girl!' and the satiated baby's eyes fluttered closed.

Meena was quite wistful. It must be so nice to be a baby she mused, having your every need taken care of and only having to think in very simple terms of I'm cold, I'm hungry, I need changing, I want a cuddle.

'Have you settled into a new routine, yet?' Dana asked, cradling the baby in the crook of her arm and wiping a spittle of milk off her daughter's soft, downy cheek.

'Yes, I suppose we have. Funny enough though, Oscar doesn't seem to be playing an awful lot of golf. Of course, I'm not there all the time during the week so I'm not totally sure what he gets up to, but whereas he used to keep his golf clubs permanently in the car, I noticed them in the garage, and they've been there for a while because there was a layer of dust on them. He's got a new hobby now – fishing.' Meena pulled a face.

'Is that not good?' Dana asked.

'I'm not sure. He's probably out of the house for longer because it's not like playing a round of golf and then going home. He's been known to sit there for ages waiting for a fish to bite – two, three, four hours.' She shrugged. 'At least it gives him something to do. I was beginning to get a bit worried that he was going to be bored, because when he's bored he's like a child, he wants attention. *My* attention. I've got enough on my plate as it is at the moment, without having to entertain Oscar.'

'Why, what's up?' Dana asked.

'It's my mum. You know she's had a couple of falls? Well, she had another one yesterday. Nothing serious, thank goodness, but I'm scared she'll really hurt herself next time. I've tried to persuade her that she'd be better off moving to a little bungalow, or preferably one of those OAP flats....' Meena trailed off.

'I take it she's not keen on the idea?'

'Not in the slightest.'

'I don't suppose you can blame her. She's lived there a long time, hasn't she?'

'Since before I was born. It was my childhood home.'

'I can see why she'd want to stay there.'

'So can I,' Meena said, 'but I'm worried it will take a very serious fall before she can be persuaded to move.'

'Let's hope it doesn't come to that, eh? Is there anything I can do? I know I'm not technically her GP, but she is a patient at the practice, so…'

'Thanks, but no. I did manage to talk her into having a stairlift fitted, so that's a step in the right direction, and if she's determined to stay there I'll have a chat with her about putting handrails up around the house and maybe changing the bath to one of those walk-in things.' Meena sighed. 'The thing is, Oscar and I are supposed to be going away for a week and I don't think I can leave her.'

'What about Anton? Can he call in?'

'I can ask him, but he's so busy.'

'So are you, yet you make the time. Ask him,' Dana urged. 'A holiday will do you both good. It'll allow you to remember what it's like to be a couple again.' She nudged the car seat with her foot, inching it closer, and placed the baby inside, then she stood up. 'I suppose I must get off,' she said. 'I never seem to have enough time in the day to do anything at the moment, and my house is looking a bit of a mess. Maybe I should ask your Oscar if he'd like to pop around and give it a clean for me?' she joked.

Meena said, 'I know a lady who's a pretty good cleaner if you're after someone.'

'You do? I might ask you for her name if I can't get to grips with it myself,' Dana said. 'It's not so bad while I'm on maternity leave, but things might get a little difficult when I return to work. I'm not quite sure how I'm going to manage. Is the cleaner through an agency?'

Meena shook her head. 'No, I know her personally. She cleans my mum's house for me, three times a week.'

'For you?'

'Sorry, I meant for my mum – she cleans house for *my mum*.'

But that wasn't what Meena had meant at all. Because if Nora didn't do the cleaning for her mother, Meena would have to do it, so in essence Nora was saving Meena a considerable amount of time and effort. Nora mightn't be cheap, but she was well worth the expense as far as Meena was concerned. And Meena had no qualms about employing a cleaner because she earned her own money and had done so for years. It wasn't as though she was expecting Oscar to pay for it.

She couldn't ask him anyway, considering she had never once told him about it. It was her secret, and what Oscar didn't know didn't hurt him.

***

Oscar wasn't a hundred per cent sure whether he wanted to go away for a week or not. He was only just getting used to his new routine he mused, as he sat staring at the far bank of the lake, and at the field beyond where several fat round sheep grazed contentedly.

Admittedly the first couple of weeks had been tough, but lately he and Meena seemed to be on a much more stable footing. She wasn't being quite so demanding, although he still sometimes caught a peeved expression on her face and occasionally he'd find her re-doing something he'd already done, but neither of them mentioned it. Instead, she'd bite her lip, and he would make a mental note of how he could improve next time. He was conscious that it was quite a steep learning curve for him; never in his life had he had to concern himself about what day the bins went out, or whether he should disinfect the bathroom. He'd never had to consider the best time or the best day to go shopping in the supermarket, or whether he needed to use that chicken up today or if he could leave it until tomorrow.

On the whole though, he thought he was doing quite well. Apart from ruining one of Meena's blouses, he hadn't made any major boo-boos on the laundry front, he was getting marginally better at cooking, and he'd even made a shepherd's pie from scratch the other evening. And, since the time when he'd realised Meena had remade the bed, he hadn't noticed her doing it lately, so maybe he was finally doing that right too.

They'd been getting on better than they had done for years (he was specifically thinking about their love-making the other night) so maybe this forced early retirement had been a blessing in disguise. He still missed playing golf – his clubs hadn't been out of the garage since that disastrous Friday when he sneaked off home – but he'd found a new and quite satisfying hobby to replace it.

Admittedly, he was still a little lonely, but he was on nodding terms with some of the other anglers. He hadn't seen Ray since the man had helped him land his fish the other week, although he'd seen his dog in the distance, and had thought how nice it would be to have some company while he was fishing, even if it was a spaniel.

He'd even said hello to a couple of familiar faces, and now and again someone would stop to have a chat on their way past, so he was getting there. Angling however was a fairly solitary business he'd come to realise; even though the other men (and they were nearly all men) seemed pleasant enough, none of them fished together, except for one pair who were obviously father and son.

He missed the camaraderie of work, of having to think on his feet, and of having to find solutions to problems. Trying to decide what he and Meena were going to have for dinner didn't stretch him much. He felt as though his brain was atrophying, seizing up like an unused engine. And not only that, he found that sitting by the side of the lake for hours on end gave him far too much time to think.

He'd tried doing a crossword, but it hadn't taken him long to complete, and he tried reading a newspaper but that only killed about an hour or so. Maybe he'd buy himself a book? The next time he was in town he'd have a look in the book shop and see if he could find an autobiography to interest him, although he'd never been much of a reader and neither had Meena, for that matter. She preferred to be doing something creative rather than reading.

She was still knitting, but he was trying not to let it get to him as much. At least if there was something interesting on the telly, she would put it to one side and watch it with him, so they were definitely making progress.

Oscar had already caught one fish today and had popped it back into the water after having recorded its length and weight in his book. He'd probably graduated from an absolute beginner and moved onto the novice stage. He still had an awful lot to learn he acknowledged, but not as much as he had done when he'd first entered the tackle shop.

Maybe it was time to try some fly fishing in the river? He got the impression there was more skill involved in catching trout, and although he had no idea whether this was true or not it might be nice to find out. He'd already set up a workstation at the back of the garage where he prepared his bait, and he'd quite happily sit there tying flies if only he knew where to start.

A thought occurred to him – could he do that indoors? Meena could sit in her chair knitting, and he could sit in his tying flies.

He sighed and looked at his watch. In another half an hour it would be time to go back. It was Meena's evening at the amateur dramatics society, so she'd only be home long enough to eat a quick meal and then she'd be off out again, and he'd be faced with another evening on his own.

Oscar felt his eyes glaze over as another thought occurred to him – maybe a dog would be company in the house. At least it would be someone to talk to...

Nah, it was a daft idea.

But there might be another solution, and it was something he would never have considered before because he'd always been too tired in the evenings when he'd been holding down a demanding job. But things were different now, and if the mountain wouldn't go to Mohammed then surely it made sense for Mohammed to go to the mountain.

CHAPTER 12

'I'm sorry,' Meena said with a puzzled expression on her face, 'I thought you said you wanted to come to amateur dramatics with me this evening.' She'd paused, a forkful of food halfway to her mouth, and she lowered it gently back to the plate and cocked her head to gaze at Oscar quizzically.

This was so unlike her husband – he'd never been interested in any of her hobbies or her societies before. He'd once tried to get her to play golf but it hadn't been her thing, and the attempt hadn't lasted more than a couple of weeks before they both realised that he was flogging a dead horse. But never once had she tried to impose any of the things she enjoyed on him.

She'd known instinctively that he wouldn't be interested, certainly not in any activities of the PTA when Anton was in school, and most definitely not in anything to do with the governing body of a school which Anton had left a long, long time ago.

Oscar had never been one to work with his hands either, preferring to use his brain and a spreadsheet or two. He liked crosswords and he did the occasional puzzle, usually in the mornings after breakfast when they were on holidays before he set off for the golf course. But he'd never *made* anything. Some men did lots of DIY, but not Oscar. If there was any DIY to be done either Meena did it herself, or she called a man in to do it for them.

He'd also never been particularly artistic: actually, he'd never been artistic at all as far as she could tell, and neither had he been interested in any physical exercise. She couldn't by any stretch of the imagination call Oscar a fitness fanatic. He didn't run, he didn't cycle, he didn't play squash, he didn't go to the gym. He played golf. And now he had fishing to keep him occupied.

Over the years he'd done his thing and she'd done hers and never the twain shall meet, as the saying goes, so when she'd joined the amateur dramatics society several years ago, it didn't once occur to her to suggest that Oscar might like to come along. Although he had watched the first night performances, often accompanied by Anton and Grace. But that was it, that was the sum total of his involvement. For him to suggest that he accompany her tonight took her completely by surprise.

'I did say that,' he said. 'If it's all right with you?'

Meena didn't know whether to be delighted or dismayed. 'Of course it's all right with me. The more the merrier. What is it you see yourself doing?'

'I could try out for some acting?' Oscar suggested.

'Do you think you'd be any good at it?' Meena asked curiously.

'I don't know, do I? Not until I give it a go. And if I'm not, I'm sure Dean can find something else for me to do. He's always muttering about how shorthanded *The First Act* is. Everyone wants to be an actor apparently, and nobody wants to paint the scenery.'

Meena tried not to wince. She couldn't see Oscar painting scenery, either. As far as she knew, Oscar had never held a paintbrush in his life, apart from maybe when he was at school.

She thought for a moment, then decided he was right – he wouldn't know until he tried, and that went for painting the scenery, too. She bit back a smile as she thought of some of the other jobs he could possibly do, and one of them was helping with the costumes which she, herself, sometimes did. She couldn't imagine the two of them sitting side by side in her workroom, both of them stitching. However... she *could* imagine him organising the ticket sales, booking the theatre, getting the best quote for the flyers that they usually had printed, and all the various admin things that needed doing which Oscar would probably be good at.

Although, saying that, when he had been working he'd had a secretary to do those kinds of things and an admin team, so maybe not.

Anyway, she'd leave it up to Dean.

The two men could hash it out together as to what Oscar could, or couldn't, do. It would be better all round if she didn't get involved.

***

'Do you mind if we quickly pop in to see Mum on the way?' Meena asked as Oscar buckled up his seatbelt. 'You can stay in the car, if you want,' she suggested.

'And how's that going to look?' Oscar retorted, then thought he'd sounded a little sharp, so he added, 'Of course I don't mind, but I think I should come in and at least say hello.'

Out of the corner of his eye he could see Meena biting her lip in the passenger seat, and he realised that she was quite worried about her mum.

'Is there anything I can do to help?' Oscar asked, feeling incredibly guilty that he had so much free time on his hands which he wasn't using in any particularly constructive way, whilst poor Meena scurried off to work every day, tried to care for her mum, whilst also struggling to keep up with all her societies and meetings. He had a feeling something would have to give, but he wasn't about to suggest what. He knew how precious she was about her hobbies and interests – she'd made that quite clear – so if there were any changes to be made it was up to her to make them and not his place to say anything.

For a second when he pulled up in front of Anita's house, he seriously considered remaining in the car as Meena suggested, but he thought back to his comment that it wouldn't look too good, and he knew he was right. Anita and he mightn't be close – that was an understatement – but she *was* Meena's mother, and she was elderly, so he should make the effort. And anything he could do to support Meena he would.

Meena let herself in, calling out, 'Hi, Mum, it's only me. I've got Oscar with me. We can't stay long, we're off to amateur dramatics.'

He followed his wife into the house, gazing around curiously. It had been quite some time since he'd ventured inside Anita's house; if he was honest, it had been quite some time since he'd set eyes on Anita herself. Meena had brought her over for Sunday lunch a little while back, not long after he'd been given the news that he no longer had a job so he hadn't been very good company and he hadn't taken a great deal of notice of his mother-in-law. He'd been too busy wallowing in his own misery.

Anita glanced up at him and scowled, giving Oscar a glimpse of the bruise on her face. He tried not to let his consternation show, but he could see why Meena was worried. There was a slight swelling around the area of the cut, which wasn't particularly large, but the bruising looked nasty.

Meena had told him that her mother had refused any medical help whatsoever, but on seeing Anita he thought Meena should have insisted.

'Don't you think you ought to get that checked out?' Oscar asked.

'Mind your own business,' Anita said.

Oscar was about to retort that it *was* his business if it concerned his wife, but Meena shot him a warning look, so instead he shrugged and let it go.

'How are you feeling today, Mum?' Meena asked. 'Is there anything you need? I'll pop in again when I come home from work tomorrow, so if there is anything just let me know and I'll fetch it for you.'

Anita's scowl deepened. 'No, thank you, I can manage.'

'This isn't about managing: I don't want you to *manage*, I want you to be comfortable,' Meena insisted.

'I'd be more comfortable if you stopped fussing,' Anita snapped.

Oscar could see that Meena was becoming frustrated, so he decided to take charge. 'If there's nothing you need and nothing we can do for you, I suppose we should get off.'

Meena turned to look at him crossly and shook her head, a tiny movement, not meant for her mum to see. But very little got past Anita.

'Don't stay here on my account,' Anita said, giving her daughter an equally glaring look. 'I don't need anything and I don't want anything. I'm perfectly fine as I am.'

Meena drew in a deep breath and let it out slowly. 'If you're sure?'

'I'm sure. You've got things to do and places to be. You don't want to be coming round here every five minutes.'

'I don't mind, Mum, honestly. It's no trouble.'

'I'm sick of you checking up on me,' Anita said.

'Someone has to,' Meena retorted sharply.

'Isn't that what Nora's for?'

'No, Mum, it isn't.' Meena turned to Oscar. 'We'll be on our way then, shall we?'

Oscar was more than happy to leave. The atmosphere in Anita's house wasn't particularly pleasant. There had always been tension between Meena and her mother, ever since he'd known her, but he had no idea why. They had an odd relationship: Meena obviously cared for her mum a great deal, but they didn't seem particularly close. In fact, now that he came to think about it, Anita had always seemed slightly resentful of Meena, and she was most definitely very uncomfortable whenever she came to their house. He could always sense the relief whenever she left, from both Anita and Meena.

He didn't delve too deeply however – if there was anything of any great importance, Meena would have told him. So he assumed it was just a typical mother-daughter relationship. Some daughters were very close to their mothers, others not so much, and he assumed that Meena and Anita fell into the "not so much" category.

'Who is Nora?' he asked when they got back in the car and he started the engine.

Meena didn't say anything, and he wondered if she'd heard him, so he repeated the question.

'Oh, no one. Just a lady who pops in to see my mum now and again.'

Oscar would have assumed that Nora was one of Anita's cronies, or maybe even a neighbour, but there was something about Meena's tone that made him wonder whether there was something more to the story.

Never mind, he thought; if it was anything important he was sure Meena would tell him.

***

Oscar felt like a spare part. *The First Act* was a well-established group of people, although they probably did have newcomers now and again. But right now everyone seemed to know what they were doing, how everything worked, who was who, and what was what – and Oscar didn't.

He wished he'd paid more attention to Meena in the early days when she'd first joined the amateur dramatics society and had come home from rehearsals eager to tell him all about it. He used to listen with half an ear, until Meena had realised that he wasn't particularly interested, and she'd stopped talking about it.

It used to irritate him slightly when he and Meena, Dean and Janet were all out for a meal, and the other three used to chat about *The First Act*. He used to feel like a spare part then too. Until Meena realised that they were excluding him, and after that they didn't talk about it all that much. In fact, Dean didn't mention it at all, apart from to complain now and again that they were shorthanded.

Maybe that had been his friend's way of trying to ascertain whether Oscar was interested in joining without coming straight out and asking him. But at the time Oscar had had too much going on.

How things changed, because right now he didn't have very much going on at all.

Oscar was positive he could be of some assistance, though; if not acting, then surely there was something else he could contribute to the group? What, he didn't know, but no doubt Dean could make use of him. At least, that's what Oscar had thought until he turned up this evening, Meena towing him behind her like a yacht with a dingy.

He felt a little awkward, even though he did know some of the people there because he'd met them at an after-performance party or two. He'd been someone then, not just Meena's retired husband.

Oscar hadn't realised how thoroughly his identity had been tied into his job. It was common practice wasn't it, that when you met someone and you got chatting to them to ask what it was they did; but now if he was asked he'd have to say he was retired. It didn't sit well. In Oscar's eyes retirement hinted at old age and decrepitude. When he'd had a job he had been someone with a purpose, someone who people looked up to. But not now – one particular Friday afternoon on the golf course had shown him that.

Now that he was in Meena's domain, he felt very much surplus to requirements once again. This wasn't his bag at all. What had he been thinking?

He tried to smile, but he was fairly sure what he wore on his face was a grimace. And Dean confirmed it when he asked him if he was feeling OK.

'Never better,' Oscar blustered.

But he wasn't OK, not really.

Perhaps it would have been better if he'd had the chance to prepare himself for retirement. He knew Dean and Janet were avidly looking forward to spending lots of time together and doing all the things that they simply couldn't do because of the constraints of their jobs. But neither Oscar nor Meena had seriously thought that far ahead. As far as he was concerned he'd had another seven or so years to go, Meena considerably more, before they needed to consider it.

'Pull yourself together,' he muttered under his breath. It was bound to take him a while to get used to being part of the amateur dramatic society. He was well out of his comfort zone, not having a single theatrical or creative bone in his body, so he was bound to be feeling a little excluded, despite everyone smiling at him and saying hello, and a couple of handshakes and the offer of tea.

'I'll make the tea!' he exclaimed. That was something he could definitely do. At least it made him feel useful.

He took a pad and a pen out of Meena's bag and worked his way around the hall, taking peoples' drinks orders, feeling like a waiter. Not that there was anything wrong with waitering – there certainly wasn't, and if he and Meena were desperate for money he wouldn't turn his nose up at applying for a job in a bar or restaurant.

That's a thought, Oscar said to himself, as he found his way to the kitchen and began opening cupboards. Although he thoroughly enjoyed his fishing, like golf there was only so much of it he could do. His life could not simply consist of housework, food shopping and fishing. Maybe he could get a little part-time job somewhere? Or do some voluntary work? That was an option. At least he'd feel useful, helping people less fortunate than himself. Or animals. Growing up he used to love animals, especially dogs. He recalled Ray's dog and the comforting feel of those silky ears under his fingers and the happy expression in the spaniel's eyes, so maybe he'd look into helping out at a dog's trust or charity.

Filing the idea away for future reference, he set about making numerous teas and coffees and when he found a tray he loaded it up with the drinks and went back into the hall.

'Who wanted tea with milk, no sugar?' he called out, and there was a show of hands. Oscar carried the tray around so people could pick up their drinks, and then he went back into the kitchen for the teas with one sugar. He repeated the process a couple more times with the coffees, finally bringing out a tea with three sugars for one little old lady who bore a striking resemblance to Barbara Cartland in her latter years.

Finally he had his own cup of tea in his hands, and he was sitting cradling it and watching as Dean directed several people, Meena included, to stand in certain positions, when a man about his own age sidled up to him.

'Meena's husband, did you say?' the bloke asked.

Oscar nodded. 'That's me. My name is Oscar.'

'Haven't seen you here before,' the man said. 'Arthur Knight.'

'Pleased to meet you, Arthur. And what do you do? In *The First Act*, I mean.'

'I'm in charge of the lighting. Not much chance to practise it in here,' he said, 'but it's handy for me to turn up. I need to know the script and I need to know all the stage directions, so I generally sit things out and take notes. What do you do?'

'I don't know yet,' Oscar said. 'I've got a bit more free time, so I thought I'd come along and see if I could help out.'

'We can always do with an extra pair of hands. No doubt Dean will find something for you. But if you don't like what he asks you to do, just tell him. He's a reasonable chap, and if something isn't for you, he'll take note.'

Oscar nodded. 'I'll bear that in mind, thank you.'

He could have mentioned that he knew Dean rather well, but he didn't. He wanted to see how he might fit in first, and he didn't want to step on anyone's toes. So he sat and watched, taking everything in.

As soon as Dean announced a break from rehearsals for another cuppa and a biscuit, he made a beeline for Oscar.

'Meena tells me you're not playing much golf these days,' Dean said, pumping Oscar's hand. 'I thought I hadn't seen you on the course recently.'

'I've taken up fishing.'

'Catch much?'

'Some.'

'I bet Meena's none too happy.'

'Why not?' Oscar was puzzled.

'My dad used to catch fish and bring them home for my mum to clean and gut. The house stank for days.'

Oscar chortled. 'It's catch and release these days,' he said.

'I'm not sure if I'd be happy with that,' Dean mused. 'I thought the whole point of fishing was so that you could bring the fish home, boast about it, then eat it.'

'Not anymore. Look, I'm quite happy to sit and watch for a while but if there's anything I can do, anything you need help with…?'

Dean scratched his chin. 'Not right now, although you could shadow Wincy?' He turned in a slow circle scanning the room. 'Ah, there she is.' He pointed to a slim woman in her thirties. 'Wincy is responsible for the music score. Or…?' Dean took a step back and looked Oscar up and down.

'What?'

'You'd make a fine Widow Twankey,' Dean said. 'I can just see you in a dress with a bonnet and lots of makeup.'

Oscar was horrified. 'No chance! Uh uh. Not going to happen.'

Dean patted him on the shoulder. 'Just kidding. We've already got a fab Pantomime Dame. Let me have a think and I'll get back to you during our next rehearsal.'

'OK.' Oscar smiled, but it was hard work because he wasn't sure whether he wanted to attend the next rehearsal or not. Far from spending more time with Meena, he'd hardly seen her at all this evening. She'd been "on stage", practising her lines with the leading lady and the leading man. The most conversation he'd had with her had been in the car on the way.

Besides, he had an uneasy feeling that Meena regarded *The First Act* as her territory and hers alone, and he wasn't sure whether she appreciated him muscling in.

He'd see how he got on after this holiday, and if he still didn't feel it was for him or that it wasn't making any difference to their marriage, he'd knock it on the head.

CHAPTER 13

'This is lovely!' Meena exclaimed in delight as she scanned the hotel room. 'And look at that view!' She walked across to the floor-to-ceiling window on the far side of the bedroom and laughed. 'You can see the harbour and right across the bay.'

Oscar smiled at his wife's pleasure, and he went to stand next to her. The view was definitely glorious.

The hotel perched high above New Quay's harbour, but not too far out of the small town that they couldn't easily walk to it. Oscar peered through the window, feeling the warm sun on his face, and he gazed down at the massive stone wall jutting out into the sea and the tiny ant-like people on it. There was also a small array of boats bobbing about in the harbour itself, and he wondered what it would be like to own one of them, to be able to just put to sea whenever he felt like it.

Of course, nothing was ever that simple, and much would depend on the weather conditions, the type of boat you had, and all kinds of things that he had no idea about.

But one thing he did know, was that Meena had promised them a dolphin spotting boat trip.

As they had travelled across country heading for their destination, Meena in the passenger seat and him driving, she had read out a list of the things they could possibly do this week. He must admit, he was greatly anticipating going out on a boat, and he idly wondered if there would be any fishing opportunities. Not when they were out looking for whales and dolphins obviously, but generally. He hadn't brought his fishing equipment and neither had he brought his clubs, as Meena had made it quite clear that they weren't going to go off and do their separate things then come together for dinner, but they were going to spend all day every day in each other's company.

It was a novelty, he admitted silently. Neither of them was used to spending so much time alone together, but he was sure it would be all right. Other couples managed it, so why couldn't they? And, if Meena's excited chatter on the journey was any indication, there were lots of things they could do to keep themselves occupied.

'I think I'll go and freshen up after I've unpacked,' Meena said.

While she was putting things in drawers and hanging clothes in the wardrobe, he made them both a cup of tea and took it over to a little table flanked by two armchairs which were strategically placed in front of the large windows, and he sat there for a moment and took in the view for the second time.

'Wouldn't it be lovely to wake up to this every morning,' he said. 'I do envy people who live by the sea.'

'Oh, I don't know,' Meena called from the bathroom where he could hear her clattering about, emptying out the contents of her toiletries bag. 'Because we don't see it every day, it means that when we do it's all the more special.'

'I suppose you're right.' Oscar took a sip of his tea and wished he had a biscuit to go with it. 'Are we eating in the hotel this evening?' he asked.

'We can, if you like, but I hadn't planned on eating here every evening,' she called back, then the sound of running water drowned out the rest of what she said.

'Pardon? I can't hear you,' Oscar shouted.

Meena stuck her head around the bathroom door, and when he glanced at her he was pleasantly surprised to discover that she was naked, and she was beckoning him with her forefinger.

'Now?' he asked, raising his eyebrows. 'It's the middle of the afternoon.'

'So it is. Do you want to join me in the shower or not?'

Oscar did want to, very much.

***

'We should come away more often,' Oscar announced as they were getting ready to go out. It was a little early for dinner, but after spending so long in the car they were both ready for some exercise, although technically he could argue that they'd already had some, and very nice it had been, too.

He'd enjoyed it so much, he'd been about to suggest seconds, but he didn't think he was quite up to it, not for an hour or so. Besides, Meena had reached for a towel and had wrapped it around herself before wandering into the bedroom and rooting through the wardrobe. So he gathered that she wasn't up for any more just yet, either.

But they still had six nights ahead of them and six afternoons, so there was plenty of time for lots more love making, if they so wished. Oscar very much did wish, and with Meena having been in a much lighter mood since the day he'd caught the fish and had come home and made love to her, he was pretty sure she would be more than happy to spend several hours in bed over the course of their week away, and he didn't mean asleep.

It was quite a steep walk down from the hotel to the main part of the little town, and Oscar caught hold of Meena's hand as an excuse to steady her, but in reality he just wanted to hold her hand. Goodness knows the last time they'd done anything like that. They'd never been a handholding couple, and he suspected it might have been as long ago as their honeymoon since they'd last walked down the street holding hands.

Why hadn't they done it more often, he wondered, relishing the feel of her soft palm in his. It felt quite intimate, and even though they'd been married for nearly four decades, he almost felt as though they were on their honeymoon once more.

They had holidayed in the UK then too, not able to afford anything more exotic. It had been a week in Torquay in a quaint little bed and breakfast, where they'd gazed lovingly into each other's eyes across a full English every morning. Anton had been nine years old before they could afford their first holiday abroad.

And that was what they'd done ever since. It almost seemed like a badge of honour to be able to say they were going abroad, and although he wasn't one for going anywhere exotic and was more than happy to go to the Canaries, or the Spanish mainland (anywhere where there was a good golf course, to be honest) and he did feel as though it was a status symbol to hop on a plane twice a year.

This week in New Quay was going to be such a change and so different to what they normally did, that Oscar almost felt as though they'd pressed the reset button. Although they weren't in a little guest house or bed and breakfast (the hotel was far from that) the culture of lazing around by the pool or going on organised trips (Meena) and playing golf (himself) wasn't there. Neither would they be staking themselves out on the beach on a sun lounger, because it simply wasn't an option. British seaside resorts weren't geared up for that kind of thing. They'd be lucky if they managed to hire a deckchair, let alone two sun loungers and a parasol. And if there was an umbrella on offer, it would probably need to be of the waterproof variety not the sunshade kind. But today the weather was glorious, warm and sunny with a gentle breeze. It suited Oscar's mood perfectly. And when the wind carried the scent of the sea, with hints of ozone and seaweed, he felt his spirits soar.

'Shall we take a walk down to the harbour?' he asked. 'We can see what restaurants and pubs there are—' His eyes lit up. 'Why don't we pop in somewhere for a pre-dinner drink?'

'That's a good idea,' Meena said, her own eyes sparkling. 'I fancy an ice-cold cider in a beer garden.'

'Cider? You?'

'Why not?'

'Do you want a pint?' he joked.

'I think I might,' Meena said, as they made their way to the first pub they saw.

It was directly on the seafront, overlooking the harbour where lots of small boats were moored. The tide was out, and the boats sat on the sand patiently waiting for water to float them once more.

The pub was busy, with most of the tables taken, but when Meena spotted an empty one she let go of his hand and hurried over to it, then she turned to him and mouthed "cider" just in case he'd forgotten. He decided to have the same, and after he'd bought their drinks he carried them carefully outside and slid onto the bench. Instead of sitting opposite her, he sat next to her so they both had a view of the harbour, and he could put his arm around her waist and cuddle her into him.

She briefly rested her head on his shoulder, then straightened up to take a drink. 'Mmm, that's lovely,' she said. 'I'd forgotten just how nice a cold cider on a warm sunny day by the sea could be.'

Oscar had to agree with her. He sniffed the air. 'Smell that,' he said.

'Fish and chips,' Meena groaned, her eyes half-closed with bliss.

'How about it?'

Meena glanced at her watch. 'It's only six-thirty: maybe a little early for dinner?'

'I don't care. Shall we?' he asked, and when he saw his wife hesitate he drove the point home by adding in a seductive voice, 'Hot, fluffy chips with lots and lots of salt and vinegar. And a piece of succulent white fish in crispy batter. I can just taste it now…'

'Oh, go on, then,' Meena said, and even though she sounded a little reluctant he could tell she was enthused by the idea.

As they finished their drinks and strolled further along the street, with the smell of fish and chips growing ever stronger, Meena said, 'I had planned on a romantic meal this evening, with candles and wine.'

'I'm sorry. Have you booked somewhere?' Oscar asked, concerned that he didn't want to scupper her plans. After this afternoon, he was very much up for a little bit of romance.

'No, I hadn't. Although perhaps I should have; I didn't realise it would be quite this busy.'

'Tell you what, let's be decadent and eat our fish and chips out of the paper sitting on a bench this evening, then we can take a stroll and if there's anywhere we fancy we can book it for tomorrow. How does that sound?'

'Fish and chips out of paper,' Meena mused, and smiled softly. 'I remember when they used actual newspaper to wrap them up in, and the grease would seep through and your hands would get covered in print.'

'Those were the days,' Oscar said wistfully. 'Life was so much simpler then. Don't you think?'

'It was, but it was also harder. We didn't have two pennies to rub together most of the time I was growing up.'

He stopped and turned to face her, catching both her hands in his.

'We've come a long way, haven't we?'

She nodded. 'We certainly have.'

'No regrets?' He didn't have any and he hoped she didn't, either.

'None whatsoever,' she said.

'I love you, Mrs Fisher.'

'I love you, too, Oscar.'

He bent to kiss her, his lips barely brushing hers, not wanting to make too much of it considering they were standing in the middle of the street with people passing on either side.

'Come on,' he said. 'Let's get those fish and chips. My stomach thinks my throat has been cut. It must have been all that exercise earlier.' He winked at her

She giggled, and it made his heart sing to hear it. He couldn't remember the last time she'd giggled; laughed, yes, but giggled like a girl? No, he couldn't.

If he could capture this moment and bottle it, he would have done.

They were going to be all right, he knew it. This holiday was just what they needed. He could almost see their bonds weaving closer together, their love strengthening – if that was at all possible.

It was also just what he needed in order to draw a line under what his life had been like before retirement, and what it was going to be like from now on.

CHAPTER 14

'Goodness gracious, I'm stuffed.' Meena slumped back in her chair and eyed her empty breakfast plate. 'I can't believe I've just eaten all that,' she said. Two rashers of bacon, a fried egg, a sausage, grilled tomatoes, baked beans, mushrooms, two pieces of toast, and before that she'd had a bowl of fresh fruit with delicious honeyed yoghurt. She wasn't quite sure where she'd managed to put it all.

She curled her fingers around the handle of a pretty teacup and gazed out of the dining room window at the view.

'I think we need to take a little stroll,' she said. 'I need to walk this lot off, otherwise I'll be going back home twice the size I arrived.'

'I can think of other ways to work it off,' Oscar said, waggling his eyebrows at her.

'Oscar!' Meena hissed at him, and she glanced quickly around the room to make sure nobody had heard.

No one was paying them any attention: they were much more interested in their own breakfasts than in two middle-aged married people.

Although calling themselves middle-aged was being a little optimistic, Meena thought. Middle-age had come and gone, technically speaking: unless Meena planned on living to one hundred and sixteen.

However, she didn't feel elderly. When Meena thought of *elderly*, she thought of her mum. Meena still worked for goodness' sake, and she was very active and quite fit. It was all that rushing around she did.

Perhaps everyone felt the same way as they aged, as though they were a younger person trapped in an older person's body.

She gave herself a mental shake. This was neither the time nor the place to be dwelling on encroaching old age.

'Wind your neck in Oscar,' she said teasingly. 'We can do that later. I'm not going to spend all day in bed, not when the sun is shining and the water is sparkling. Come on, where's your sense of adventure?'

'How adventurous would you like me to be?' he teased, waggling his eyebrows again.

She sighed theatrically. 'I was talking about getting out and doing something on this lovely day. Not spending it in a hotel room. If it rains later on in the week, we don't have to go out at all, but now I'm here I want to go exploring.'

'OK,' he sighed.

But he was smiling, so she knew he wasn't bothered about her rejection. Anyway, it was more of a promise than a rejection. No doubt they'd come back after their day out, and would want to relax for an hour or two before dinner.

'What is it you want to do?' Oscar asked, finishing his coffee and patting at his lips with a napkin.

'I want to take a stroll across the beach first,' she said, 'and dabble my toes in the water.'

'I think we can manage that,' he agreed. 'Then what?'

'We can take a walk along the coastal path, so wear your trainers.'

Oscar tilted his head to the side. 'Um…' he said. 'Is there a golf course nearby?'

Meena sucked in a sharp breath and glared at him. Then she realised he was teasing her, and she swatted at him with her hand.

'I could change my mind about going back to bed later,' she warned, and Oscar held his palms up in surrender.

Meena fairly waddled out of the hotel, still feeling rather full, but pleasantly so. She hadn't indulged in a cooked breakfast for some considerable time, and she couldn't remember the last time she'd been tempted by bacon and eggs.

When they were on holiday abroad it was normally an all-you-can-eat buffet, but the bacon just wasn't the same somehow, and neither were the sausages. So she tended to stick to fruit, fresh bread with jam, or the occasional light omelette. But when you came to the British seaside, you simply had to have bacon and eggs for breakfast, she decided. It was the rule. At least it would set them both up for the rest of the day, because she couldn't imagine being hungry at lunchtime, but maybe they could stop off for a coffee and cake somewhere?

As they began to walk down the hill towards the harbour and the little beach next to it, she felt Oscar slip his hand into hers again and a warm feeling of contentment spread through her chest. She'd been quite shocked when he'd held her hand yesterday evening. It wasn't something they normally did but it had felt so right, and she was pleased that he had. My, she was getting romantic in her old age. But she wasn't complaining. This was the happiest she'd felt in a long time.

'Come on,' she called as they dawdled down the concrete walkway to the beach.

As beaches went this wasn't a very big one but it did have lovely soft sand. And the tide was going out; or was it coming in? She wasn't quite sure, but there was an expanse of damp glistening sand for her to wiggle her toes into, so she slipped her trainers and socks off and walked towards the little wavelets.

The sea was incredibly calm, with only a gentle breeze blowing towards the shore, and Meena turned her face to the sun, feeling the heat of it already. It was going to be a warm day, perhaps not ideal for hiking along the coastal path; nevertheless they'd come here to explore and that was what they were going to do.

She waited for Oscar to take his own trainers off, then once again he took hold of her hand and they sauntered towards the water's edge. 'Oh!' Meena squealed. 'It's cold!'

Oscar chuckled. 'What did you expect? It's hardly the Med, is it?'

She nudged him with her elbow. 'Silly, I know that. It's just a bit of a shock, that's all.' She splashed around a little, going slightly deeper up to her mid calves. 'Once you get used to it, it's quite pleasant,' she said.

'I bet you any money that you won't go for a dip,' he teased.

Meena looked at him. 'Challenge accepted,' she replied.

'When?' Oscar was taken aback.

'Tomorrow, if the weather is like this.'

'Shall I find you outside in the middle of the night, doing your rain dance?' He chuckled.

'Most certainly not,' she said. 'But what I want to know is, what will you forfeit if I do go for a dip?'

'I'll treat you to an afternoon in the spa?' he suggested.

'I was going to do that anyway,' Meena countered.

'Did you have something in mind?'

'Yes, the attic needs cleaning out.'

Oscar groaned. 'You can't be serious?'

'I can.' She kicked, sending a spray of water into the air and watched it fall back, the droplets glistening in the sunlight. 'It needs doing, and it's something I've been putting off for a while.'

'When you say "a while", how long do you mean?'

'About five years.'

'Great, I'm going to be the one who's out there doing a rain dance now. Because if you do go for a dip, and I mean a full dip with your head under and everything, then I'm going to have to sort out the attic.'

Meena stood on tiptoe and kissed him, and she felt his arms slip around her waist and pull her close.

'This is nice, isn't it?' she said, and Oscar murmured into her hair and kissed the top of her head.

As one, they turned and dawdled back up the beach and onto the walkway to find a bench where they could sit to dry their feet and brush the sand off before putting their trainers back on.

'Are you ready for this?' Meena asked, getting up.

Oscar pulled a face. 'How far are we going?'

'It's about four miles. I looked it up on the map. It's a tiny little place called Cwm-something-or-other, and it's got an old limestone kiln.'

'Anything else?'

'Not really.'

'Why are we going there?'

'Because we can,' Meena said, grabbing hold of him and yanking him to his feet. 'I'll race you to the road,' she cried. 'The last one is a ninny.'

She dashed up the walkway until she reached the road. It wasn't far, but she was panting anyway. It seemed that both of them were in dire need of the exercise: she'd thought she was fairly fit, but she wasn't.

Meena lifted her chin and straightened her shoulders as Oscar caught up with her, and she tried not to let him see how winded she was.

'Lead on, 'he said, falling into step beside her. 'But I warn you, if you get tired I'm not carrying you back.'

'I was kind of hoping that we would both be tired by the end of this,' she said with a glint in her eye. 'I was thinking we could have an afternoon nap.'

Oh yes, this holiday was definitely what they needed.

'Thank the lord for enterprising people,' Oscar said as he sank gratefully down onto a patio chair. Cwm-whatever-it-was – he couldn't pronounce it either – did have a lime kiln, although it hadn't been operational for goodness knows how long. Apparently, it had been used to roast limestone from Pembroke, and the resulting mixture was spread on the fields to counteract the acidity of the soil, and it was also used to make mortar.

Oscar, if he was truly honest, could have quite happily lived the rest of his life without knowing this little snippet of information and he couldn't believe they'd walked over four miles from New Quay just to see it.

He had to admit though, that the scenery was absolutely stunning, if somewhat taxing. The whole walk had consisted of relatively narrow paths, some kissing gates, the odd stile or two, and more up and down than was good for his hips or his knees. By the time they'd crossed a little wooden bridge at the end of their walk, Oscar felt he'd more than earned the coffee and cake Meena had promised him. Breakfast seemed like an awfully long time ago.

The enterprising person was the owner of a cottage situated on a narrow lane leading up from the little cove. It was one in a row of about ten houses, and the owner had seen an opportunity to offer refreshments and homemade cakes to weary walkers, so they'd popped a couple of tables and chairs on the bailey at the front of the house, and had propped up a chalkboard with a selection of cakes and drinks written on it by hand.

Meena took her sunglasses off, dropped her bag at her feet and relaxed into her seat. Oscar was thankful that she'd had the foresight to bring a couple of bottles of water with her. It hadn't even occurred to him, and he realised that he still wasn't stepping up to the mark as much as he should.

It had always been Meena's responsibility to make sure that the family had sun cream and hats, plasters, and a spare T-shirt for Anton because he nearly always dropped something down his. And later on, when Anton no longer wanted to accompany them and Oscar and Meena were by themselves, she'd still made sure she packed everything they needed, even if it was just for a day out.

If he'd realised she had been carrying two bottles of water in her bag, he'd have offered to carry it for her. He felt remiss that he hadn't had the foresight to think of such a thing.

However, he asked if the café's owner would refill their water bottles for them, because it was going to be even warmer on the return journey, and he'd make certain he was the one carrying the bag on the way back.

'I think we've earned this,' Oscar said when the lady bustled out with a tray laden with a cafetiere, a teapot, a jug of milk, a couple of mugs and, to Oscar's delight, two huge slices of cake. They'd each chosen a different variety, with the intention of sharing.

'This is very pleasant,' Meena said, tucking into her half of one of the slices. 'We should do it more often.'

'Go on humongous walks with cake and coffee at the end of it?' Oscar joked.

'I'm serious,' Meena said. 'We don't make enough use of the time we have off.' Then she realised what she'd said and looked guilty.

'I agree,' he said mildly. 'We didn't, did we. But we were both busy people. You still are. And there are only so many hours in the day.'

'From now on, we must make a resolution to spend more quality time together,' she announced.

Oscar couldn't fault that. But the question was, just how much free time did Meena have? She still worked full time, and with all the other activities she did, it meant that her only free day was Sunday, and although they didn't see Anton, Grace and the children every Sunday, it was often twice in a month. So that left just two Sundays to themselves.

It was better than nothing, Oscar thought, trying to look on the bright side.

He'd been just as guilty as Meena of letting their precious Sundays slip by without doing a great deal. Actually, that was a lie; he'd often gone out for a game of golf in the morning, regardless of whether their son was coming for lunch or not.

But now that he had more time than he knew what to do with, he could fish whenever he wanted, which left Sundays free to spend with his wife.

He couldn't believe how much he was looking forward to it. Of course, they wouldn't be doing things like this every day because the coast was a fair distance away, but they could certainly go for some nice walks along the canal, or visit a castle or two, or take a stroll in the woods. Autumn would be here before too long, with all its brilliant colours, so why shouldn't they go for a lovely long walk on a bright autumn day and kick through the leaves. And he wouldn't expect Meena to plan it or decide where they were going. This was now down to him.

Hopefully, with Meena not having to do anything around the house unless she wanted to, she might have more free time to spend with him.

***

'Having an afternoon nap is getting to be a habit,' Oscar said as they left the hotel later that evening to go in search of dinner. Although, there was no searching involved because Meena had spotted a nice little restaurant as they staggered back from their long walk earlier, and had made sure to book a table.

When they'd arrived back at the hotel, both of them hot, thirsty, tired and with aching legs and feet, they'd had a quick shower (separately, not together) and then had relaxed on the bed.

Two hours later Oscar had woken up to find Meena still asleep, curled up next to him. She'd looked so cute lying there, with a slightly pink nose from being out in the sun, the towel she'd wrapped herself in after her shower falling away to reveal the curve of a breast, that he'd woken her gently with kisses, and what they had subsequently done had warranted yet another shower. And now they were heading out for dinner.

This was only day one of their holiday, and Oscar already felt like a different man. He was much more relaxed and contented; happy even.

They passed the harbour on the way to the restaurant, and Oscar almost felt like a local because the site was becoming so familiar to him, and he gazed around, taking it all in, trying to commit it to memory.

He spotted a brightly coloured kiosk and guessed it must be one of the places where you could book the dolphin-watching trips that Meena had been talking about. He was looking forward to getting out on the water. It would be quite an adventure. Then something else caught his eye – something equally as exciting. It was a sign for fishing trips. Wreck and reef fishing, he read, and he also saw that tackle was included as well as tuition.

His eyes lit up. Half a day's fishing, in the sea no less. It was a thought. Then he realised he'd better put it on the back burner because Meena wouldn't be all that keen. Although… she did say she was going to book herself into the spa. He didn't fancy any of that hot stone and aromatherapy stuff, so he could always go out for a morning's fishing while she was getting her back pommelled and her face de-wrinkled – not that she had any wrinkles, just the occasional line, he thought diplomatically.

He only realised he'd stopped walking when Meena tugged at his arm. This time they weren't holding hands, but she'd slipped an arm through his instead, and now she was getting impatient.

'I've booked our dolphin-watching trip with another company just around the corner,' she said, thinking that was what he'd been staring at, and not the sign next to it about fishing.

Oscar cleared his throat. 'When are we doing that?' he asked.

'Tomorrow, in the morning, because apparently the sea can pick up a bit more in the afternoon and I didn't want either of us to feel seasick. I've booked us into the spa for the afternoon.'

'I thought you were supposed to be having that dip in the sea you promised?'

Meena pulled a face. 'Maybe another day?'

'Chicken.'

She clucked and said, 'I haven't forgotten, just not tomorrow, eh?'

'*Us?* You've booked *both of us* into the spa?'

'Yes. That's OK, isn't it?'

Damn, Oscar thought; he wasn't going to go fishing tomorrow after all. Oh, well, it was probably a good thing. They were supposed to be spending this holiday together, and not going off and doing their separate things like they normally did. Oscar could forgo doing a spot of fishing if it meant being this close to Meena, and he didn't just mean physically. He felt like he'd fallen in love with his wife all over again, and at the moment he had eyes only for her and she for him. There was no way he was prepared to jeopardise that.

CHAPTER 15

Meena allowed herself to be helped down from the quay into the boat. For some reason she'd been imagining a significantly larger vessel, but this one only held about twenty people and it bobbed around a lot, even in the harbour, so she was a little concerned.

Oscar must have sensed her nervousness because he slipped his hand into hers and squeezed it.

'It'll be better once we get underway,' he said.

He seemed to know what he was talking about, and she was a little surprised because she didn't think he knew an awful lot about boats. But he was soon proved right because once everyone had boarded and was seated, the engine throbbed into life and the boat made its way slowly into the water beyond the harbour wall, and she immediately felt better.

Meena paid attention as one of the crew demonstrated how to use a life vest and told them where they could be found, and she fervently prayed that there was enough for everyone in case the worst should happen. Which it wouldn't, of course. She hoped.

She'd never been on a boat before, apart from a rowing boat on a pond many years ago, which she had forgotten about until now, and didn't think counted. She hadn't anticipated being quite so nervous: however, everyone else seemed to be taking it in their stride so she supposed she'd have to as well, otherwise she'd make a fool of herself.

The boat moved out beyond the harbour wall and into the sea proper, and as it headed into the wind it picked up speed. It still wasn't going particularly fast, but she could feel the rise of the bow as it ploughed through the waves, and she swivelled around to stare back at New Quay.

She hadn't realised quite how steep the town was, until she saw it from this angle, and her eyes sought out their hotel. No wonder it had such fabulous views, she thought – it was perched quite high up and seemed to tower over the streets below. Thankfully it didn't stick out like a sore thumb and it blended in with the rest of the town, although it lacked the bright colours that many of the houses were painted. From this angle the town reminded her little of Tenby, where she used to holiday when she was a child.

New Quay gradually became smaller until the boat rounded a headland of sorts and disappeared from view completely. When she could no longer see it, she turned her attention to where the boat was headed and saw that the open sea was to the right and towering cliffs were on their left.

When Meena realised that she and Oscar had walked along the tops of those very cliffs only yesterday, she gasped. 'Crumbs,' she said. 'I didn't realise we were so high up.'

'That's because we were quite a distance from the edge,' Oscar said, looking at where she was pointing. 'From up there it slopes off gradually, you don't see how steep it is or how long the drop.'

Thank goodness, Meena thought, because if she had known, she would never have suggested such a dangerous walk. Saying that though, she hadn't felt in any particular danger at all. The track had been steep in parts, both up and down, but she hadn't worried about losing her footing or falling. It was because she was seeing it from this angle that it made her realise just how wild and impressive the landscape in this part of Wales was.

As the boat sped through the water, she noticed everyone turning their heads from side to side trying to spot a dolphin, and she did the same, hoping to catch a glimpse.

There weren't any at the moment and there was no guarantee they would see some, so she settled back to enjoy the trip and listened to the skipper's commentary as he pointed out various sea birds. There weren't as many now as there had been earlier on in the year because the breeding season was over, but there were still plenty of gulls around, some of them very curious as they swooped down low to see if there was any food on offer. One even landed on the top of the canopy and peered down over the edge at the human occupants.

'Oh, look a seal!' Meena cried, when a sleek black head broke the surface and bobbed up and down, looking at them. It was only after she'd spotted the first one did she realise there were quite a few. Grey Atlantic seals the passengers were informed, and the skipper shared a few interesting facts about their feeding and breeding habits. He then pointed out the sedimentary rocks that formed the cliffs, and gave them some background information, which Meena found fascinating.

When the boat arrived at the limit of its outward journey and had started to swing around to head back the way they'd come, Meena felt quite disappointed. She'd thoroughly enjoyed being out in the open water and didn't want the trip to end, especially considering they hadn't seen a single dolphin yet.

It couldn't be helped; they were wild animals and didn't appear on command, and she'd resigned herself to not seeing any when a shout had her craning her neck and peering over the other side of the boat.

'Oh my God, there's a whole pod of them!' Meena cried, her voice lost amongst the excited chatter of the other passengers. Everyone tried to take a photo, but not Meena. She wanted to live in the moment, rather than vicariously through the lens of a phone. She knew she wouldn't forget this, and she wouldn't need a photograph to remind her of it, so she lost herself in watching the magnificent creatures as they powered through the water, their fins and the tops of their backs breaking the surface before disappearing under it again. They took absolutely no notice of the boat which was a respectful distance away.

Very soon the animals had outstripped the boat, swimming faster than Meena thought possible, and she watched them until she could see them no more, joy in her heart. It was only when they finally disappeared from sight that she realised Oscar had his arms around her and she was leaning back into him. His chin was resting on his shoulder, and when she turned her head to kiss him on the cheek, she saw her own sense of wonder reflected in his eyes as he dropped his gaze to her.

'That was wonderful,' Oscar said slowly. 'Thank you so much for suggesting this.'

'Magnificent, weren't they?' she said. 'I could watch them all day.'

'So could I,' he murmured, 'so could I.'

***

Oscar was still buzzing during lunch, which they ate in a small cafe a couple of streets back from the harbour, before making their way back to the hotel and the spa treatment Meena had booked for them.

He wasn't sure about having any kind of treatment, but Meena had insisted that he'd enjoy it. They were to have a massage each, hers was aromatherapy and his more of a sports massage because he'd complained once or twice about his shoulder aching. Meena thought a massage would do him good. Whilst she was having a facial, he'd relax in the sauna. Afterwards he'd join Meena in the pool and they could have a swim about, and maybe a sit in the hot tub with its soothing jets of water.

They were shown into their respective changing rooms and were given complimentary robes to wear and slip-on plastic shoes. Oscar felt a bit of a prat wearing disposable shoes, swimming trunks and a fluffy robe over the top, and he reluctantly followed a rather small lady as she showed him into a room.

Soft music played throughout the treatment rooms, and the ambience was definitely relaxing with its subdued lighting and soothing scents.

Oscar didn't feel relaxed, however. He felt on edge, not knowing what to expect, and when he was instructed to take his robe off and lie face down on what appeared to be a hospital trolley with a hole in the middle for him to put his face into, he was as far from relaxed as it was possible to get.

'Relax,' the woman told him, which made Oscar tense even more, and he almost leapt out of his skin when he felt her warm hands on his back. But as she got to work on him, it didn't take very long before he had reached the stage of ragdoll floppiness which reminded him of Anton when he was asleep as a baby.

Gosh, that woman had incredibly strong hands, he thought, as she dug her thumbs into the muscles around his shoulder blade. He didn't know whether he wanted to cry out in delight, or whimper at the pain of it. It hurt, but it was a nice kind of hurt, and he could feel his muscles loosening as she concentrated on his back and shoulders.

'Oh…' he groaned when she found a particularly knotted area. He could hear the muscles crunching underneath her fingers and he prayed she wasn't doing him any permanent damage.

He groaned again and hoped nobody could hear him. These weren't noises that he generally made outside of the bedroom and he began to feel a little embarrassed, although his therapist didn't seem to mind. She said very little apart from "move your arm" or "I'm just going to do your legs". There was only the sound of his breathing, the glide of soft hands on skin, and the occasional rustle of her clothing as she moved around the massage bed to reach different areas of him.

By the time she'd finished, he felt like a new man. He had also lost his embarrassment. If he could afford it, he would have suggested that she came home with them so she could give him a massage like this every evening. No wonder people raved about them.

She left him to lie there for a short while to compose himself, and Oscar managed to compose himself so successfully that he was almost asleep when she came back into the room.

He slipped his robe back on, shoved his feet into the disposable shoes, and headed for a shower to wash the oil off his skin before he ventured into the sauna.

When Meena stuck her head around the door sometime later, Oscar was leaning back against the wooden side of the sauna, his eyes closed and sweat dripping from every pore. He was so hot he didn't know what to do with himself, but he was also so chilled out that he couldn't make a move.

'You look as if you've had a good time,' Meena said. 'You've got a blissful expression on your face.'

Oscar opened an eye and squinted at her. 'You look pretty pleased with yourself, too,' he murmured. She was glowing and looked rather radiant.

'Oh, I am,' Meena said, stepping inside and closing the door behind her to keep the heat in. 'I always feel rejuvenated after one of these sessions, and the facial was to die for. She even gave me a head massage… mmm.'

Oscar used the towel he'd been given to wipe the sweat from his face. 'I think I'm just about cooked,' he announced, getting slightly unsteadily to his feet, his head spinning. 'I need a cold shower.'

'The Scandinavians swear by it,' Meena said, as he followed her outside. 'But I think they like to roll in the snow or something afterwards.' She shuddered. 'No thank you: a dip in the pool will be enough for me.'

She waited for Oscar to rinse himself off, and while she did so she put two fresh towels on a couple of sun loungers.

'Would you like a drink first?' she asked him. 'I can get us a glass of cold water, or you can have something sparkly if you like.'

'Water is fine, thanks,' Oscar said, panting slightly. He needed to rehydrate after spending so long in the sauna, so he waited for her to fetch some drinks and he downed his in one before he slid into the pool.

He did a couple of lengths of breaststroke then turned over onto his back and floated about for a bit, his hands wafting through the water to keep himself steady. Meena treaded water next to him.

'I could get used to this life,' she said, and Oscar agreed with her.

'This is only day two,' he said. 'We've still got four more days to go.'

His wife grinned at him. 'I know! Wonderful, isn't it?'

'Have you got anything planned for the rest of the week?' he asked, although knowing her, she probably did.

'As a matter of fact, I have,' she told him.

'Are you going to enlighten me?'

'Nope, I don't think I shall. Not until tomorrow. It involves a short drive, so don't drink too much at dinner tonight or this evening.'

Oscar twinkled at her; he had no intention of drinking very much at all, because he had every intention of making love to her. All night, if he could manage it.

CHAPTER 16

'Well?' Oscar asked, after breakfast the following morning.

Meena had just put her knife and fork down and was contemplating another cup of tea. She'd eaten her second enormous breakfast of the week, but with all the calories she'd been burning lately, she felt she could get away with it. She'd better not get too used to eating this amount though, because when she returned home she didn't think she'd be half as energetic as she was currently. She would like to be, but life had a tendency of getting in the way and she knew that once she was back in work she'd probably be too tired to do much more than sleep when her head hit the pillow, and their bedroom antics would dwindle to what they had been pre-holiday.

'Now,' she said in a warning tone. 'Don't get on your high horse, but I've booked us in for a pottery class.' Then she watched the expectant look on his face fade.

'A pottery class.' It wasn't a question, it was a statement, and he didn't sound happy about it.

'That's right. There's a craft centre about a ten-minute drive away and they do all kinds of things, but I thought we'd have a go at pottery. We throw down our pots today, they'll be fired overnight and I think we can pick them up tomorrow, or the day after – I'll have to check.'

'Wonderful.'

Oscar was saying the right thing but not in the right tone of voice, and she knew he wasn't enthused. She hoped he'd change his mind once he got into the swing of it. At least pottery wasn't something she'd tried before, so she wouldn't be any better at it than him.

If she was honest, she didn't particularly like getting mucky, so the odds are she'd probably be worse because she'd be a bit squeamish about all that damp clay on her hands.

Oscar's mood didn't appear to be any better when they arrived at the craft centre, but at least he hadn't refused to accompany her, so she took some heart from that.

They were shown into a small room, where a few other people were already gathered, and were given some basic information such as what to do if the fire alarm went off and where the loos were. Then they were given an overall to wear. Meena's was too big, but she preferred it that way because it covered more of her clothes, so she buttoned it up, rolled up the sleeves and prepared to get dirty.

Oscar just stuffed his arms into his and shrugged it on, then he stood there with a guarded expression on his face.

They were led into the main workroom, where their tutor introduced herself, and she asked them to gather round to give them a quick talk on what to expect, followed by a demonstration.

Meena was fascinated, Oscar not so much. He held himself quite stiffly and didn't say anything, and she knew he wasn't at all happy about being landed in this situation. But she also got the feeling that if he gave it a go, a proper go and not a half-hearted one, he might actually enjoy himself.

Demonstration over, each student went to stand by their respective workstations, on which a lump of damp clay already sat next to the wheel.

Meena picked hers up and slapped it down onto the wheel, the way she'd watched the tutor do it, then she turned it slightly whilst she patted it into some semblance of a ball.

Out of the corner of her eye, she noticed that Oscar had picked his up and had put it on his own turntable, his attention on what he was doing. And, as the tutor issued instructions such as advising them to wet their hands, where to place them, and how much pressure to use, Meena saw Oscar start to loosen up, and she knew that as long as his pot didn't fall apart or collapse, he'd probably have a good time.

Soon though, she forgot about Oscar and his slightly grumpy attitude, and she concentrated on making as good a bowl as she possibly could, and when she was finally finished she looked up to see that most of the others had finished theirs, including Oscar. He was looking awfully pleased with himself.

Wiping her hands on one of the old cloths provided, she walked over to his workstation and examined his pot.

'That looks good,' she said. 'I'm impressed.' He'd even glazed it in a soft shade of green.

'So am I,' Oscar admitted, his surprise evident.

'Was that as bad as you thought it was going to be?' Meena asked.

'No, it wasn't. I rather enjoyed it.'

Meena laughed then lowered her voice. 'I doubt if you would have enjoyed it as much if your pot had collapsed,' she muttered, scooting her eyes over to the left where one of the ladies had had an unfortunate accident with her bowl.

'Come on, let's get cleaned up,' Meena said, after they'd placed their bowls on a shelf. 'We'll have some lunch on the way.'

'On the way to where?' Oscar asked.

Without answering, Meena smirked to herself when she thought about what she'd lined up for her husband next.

Lunch was in a pretty little pub a short drive away, and Meena had a wonderful rainbow salad with a seafood platter while Oscar opted for a steak and ale pie with chips. She encouraged him to eat it all because he'd need a hearty meal inside him to line his stomach for what was to come.

'Are you going to tell me what you've got planned?' he asked after they'd finished eating and had ordered coffees.

'Artisan ales,' Meena announced. 'We're having a tour of a brewery this afternoon,' she added, and she laughed as his face lit up.

'Perfect,' he said.

'Better than the pottery this morning?'

'Much,' he agreed. 'Although, pot-making wasn't as bad as I thought it was going to be. I'm not sure how my pot is going to turn out, though.'

'Does it matter? As long as you enjoyed the process, that's the main thing.'

'Bit like fishing, I suppose,' he said. 'It's the activity, more than anything, although catching a fish is good fun and a bit of a thrill. You ought to try it sometime.'

Meena gave him an incredulous look. 'I don't think so,' she said with a shudder. She couldn't imagine anything worse than sitting beside a lake or a river for hours on end, with nothing to do apart from stare at a long pole with a bit of wire dangling from it, and hope that some poor fish would get the hook caught in its mouth.

'Don't knock it until you try it,' her husband said. 'I tried your pottery class, didn't I? Besides, I didn't think I'd like fishing either until I tried it. You might be surprised.'

Meena didn't think she would be surprised. She didn't do sitting still all that well – maybe she could take her knitting? It was a thought and she wondered how Oscar would react if she suggested it.

She didn't say anything further on the subject, instead she asked for the bill and then they were on their way. As far as she was concerned, the subject was closed. There was no way her husband would get her to go fishing with him. It might be hypocritical of her considering she'd insisted that he go to a pottery class with her, but she didn't see it as quite the same thing.

His reward for attending the class was this visit to the brewery, which Meena wasn't at all keen on but she'd booked it because she knew Oscar would enjoy it.

To her surprise though, she found the tour to be quite interesting. She'd never considered how beer was brewed before, or any other alcoholic drink for that matter, and she was incredibly impressed with the high tech, industrial look of the place. She was more interested in the process, whereas her husband, bless him, was more interested in the end result. Luckily for him there were plenty of opportunities to taste the various ales.

Meena sampled one or two herself, but she only had the tiniest of sips because she was driving, and she enjoyed the flavour of the two she tried, although ale would never be her go-to drink, she decided.

Oscar, on the other hand, was in his element, and by the time they had completed the tour he was well on the way to being tiddly. He emerged from the brewery with a cardboard carrier full of artisan ales and a rather drunken vow to do some home brewing, which Meena knew would be unlikely to happen.

By the time they arrived back at the hotel, Oscar's eyes were closing and his head was lolling. He woke up enough to get out of the car and go inside, but once they reached their room it was clear he would need a nap before dinner.

Meena wasn't tired, so she left him to it and popped down to the hotel's lounge for a cup of tea and a skim through the papers.

It had been a good day, she thought, a very good day indeed. She didn't want this holiday to end. She wasn't looking forward to going home because they were having such a lovely time, and she felt quite sad that they only had two more full days to go before they'd have to head back to reality.

This week away was doing them the world of good. She almost felt like they were on a second honeymoon, and she made a promise that they wouldn't slip back into their old ways.

It was a new beginning for them, and she was convinced that now they'd settled into some kind of routine at home and both she and Oscar were becoming more used to their new status quo, that everything would be absolutely fine from now on.

***

Oscar's mouth felt like the bottom of a parrot's cage when he woke with a thumping head and a feeling of complete disorientation. It took him a moment to realise where he was, and then another moment to work out what day it was, what he'd been doing, and the time.

It was just gone six o'clock in the evening, he was in a hotel in New Quay, he'd had a bit too much to drink this afternoon, and his wife was nowhere in sight. He guessed she'd probably left him to sleep it off, but he was still a little disconcerted that she hadn't stayed in the room. He thought she'd probably gone for a walk, and the likelihood was that she was mooching around the shops, an activity she enjoyed but he wasn't too keen on. He thought about phoning her to ask where she was, but realised her phone was sitting on the table next to the picture window. Never mind, he guessed she wouldn't be long.

Oscar had a quick shower to freshen up, but Meena still hadn't reappeared by the time he was done and he debated whether to make himself a cup of tea in the room or take a stroll to clear his head.

He decided on the latter because he was feeling a little stewed and the fresh air would do him good, so he left the key card in reception and ventured outside, keeping his eyes peeled in case he spotted his wife heading back to the hotel.

His feet took him down towards the harbour and as he walked he breathed deeply, enjoying the smell of the sea on the breeze and the sun on his face. It was still relatively high in the sky and wouldn't set for another three hours, and he squinted as he stared out to sea, shielding his eyes. The sun danced off it and he marvelled at the different colours of the water, from deep navy, to grey, to bright blue and even turquoise in places, and the waves were flecked with white. He realised it was probably quite choppy out there as he studied the boats beyond the harbour wall and the spray from their bows, and he was thankful he wasn't out there right now. He'd enjoyed his boat trip the other day, but he wasn't so sure how he would have fared if the sea had been rougher.

He turned his gaze away, feeling a little nauseous. That would teach him to drink so much. He hadn't intended to, but when it was on offer it would have been rude to say no.

Meena's thoughtfulness in booking a tour of a brewery made him smile, and the pottery session hadn't been too bad either, he admitted.

He'd meant what he said when he'd suggested that Meena tried fishing. Apart from the fact that she hadn't been able to drink much this afternoon because she was driving, she'd seemed to have had a good time at the brewery, so she might enjoy fishing if she'd just give it a go.

It was only when he found himself standing right in front of the little kiosk advertising fishing trips, did he realise what he intended to do.

He knew Meena hadn't planned anything for their last day because she'd told him so, saying that they might just want to chill and relax and maybe go for another walk, so he was confident he wouldn't be disrupting her plans if he booked a fishing trip for a couple of hours for the last day.

Despite today's white-topped waves and the blustery sea, Oscar was keen to get back out on the water, but this time he wanted a rod in his hand. And the dolphins might also make a reappearance, which would be the icing on the cake as far as he was concerned.

Meena had loved seeing them, so even if she wasn't thrilled by the thought of fishing she'd probably welcome a chance to get on a boat if there was a possibility of spotting dolphins again.

With that in mind, he booked a two-hour trip for Friday. Two hours was long enough for Meena's first taste of fishing, he thought, especially when the bloke manning the booth informed him there was a very good chance of catching some fish.

Hangover gone, Oscar hurried back to the hotel. He wouldn't tell Meena about the fishing trip until Friday morning – she wasn't the only one who could spring a surprise.

***

Meena treated herself to a second pot of tea, then when she'd finished reading the papers she returned to the room, only to discover that Oscar wasn't answering the door. Concerned, she went back downstairs to ask reception if they could ring up or maybe even let her in, and was informed that the key was behind the desk and that Mr Fisher had gone out.

Cross because he hadn't told her, her irritation faded when she realised that her phone was still in the room so he wouldn't have been able to call her anyway, and she wondered if he'd gone looking for her, guessing that he probably had.

Whilst she waited for him, she had a soak in the bath, revelling in the complimentary bubbles, and was drying herself off when she heard a knock at the door.

'Where have you been?' Meena asked as she let him in.

'I could ask you the same thing,' he said. 'I woke up and you were nowhere to be found.'

'I was in the lounge, reading the papers.'

'You didn't take your phone with you,' he pointed out.

'I forgot.' She picked it up and quickly checked for messages. There was one from Nora to say she'd been in to see to her mum earlier and everything was OK. That was a weight off her mind, and Meena breathed a sigh of relief.

'How are you feeling?' she asked Oscar.

He grimaced. 'Fine now, although when I woke up I had a bit of a headache.'

'I'm not surprised,' Meena laughed. 'Will a hair of the dog make you feel better?'

Oscar groaned. 'Definitely not, although I expect you could do with a drink.'

'And some dinner?'

'After that huge meal at lunchtime?'

She shrugged. 'It's all this sea air; it's giving me an appetite.'

Oscar pretended to leer at her. 'It's given me an appetite, too. Shall we order room service and retire to bed?'

'I'm not tired,' Meena said, primly.

'Neither am I!

CHAPTER 17

'Dress warmly,' Oscar advised his wife as he made her a pre-breakfast cuppa. It was their final day in New Quay, and he was looking forward to their fishing trip. He still hadn't told her, and if he was totally honest he wasn't looking forward to her reaction.

They'd had a lovely day yesterday, walking along the coastal path – in the opposite direction this time – despite the weather being blustery, followed by a trip to Cardigan Castle which was a short drive down the coast, and had called in to pick up the bowls they had made on the way back. Meena's had turned out well: Oscar's not so much. His pot had collapsed on the one side and when he looked at it from a certain angle it reminded him of saggy buttocks.

He'd tried to tell her about their fishing trip several times throughout the day, but there hadn't seemed to be the right time or the opportunity, and if he had thought about it logically, he should have realised that his reluctance to say anything to her indicated that he knew deep down that she wasn't going to be thrilled at the prospect.

Meena tilted her head as she accepted the mug from him. 'Oh? Why's that?'

'I've planned a little trip,' he admitted.

'Where?'

'That would be telling. If you can be mysterious, then so can I.'

When she narrowed her eyes at him, he could tell she knew he was up to something, and he recalled she'd been just as elusive when she'd sprung the pottery class on him. However, despite being sceptical initially, he'd enjoyed it. He just hoped that Meena would feel the same about fishing. She'd loved being out on the boat the other day – she'd love being out on one today, he was certain of it, and even if she didn't like catching fish, she could watch the sea for fins and seals.

'I'm going to miss this,' Meena said as they were tucking into yet another cooked breakfast.

'I can make you a full English before work, if you like?' Oscar offered.

'It wouldn't be the same, but thanks anyway. Besides, I'm always in a rush in the mornings.'

'You don't have to rush on the weekend,' he pointed out. 'Not with me doing more around the house.'

'True, but it still wouldn't be the same. I like sitting here with this view and having our breakfasts brought to us.'

The dining room had a fabulous view out over the bay, and Oscar had to agree with her that having breakfast served to them was far more pleasurable than having to cook it. He'd miss the view more than the full English though, he decided as he studied the boats in the harbour.

But when his eyes were drawn to the horizon, his heart sank.

On peering through the curtains this morning he'd been delighted to see that the sky was blue and the sea was calm, which boded well for bobbing about on it. But now the breeze had picked up, evidenced by the white tops, and clouds scudded across the sky.

Oh, dear, it was going to be choppy he guessed, but he took comfort from the thought that Meena hadn't felt at all unwell the last time they'd been on a boat, so she'd probably be fine today.

He hoped she'd join in with the spirit of the trip and have a go at casting her rod in the water. If she caught a fish or two she might be bitten by the fishing bug the way he had been, and it would be something they could do together, because for him the jury was still out on the amateur dramatics thing. Maybe if he and Meena had joined at the same time things would be different, but as it was he felt like an outsider. *The First Act* had always been something Meena did by herself, and Oscar wondered if she thought he was trying to muscle in. But that wasn't the only reason he felt uncomfortable about it – he had no idea how he fitted in. Everyone else had a role to play and knew what they were doing. What had Oscar done? Made the tea and lingered around like a bad smell.

When he had been working, he hadn't noticed just how little time he and Meena spent together, but since he'd been forced to retire, he had also been forced to re-evaluate his life. And the wonderful time they'd had this week had made him realise that they needed to find a hobby they both enjoyed and that they could do together.

The problem was… what?

***

Meena felt like screaming. It wasn't catching sight of the craft they were about to board that sent her spirits plummeting, but what they were about to do on it. No way did Meena want to fish. She might enjoy a piece of cod in batter but she didn't want to see it in its raw, dead state. And neither did she want to play any part in the process of it going from alive and flapping, to being dead and slimy. Just seeing the whole fish at the fish counter in Sainsbury's was bad enough. And as for the smell…

A shudder went through her as she drew in a shallow breath. The boat stank strongly of fish, and it was decidedly unpleasant. She had a suspicion she'd be able to smell the stench of it in her hair for days.

The two men operating the boat seemed friendly enough, and they did their best to make her feel safe and comfortable, but the vessel hadn't left its mooring yet and she was already starting to feel nauseous. Combined with the stiff fresh breeze, she wasn't at all happy.

'You might see a dolphin,' Oscar coaxed, his voice full of false cheer.

He was trying to jolly her along, the way Meena herself had done when Anton was a child and he hadn't wanted to do something, and resentment began to simmer. She didn't want to see a damned dolphin. Or rather, she *did*, but not as a side-product of watching Oscar fish.

She was strongly reminded of when he'd first taken up golf and had discovered a course not far from the hotel they were holidaying at on the Costa del Sol. He'd persuaded her to go with him, and she'd trailed behind him like a caddy pulling the damned rented set of clubs. He'd gone from green to green, lamenting the fact that he hadn't had the foresight to bring his own set.

That had been before Anton was born, and once their son was on the scene Meena had the perfect excuse not to accompany Oscar on the golf course. By this time it was clear that Oscar was addicted to the game, so Meena had found other ways to occupy herself and their son.

But now Oscar seemed to think she'd like fishing, in the same way he'd thought she'd like golf. Would he never learn?

She took a seat and huddled into her coat. It was chillier today than it had been the last time they were on a boat, and she had a feeling it was going to be even chillier once they cleared the harbour.

She was still grumbling silently to herself when they cast off and the boat sprang into life. It was at that moment she realised she'd ambushed Oscar in exactly the same way with the pottery class. She knew he wasn't particularly creative and that arts and crafts had never been something he was interested in, yet she'd gone ahead and booked him into a pottery taster-class regardless.

Wasn't Oscar doing the same thing to her with fishing?

They were both trying to shoehorn the other into boxes they didn't want to be in.

She was no better than he.

It was probably best if they agreed to disagree when it came to their respective interests. The only activity they seemed to enjoy doing as a couple was walking. Maybe they should stick to that? It was a thought... A nice long walk on a Sunday morning if Anton wasn't coming for lunch would be something she and Oscar could do together.

She smiled ruefully to herself – if anyone was able to listen in on her thoughts they'd get the impression that Oscar and she lived totally separate lives. That wasn't the case – they were busy people, that was all. Or rather, she *was* and Oscar *used* to be.

Meena caught Oscar's eye and he grinned. She realised he thought she was smiling because she was enjoying herself, and she shook her head and sighed. He was trying so hard to get her interested in his world, bless him, that maybe she should give it a go and try not to be so negative. After all, Oscar had made a good attempt at throwing a pot. He hadn't sulked, but had made the best of it and although she knew he'd quite enjoyed the experience, she also realised that he didn't particularly wish to repeat it. But at least he'd given it a go.

So it was with a degree of false joviality that Meena joined in when the boat drifted to a halt and she was given a rod. She listened to and tried to implement the advice given to her (all the while secretly hoping that she wouldn't catch anything) but her heart wasn't in it. And when the continual roll and bob of the boat began to make her feel queasy, she struggled to maintain her false enthusiasm.

Oscar, on the other hand, was having a fantastic time. When he landed his first fish after a bit of a struggle, his face glowed with excitement.

'Look!' he cried, holding it up for her to see.

It flapped and flopped weakly, and Meena felt incredibly sorry for it. Assuming it would be thrown back the way Oscar did with his lake catches, she let out a gasp of dismay when the skipper took it from Oscar and conked it on the head.

There was a brief tussle in Meena's tummy as she tried to hang on to her fried breakfast – then she threw up.

At least she managed to aim over the side of the boat, she thought weakly, as she wiped her mouth, her eyes watering. But she promptly vomited again when the skipper announced in a hearty voice, 'Keep it up, love! Nothing brings the fish in like some sick in the water. You'll hook one in no time.'

****

That went well, Oscar thought sarcastically. It had been clear right from the very start when he'd told Meena he'd booked a fishing trip, that she'd had absolutely no intention of even trying to enjoy it. She'd made her mind up she was going to hate it, and so she did, despite the polite smile she'd plastered on her face for the benefit of the crew.

But he hadn't been fooled: he knew Meena too well.

She'd spent the first half of the trip huddled in her coat, her cheeks pink from the raw wind, and the second half hanging over the side as she lost her breakfast.

Oscar felt quite sorry for her; she couldn't help being seasick, and if he had got the tiniest inkling the last time they were on board a boat that she might suffer from it, he never would have sprung this on her.

Admittedly, the sea had been calmer then and there hadn't been the constant whiff of fish…

Despite his concern for his wife's indisposition, Oscar had managed to land two mackerel and one bream, and had thoroughly enjoyed himself. It was a real treat to keep what he had caught, and when the skipper recommended that he give the fish to the hotel to cook for tonight's dinner, he was over the moon. Cooking what he'd caught appealed to the caveman in him, and he felt like a proper fisherman.

Meena had been very quiet on the way back to the hotel, and she'd kept her eyes firmly averted from the bag of fish he had been holding, only perking up a little when they'd arrived in reception and she'd been given the room card.

When Oscar handed the bag over and enquired whether they were able to cook his catch (he'd hoped the skipper hadn't been having him on) the man behind the desk said, 'Of course, sir. Chef will be delighted to prepare these for you to eat this evening. Do you have any preference in the way they are cooked, or do you want to leave it up to Chef?'

'Let's leave it to Chef, shall we?' Oscar said. 'I hook 'em, he cooks 'em.'

Meena shuddered delicately, but Oscar knew that she'd feel differently when she was faced with a beautifully cooked mackerel for dinner. She liked fish, did Meena, and you couldn't get any fresher than that.

***

'I think I'll have the pan-fried chicken,' Meena announced at dinner that evening, shaking a white napkin open and draping it across her lap.

She reached for her glass of white wine and took a big mouthful. It was the first thing she'd been able to stomach since they'd returned to their hotel several hours ago. She hadn't even been able to face a cup of tea.

All she had wanted to do was to lie down – after she'd had a much-needed bath to rid herself of the lingering smell of brine and fish, of course.

She'd even managed to drop off to sleep for a while once the sensation of bobbing about on the boat had left her. But when she'd woken, she'd still not felt like eating or drinking anything apart from a couple of sips of water.

She wasn't unduly hungry now, but she knew she'd better have something, and pan-fried chicken with a small side salad was the plainest thing on the menu. The chicken came with a wild mushroom sauce but she'd ask if it could be cooked without. Meena was sure they'd be happy to do so once she explained she'd been unwell and couldn't stomach anything rich or fancy.

'The chicken?' Oscar asked. 'But we're having the fish I caught.'

She'd forgotten that Oscar had proudly brought his catch back to the hotel, and she'd forgotten that the kitchen

205

was going to prepare it for their evening meal. Or had she deliberately pushed the memory from her mind because she was hoping that it wouldn't happen? It had been bad enough watching the poor things being despatched, without having to eat them as well. It was almost enough to make her become a vegetarian, she thought; then the irony of her wanting to order the chicken made her roll her eyes at her own silliness. Even so, she didn't intend to eat the damned fish.

'There's no need to be so sniffy about it,' Oscar said, taking offence where none was intended.

'I'm not being sniffy,' she argued.

'I saw you roll your eyes. If you don't want to have the fish, all you needed to do was say so.'

'I thought I had.'

'And I was just checking that you hadn't forgotten that Chef was cooking our fish,' Oscar shot back.

'*Your* fish.'

Oscar chortled. 'Are you annoyed because you didn't catch anything?'

'Hardly.'

Her husband wasn't convinced. 'Never mind, what's mine is yours,' he said. 'So they are your fish, too.'

'I don't want them to be my fish. They're nothing to do with me and I'm not eating them. I want chicken.' Why was it so hard to understand, she wondered.

They fell into an awkward silence which was only broken when their respective meals arrived, and only then because Meena winced when she saw the fish's dead eyes stare accusingly back at her from Oscar's plate.

'Good grief!' she exclaimed. 'You might have asked the kitchen to remove the heads first.'

They finished their meal without saying another word, Meena picking at hers, Oscar devouring his as though to make a point, and she was glad when the ordeal was over and she could retire to their room. She'd been hoping that their last night in New Quay would consist of a romantic meal in one of the nice restaurants in the town, followed by leisurely lovemaking; not the awkwardness it had turned out to be.

'Sorry,' she heard Oscar mutter later, as they watched the news.

Meena had been lying under the duvet in rigid irritation, but she softened at his apology. He had miscalculated, that was all.

'It's OK,' she replied, turning towards him. He was propped up on one elbow, looking at her with a woebegone expression on his face. 'At least we know that fishing isn't for me.'

He brightened. 'Maybe not *sea* fishing—'

'Hold it there! I don't want to do *any* fishing, thank you. You're welcome to sit on a muddy bank for hours on end, but don't expect me to join you.' She'd be bored out of her mind watching nothing happening.

Seeing his face fall, she said, 'I'm sure we can find something else we can do together instead...?'

What they found to do that evening kept them occupied for a good long while, much to the delight of both of them.

CHAPTER 18

Oscar scowled. It hadn't taken very long for things to return to exactly the same way as they had been before they went on holiday, and they'd only been back a few days yet New Quay felt as though it had been months ago. He didn't know what he'd been expecting, but he had been hoping that at least some of the magic they'd re-kindled would have continued.

It hadn't. Meena was at work all day and occupied with her various activities in the evening, plus calling in to see her mum, and he was left at home to do the housework and a spot of fishing. The housework he could do without and, as enjoyable as fishing was, he couldn't be expected to sit on the lakeside for hour, after hour, after hour.

He made himself a coffee and took it into the garden. The bushes were starting to grow back after he'd hacked at them, he noticed with satisfaction, and although it would be a while before they returned to their former glory, they didn't look as chopped about as previously. The lawn also looked better, the former bald patches now covered with lush grass. It could probably do with another mowing, but he wasn't in the mood.

'Pull yourself together,' he muttered under his breath. This despondent attitude of his simply couldn't go on. He had to get a grip and decide what he wanted out of this new life of his. He'd not wanted to retire, but it had been thrust upon him anyway, so it was down to him to make the best of it. Moping around and feeling sorry for himself wasn't going to get him anywhere. Waiting for Meena to come home and throw him a few crumbs of attention wasn't ideal, either.

What he wanted was his old job back, but as that was impossible the next best thing was to get another job – which was easier said than done. He'd scoured the internet relentlessly during those first few days and weeks after he'd been told he was being given the push, and had even fired off a few applications.

Those companies who had bothered to reply had politely said "thanks, but no thanks" but he'd not received a response from the majority of them. He'd spoken to a couple of employment agencies too, but when they knew how old he was they'd not held out much hope.

So what was he supposed to do? He didn't want to sit at home twiddling his thumbs for the foreseeable future. Being bored to death wasn't the way forward.

His sole topic of conversation these days was what the best deals in the supermarket were and what he'd planned for dinner. It was hardly riveting, and he could feel himself becoming duller and more uninteresting by the day.

Not just that, resentment that Meena's life was carrying on just the way it had always done, despite the wonderful week away (it was as though it had never taken place for all the good it was doing them now), bubbled inside him and he was frightened it might boil over.

It wasn't his wife's fault that his life had been turned upside down, he reasoned in one of his more sensible moments – on the other hand, he did feel that she could be more supportive and spend a little more time at home, with him.

But perhaps that was the problem – maybe she *didn't* want to spend time with him?

After all, it would be a novel experience for both of them. The holiday in New Quay had been an aberration, a fluke, a one-off. He'd been kidding himself, thinking that this was what retirement could be like – long walks, lots of lovemaking, meals out…

Real life wasn't like that, especially since one of them still had a job and a social life. And a needy mother. He knew Meena felt duty-bound to pop in to check on her most days, but it was taking its toll on her already and they'd only been home five days. Meena was running herself ragged, stretching herself too thin.

Despite him taking over the household chores (he still wasn't convinced he was doing things the way she liked them done) she looked tired.

There wasn't a great deal more he could do in terms of housework, but it suddenly came to him that there was a task he could take off her shoulders – he could help out with Anita.

Anita probably wouldn't thank him for it, but she'd have to put up with it. If he popped in three times a week, it would mean Meena wouldn't feel obliged to. He'd do Anita's shopping for her and run the vacuum cleaner around if needs be, and anything else the old lady wanted doing; although to be fair to her, she managed most things herself. She didn't have Meena's exacting standards (who did?) but her house was always clean and tidy, and she seemed to be keeping on top of things.

Maybe he could make his mother-in-law see sense when it came to downsizing? Meena was right – the house was too big for her and there would come a time when Anita would be unable to cope with it, despite the stairlift she was having fitted shortly.

Failing that, he might be able to talk her into having some home help, or meals delivered – anything to help put Meena's mind at rest. Of course, none of these measures would do much to prevent Anita from having another fall, but if that happened they'd just have to deal with it. He'd meant it when he'd told Meena that her mum was welcome to move in with them, but he knew Anita would hate it.

How did other elderly people cope, he wondered. Anita was lucky in that she had Meena (and him) plus Anton and Grace. How did people without families manage? Was there a volunteer service of some kind? Generous souls who checked up on old people—

Oscar stilled, his hand halting in mid-air as it reached for his mug on the wooden patio table, when he remembered something he'd thought of a while ago.

He could be a volunteer!

Not only would it keep him busy and give him something to do, it would also be worthwhile and rewarding.

Hastily, he fumbled his phone out of his pocket and started to search.

***

Crikey, who knew there was so much out there? Oscar was feeling rather overwhelmed with the number of charities and organisations which needed help, and it had taken him some considerable time to whittle down what he *could* do, compared with what he *wanted* to do.

But it was the photos of all those poor dogs and their mournful little faces which convinced him that he definitely wanted to work with dogs. How could he resist? And the information on each poor pooch and why they had ended up in a shelter pierced his heart, and one or two of their stories even reduced him to tears.

Oscar shot off a quick email with his details to the nearest rescue centre, then sat back and thought about what he'd done. He wasn't sure how Meena would react, but he was confident that she wouldn't mind what he did as long as he wasn't moping around waiting for her to come home.

If *Pawprints on Your Heart* accepted his offer of help, he hoped he'd be too busy to pine and pout, and it would give him something to talk about other than the size of fish he caught, or whether he'd managed to dry the washing outside or not.

He couldn't wait for her to come home so he could tell her what he'd done and at the same time he'd also suggest taking some of the burden of calling in to see to her mum off her shoulders.

He was about to take some chicken breasts out of the fridge for their dinner, when he remembered something that made his own shoulders slump – Meena was going out for a meal tonight with her Knit and Natter friends after dropping in on Anita, so she wouldn't be home until later.

With a sigh, he closed the fridge door and leant against it.

Tonight was another evening where he would eat alone and watch TV alone, and he found himself wishing that his wife would make him a priority for once.

***

Meena's Knit and Natter group met up about once a month, although in between meetings most of the members were quite active online and they had a WhatsApp group where they posted photos of how far they'd got with their projects, and shared hints and tips. Occasionally someone would say they were stuck, or they needed more yarn or some other such problem, and everyone jumped in to help. It was a nice little group, and Meena didn't mind going to the meetings because they only happened twelve times a year. Scratch that, it was more like eleven, because no one wanted to meet during December as there were so many other things going on.

They always met in the pub, and everyone took their knitting with them, both current projects and recently completed ones. They ignored the looks they got from some of the other clientele, and the bar staff were well used to them by now and didn't bat an eyelid when one or two of the members whipped out their knitting needles in between courses.

Meena felt a little guilty that she wouldn't be eating with Oscar this evening. Since he'd retired he had been at home for dinner every evening (and so he should be considering he was the one cooking it) and they generally ate together, then they either sat in the living room and watched some TV, or Meena went out again. Sometimes she occasionally disappeared upstairs to her workroom instead – which reminded her, she still had quite a bit left to do on the quilt she was making. However, it was a labour of love, so she didn't mind how long it took, but she nevertheless made a mental note to spend an hour or so on it tomorrow to keep the momentum going.

'Meena, how the devil are you?' One of the ladies, who was the driving force behind the Knit and Natter group stood up as Meena walked into the bar, and held out her hands. Taking both of Meena's in her own, Fiona pulled her into a hug.

'I'm good thanks,' Meena said, hoping no one realised she wasn't being totally truthful. 'How are you?'

Fiona grinned. 'Never better,' she said. 'Especially since we seem to have a full house this evening.'

Meena counted heads and arrived at nine. They were indeed all there, and she smiled and said hello and gave little waves across the table as she sat down.

She turned to the guy behind the bar and held up a finger. He nodded, knowing what she drank, and whilst she waited for him to bring her wine, she told the group all about her lovely week in west Wales.

And it had been lovely, despite the last day.

However, now that she and Oscar were at home once again, things were back to normal. They hadn't been back a week yet, and she could already sense Oscar's resentment at her going out to work during the day and then out again in the evenings. But, darn it, this was her life and it had been this way for such a long time, she didn't see why she should stop doing what she enjoyed just because Oscar was bored.

Recently that enjoyment wasn't as in evidence as much as it used to be. She felt restless and out of sorts, and guilt continually hovered around the edges of her mind.

Suddenly her mother's words flashed into her head and Meena realised her mum was right – she *wasn't* happy.

She had been, before Oscar had been forced to retire.

But she wasn't now.

She felt as though Oscar didn't want her to have a life of her own now that it no longer suited him, and resentment rose up to form a lump in her throat.

Feeling as though she might cry, she lowered her head and blinked hard to drive the sting of tears away. Her marriage, which she'd once thought of as rock solid, now felt fragile and friable; she was worried sick about her mum, well aware that if her mother had another fall it could mean a broken hip; and she was also trying to juggle work and a busy social life.

Something had to give.

With a deep sigh, she glanced up as her wine was placed in front of her and she made a grab for it, gulping it down in one. Sod it, she'd get a taxi home and Oscar could drive her to fetch her car in the morning.

As she signalled for another drink, she made a decision. For the sake of her marriage and her sanity, she'd resign from the school's governing body at the start of the new academic year. She'd also jack in the WI. As for *The First Act*, she'd wait and see whether Oscar would continue to attend; he'd not said anything, but she had a suspicion he wasn't enjoying it. She wouldn't do anything drastic yet because Christmas was less than five months away and she had a substantial part to play in the pantomime so she didn't think it fair to leave them in the lurch. The time to leave the society would be after Christmas – a fresh start, and all that.

Two impending resignations were enough for now, so she'd see how things went and whether there was any improvement at home before she resigned from the amateur dramatics society. Maybe she wouldn't have to? Maybe Oscar would settle down and discover that he enjoyed it as much as she?

She wasn't going to hold her breath, though…

CHAPTER 19

Meena hurried home from work, conscious of the time. Rehearsals were in an hour and a half, and she hadn't had dinner yet. She'd spent longer at her mum's than she'd intended (she'd called in on the way) and she was now running late.

Thankfully Oscar informed her that the meal would be ready in minutes, and some of the tension drained out of her. Meena hated being late; it was one of her bugbears.

She slipped into her usual seat and sniffed appreciatively as Oscar placed a steaming plate of tagliatelle in front of her. A bowl of salad was already on the table, along with a sizeable chunk of Parmesan cheese and the grater.

Oscar was turning into a real whizz in the kitchen, she mused as she picked up her fork and dived in. She hadn't had time for a proper lunchbreak today because the practice was short-staffed and eating at her desk generally killed her appetite. She was starving now though, and she ate eagerly, enjoying the simple pleasure of eating a meal she hadn't had to cook herself.

Meena realised she'd grown quite used to that in the weeks since Oscar had retired. It was one less thing on her daily to-do list, one less thing to have to think about.

However, considering that Oscar did nearly everything around the house, Meena seemed to have less time – which was odd. She was constantly rushing here, there and everywhere, and she'd recently begun to wonder how she had managed to fit all the household chores in as well.

'I've been thinking of doing some voluntary work,' Oscar said, joining her at the table. He looked very domesticated with a tea towel slung over his shoulder.

'That's a good idea,' Meena said, around a mouthful of food. She put a hand in front of her lips as she spoke.

'I sent them an email today asking whether I could be of any use.'

Meena was pleased to hear he wanted to do something constructive. It would give him an interest, as well as helping those less fortunate than themselves. And with him busy, she wouldn't feel so guilty about all the interests she had. It was an ideal solution.

'I've also been thinking about something else I can do…' he said slowly, his expression expectant, and she wondered what he was about to tell her. 'How about if I call in to see your mum a couple of times a week? It'll take some of the pressure off you and give you more time to yourself.'

Meena froze, her fork halfway to her mouth. That was the last thing she'd expected him to say. Oscar and her mum weren't exactly pally.

Meena felt a frisson of guilt as she thought of the reason why. From the moment she and Oscar had started dating,

Meena had made sure to keep her boyfriend and her mother at arm's length from each other. She'd rarely invited him back to the house, worried about the state it might be in even though she'd always, *always* made certain the place was spotlessly clean and tidy. She knew it wasn't logical and that her fears were a holdover from her childhood, but her behaviour was ingrained, and she'd been that way ever since she'd heard Caroline and Wendy's mothers discussing her own.

And to be honest, Oscar had been so busy working his way up the corporate ladder that he hadn't wanted to play happy families with her mum. Meena didn't think he'd noticed that they rarely visited her mother's house as a couple, or that Anita always came to theirs. It was just the way they did things, and he never questioned it.

So it was a complete shock to hear him offer to look in on her mum.

Then a thought occurred to her – all this talk of doing voluntary work… Did he think he was going to start with her mum? Did he see her as a charity case?

If so, it wasn't going to happen. Meena was coping just fine – she didn't need Oscar's help when it came to her mother. And her mum didn't need his help, either.

And what was that about giving her more time to herself? Was he offering to help with her mum purely for his own selfish reasons, because he wanted Meena to spend more time at home with him?

'Thanks, Oscar, but I can manage,' she said through stiff lips. 'Anyway, I've been thinking about packing in the WI and resigning from the governing body, so that'll give me quite a bit more time to myself.' She said this last sentence with a degree of sarcasm, but Oscar didn't seem to notice.

'OK, but the offer is there if you want to take me up on it,' he said, getting to his feet to gather up the empty plates. 'Fancy watching a film tonight?'

'We've got rehearsals, don't forget,' she reminded him, and although he tried to hide it, she couldn't help noticing a flash of glumness cross his face.

Oscar, she thought, wasn't looking forward to this evening one little bit. She had been right not to hold her breath.

***

Oscar wasn't looking forward to rehearsals in the slightest. A fish out of water didn't begin to describe how he felt when he and Meena entered the community centre later that evening.

Everyone greeted everyone else enthusiastically, catching up with events, comparing how well they were getting on with learning their lines, or the trouble they were having with costumes and whatnot, and all Oscar could do was wonder why he was putting himself through this.

It didn't help that the woman who he had "shadowed" the last time was unwell, so he found himself making teas and coffees again and wishing he'd stayed at home in front of the telly.

'Oscar, do you think you can put the next track on?' Dean asked.

Actually, Dean didn't ask as much as barked out the instruction, and although Oscar nodded and did as Dean requested, he felt uncomfortable to be taking orders from a bloke who he was friends with.

He knew he was being silly (Dean was the production's director, and that's what directors did) but it was awkward, as though Dean was his superior: Oscar felt they weren't as equal as they had once been. The dynamics of their relationship were altering in front of his face, and he didn't like it. He was getting the impression that their previously easy camaraderie had changed slightly but he couldn't put his finger on it.

This, combined with the realisation that he didn't fit in and that he had nothing to contribute, plus his growing awareness that this was Meena's domain, drove him to make the decision that he wouldn't come again. *The First Act* wasn't his thing at all and if it hadn't been for wanting to spend more time with Meena, he never would have considered it.

During the break – where Oscar once more supplied the hot drinks – he took Dean to one side.

'I don't think I'll be coming again,' he said. 'What *The First Act* does is marvellous, but it's not for me. I'm going to knock it on the head.'

'That's a shame. Janet and I were so pleased you wanted to join us.' Dean appeared to be genuinely regretful.

That might well be the case, Oscar thought, but he was under the impression that Meena didn't feel the same way about his presence in the group, and he knew he'd made the right decision to quit.

Dean changed the subject and asked about Oscar's fishing, and that was the end of that.

The only thing left was for Oscar to breathe a sigh of relief and tell Meena what he'd done.

Undoubtedly she would breathe a sigh of relief, too.

***

The pub was loud and busy. Most of the amateur dramatics lot had piled into it after rehearsals, as they so often did. It was because the pub was only a stone's throw from the community centre and Meena often thought that having a pint (or a gin, in her case) was people's way of rewarding themselves after rehearsals. Of course, there was the alternative explanation – that attending rehearsals was merely an excuse to go to the pub afterwards!

Whatever the reason, Meena was glad to have a gin in her hand and Janet sitting next to her. She'd been acutely conscious of Oscar's discontent all evening, although he had lightened up now that he was propping up the bar with Dean and a couple of the other men.

'How are things?' Janet asked. 'You seem a bit down.'

'So, so. I was hoping the holiday would reboot our marriage, and it did whilst we were there—' Meena blushed at just how much rebooting had taken place '—but everything has gone back to how it was before.' She took a sip of her gin, feeling the alcohol hit her stomach.

'In what way?' Janet tucked her hair behind her ear and leaned closer. The noise was quite loud.

Meena didn't want to shout in case Oscar overheard, so she shuffled her chair nearer to Janet's. 'He's not happy that I've got a life and he hasn't,' she replied, shortly.

Janet's eyes widened.

Meena continued, 'He's made it clear he doesn't like me being out several evenings a week, and to top it off I'm having to call in to see Mum every day on the way home from work, and check on her on a Saturday, too. There is a glimmer of light, though – Oscar has decided he wants to do voluntary work. Hopefully it'll keep him out of my hair.'

Janet pursed her lips. 'Do you think you might be a little unreasonable?' she asked, her tone hesitant. 'It must be difficult for him after having worked all his life. He's probably finding it as hard to adjust as you are. At least he's trying to support you.'

Meena tensed. 'So he should, considering he's at home all day. I can't be expected to do *everything.*'

'I was referring to him joining *The First Act.*'

'Oh. That.' He might have been there tonight in body, Meena thought, but she didn't think he had been there in spirit. He'd looked positively bored to death.

'He's trying to join in, surely that counts for something?' Janet pointed out.

Meena wasn't so sure, and she pulled a face.

'I think you're being unrealistic,' Janet added, and Meena bit back a gasp. 'You have to work at a marriage. Oscar seems to be trying to work at his, but are *you?*'

How dare Janet say such a thing! *Of course* Meena was working at her marriage – why else had she booked a week's holiday for them?

She was about to give Janet a piece of her mind, but Meena abruptly realised that maybe Janet had a point. Oscar *was* putting himself out to come to *The First Act*, when he was clearly not loving it.

What was Meena doing to help their marriage?

Ah yes, she was going to shortly resign from two of the organisations she'd been a member of for years – that was her contribution. She'd have more time to sit on her backside in the evenings and watch TV with Oscar.

But if it made him happy, she was prepared to do it for his sake and for that of their marriage. If he could put himself out and make compromises, then so could she.

'We're going to miss Oscar's tea-making,' Dean said, intruding into her thoughts as he pulled up a chair and sat down at their table.

Meena glanced around for her husband and spotted him heading in the direction of the loos.

'Pardon?' She had no idea what Dean was talking about.

'He's not told you?'

Meena shook her head, her eyes on her husband as he made his way across the room. He was stopped by one of the society's members and he paused to speak to them.

'Told me what?' she asked, but she already guessed what Dean's reply was going to be before he opened his mouth.

'He's decided *The First Act* isn't for him. I don't blame him – amateur dramatics isn't for everyone and it's a big commitment. I hope you're not quitting, as well?' Dean patted her arm jokingly.

'No, I'm not quitting anything,' she said, irritation sweeping through her. She had been a hair's breadth away from resigning from the WI and the governing body, all in the name of compromise, yet Oscar had given her the token gesture of accompanying her to a couple of rehearsals and had then packed it in.

So much for wanting to spend time with her! He knew how much she loved performing, yet he couldn't be arsed to give it his best shot.

Damn him. There was no way she was going to resign from anything after this.

CHAPTER 20

It was Monday before Oscar received a reply from the dog shelter and he'd been on tenterhooks all weekend.

He surprised himself by how much he wanted this, and he hadn't visited the place yet! He might hate it, for all he knew, or he might find it difficult to cope emotionally; at least, that's what he kept telling himself each time he checked his emails, only to discover that *Pawprints on Your Heart* hadn't responded.

Eventually, someone from the charity did, but Oscar was then scared to open it in case it was a "thanks, but no thanks" reply.

When he plucked up the courage, he was delighted to read that he was being invited down for a chat and a look around, so he rang the number they provided and spoke to a very nice lady by the name of Yvonne, and she arranged for him to pop along later that day.

Oscar finished his chores (cleaning the windows and defrosting the freezer – riveting stuff!), had a quick spot of lunch, then changed into some old clothes and set off.

As soon as he got out of the car, he heard barking; the noise was incessant and rather loud, and he began to wonder what he was letting himself in for, but as he stepped inside the main building where the reception area was situated, the volume turned down a tad and he could hear himself think again.

'Can I help you?' the young woman behind the desk asked. She looked about eighteen and had numerous piercings.

'I'm Oscar Fisher and I'm here to see Yvonne,' he said.

'You're our new volunteer!' the girl declared happily. 'I'm Skylar.'

'Erm, I'm only here for a look around,' he said. 'Nothing has been decided yet.'

'You'll stay.' She seemed very confident of that. 'Everyone does – they take one look at those sweet little faces and they're hooked.'

'Right...'

That's what he was afraid of. But it was also why he was here. He'd get to spend time with dogs, he'd feel he was contributing to their welfare, and he'd be keeping himself busy. It was a win-win situation for everyone – Meena, included.

Yvonne turned out to be a no-nonsense lady in her mid to late forties, with a ready smile and a gung-ho attitude. She reminded him of Meena and he simply knew he'd get on with her.

The dogs seemed to adore her, he discovered after he and Yvonne had a quick chat during which she grilled him about his experience with dogs and animals in general, what he thought he could contribute to the shelter, and what he was hoping to get out of the experience.

When she eventually rose to her feet and suggested he take a look around before he made a final decision, Oscar felt wrung out. He'd had job interviews that had been less intense than this.

He hoped that by her offering to take him on a tour of the rescue centre that she'd found him acceptable volunteer material.

The buildings where the dogs were housed appeared to be purpose-built. They were ugly and functional, but he could tell that they served their purpose in keeping the dogs warm and dry, whilst giving them some outdoor space. He was surprised to see that the indoor area of each kennel was heated, and he understood that the centre staff were doing their best to make the dogs as comfortable as possible.

Each pooch had a comfy bed, which was raised off the floor, water and food bowls, and toys were strewn around, although none of the animals were playing with them as they seemed more interested in him and Yvonne.

Attached to the outside of each pen was some basic information regarding the dog it housed – such as their name, age, the breed if known and its gender, along with any special requirements and other notes that the staff and volunteers needed to be aware of.

Oscar read a few with interest. *Simba, three-years-old, Staffie-cross, male, needs lead training. Bessie, five-years-old, German Shepherd, female, nervous and very anxious. Mike, possibly ten, terrier-mix, male, deaf.* Bless him.

There was also a chart attached to every kennel specifying when the dog was last fed, when it was exercised and for how long, and loads of other snippets of information essential to the animal's welfare, such as when it was wormed, was it neutered, and so on.

Oscar was impressed at how organised the place was, and how well it was run. Even if it wasn't for the dogs, volunteering here would appeal to him for that reason alone. Despite Meena's opinion of his capabilities on the home front, he was a stickler for doing things properly and by the book when he was at work. *Had* been at work…

Occasionally, Oscar forgot himself and thought of work in the present tense. Being here, surrounded by calm efficiency and an ordered way of doing things was one of those times. But instead of finding it upsetting or disturbing, he found it oddly comforting and familiar, and he knew he was in the right place for him.

Suddenly fearful that Yvonne was going to tell him she didn't think he was the right fit for the rescue centre, he blurted, 'Can you use me?'

'We most definitely can,' she told him, holding her fingers out to a large fluffy dog with the most doleful expression Oscar had ever seen. 'This is Tiger, but he's the biggest softie going. He hasn't had his afternoon walk yet, so would you like to take him out?'

'Me? On my own?' Were they going to trust him with the dog? He could be anyone. He could run off with—

'I'll come with you to show you where to go, and if you are serious about volunteering, I'll assign you to one of the more experienced helpers for the first few weeks until you get to grips with how things work.'

'I'm serious,' Oscar said firmly. He'd never felt more serious in his life. One look at the hopeful furry faces had convinced him he was doing the right thing. The trick was, he realised, not to get so attached that he wanted to take each and every one of them home with him.

Yvonne lifted a leash off a hook and opened the kennel door. The dog barely gave her a chance to sidle in before he was flinging himself at her, his tail sweeping from side to side, his paws on her shoulders as he stood on his hind legs and tried to lick her face.

'He's a friendly boy, just over-enthusiastic,' she said, pushing him down.

The dog immediately jumped up again.

Tiger was a uniform black colour, with a vibrant pink tongue and dark brown eyes. He was similar in size to a small pony, and Oscar wondered how Yvonne managed to control him. The animal looked as strong as an ox and Oscar was doubtful whether he'd be able to hold him if Tiger decided he wanted to go somewhere.

Yvonne slipped the leash over the dog's head and to Oscar's astonishment the animal immediately settled down.

'He gets excited, but he's a good boy and we've been working on his leash behaviour,' she explained. 'It won't be long before someone adopts this fella, although he might be too large for some people.'

As soon as they were outside, Oscar fell into step beside her and gazed around with interest as Yvonne opened a gate and led him into a field.

'We're fortunate this field is secure, so we can let the dogs off. If we can, we try to walk two or three dogs together so they can socialise, and we also train them on their recall here. They can play with balls or frisbees, or just have a sniff around. And two to three times a week we take them on longer walks and expose them to as many things as possible. In some cases a dog will go to a foster home before they are put up for adoption if they need help with learning to live with people in a home setting. Some of the poor little mites have never been inside a house and you wouldn't believe how scary a washing machine can be, or how frightening a doorbell is if you've never heard one before.'

Oscar wanted to cry, and he had only been there an hour. What was he going to be like when he came here day after day? He'd probably be an emotional wreck. But he found he didn't care. He was more interested in helping these innocent little dogs more than he cared about his own emotional health.

He could make a real difference here, he knew he could. Even if it was just to make an animal feel loved. He suspected it might also be hard work, but he didn't mind. He was looking forward to it. For most of his working life he had been deskbound, so it would be a complete change of direction for him to do anything physical. The only thing he wasn't too keen on was picking up poop, but that was part and parcel of the role so he would have to get used to it.

Walk over, Yvonne led him back into the office once again, made them both a hot drink, then gave him some forms to fill in, and once all that was completed she asked him when he would like to start.

With a big grin on his face, Oscar said, 'How about right now?'

***

Meena sighed irritably when she stepped out of the office and into the surgery's reception area, and noticed the queue of patients wending its way to the main doors. She immediately went to one of the stations, typed her password into the computer, and called, 'Next!'

She instantly recognised the old lady who approached the desk. 'Are you here to see the nurse, Mrs Phelps? How is your leg?' With a few clicks of the mouse, she'd confirmed that Mrs Phelps had arrived, then she glanced up from the screen again.

The poor woman didn't look well. 'It's taking a long time to heal,' Mrs Phelps said. 'I'm getting fed up.'

'I expect you are,' Meena sympathised.

Mrs Phelps had caught her leg on a nail in her kitchen, and it had caused a nasty wound. In the elderly, wounds could often take longer to heal than they would in younger patients, and Mrs Phelps had been hobbling back and forth to the doctor's surgery every other day to have the wound dressed. It couldn't have been easy for her and Meena wished she could do something to help, but she didn't have a spare minute to herself as it was, and there were so many people who needed help, she wouldn't know where to start or who to prioritise.

She wondered how Oscar was getting on. He'd sent her a quick text to say he was off out this afternoon because he'd had a reply to his email about volunteering, and she wondered which charity or organisation he'd chosen, thinking that perhaps it might be one of those devoted to the elderly, considering he'd offered to call in to see her mum. Besides, Meena acknowledged they were both getting older themselves and they might need help in the future, so paying it forward might be a prudent thing to do—

Dear Lord! Meena caught herself and rolled her eyes as she realised she'd just wished twenty or so years away. But time flew by so quickly that she knew that the next two decades would be gone in a flash. The previous two certainly had. It seemed like only yesterday she was dropping Anton off for his first day in secondary school. Which reminded her, she still hadn't decided whether she was going to resign from the governing body, and she wondered whether she would actually go ahead with it. She should make a decision before the AGM in two weeks' time, but she'd been putting it off, reluctant to give it up.

As she booked the next patient in, she snorted to herself. Oscar hadn't been reluctant to give up *The First Act*, had he? He'd done it the first chance he'd got. Which was one of the reasons why she hadn't resigned from anything yet. She knew she'd have to at some point because she couldn't go on like this indefinitely, but not just yet.

The rest of the afternoon was equally as busy, and Meena was drained by the time she finished work. There were still patients waiting and there were still doctors on site, but her shift was done and it was up to one of the others to lock up.

The glorious aroma of roasting beef wafted up her nose as soon as she stepped into the house, and she guessed Oscar was cooking a roast for dinner and wondered what the occasion might be.

He'd only attempted a roast a couple of times and each time had been a success of sorts, although he'd been a flustered wreck at the end of it having been too ambitious in trying to cook more varieties of vegetables than was needed, as well as roast potatoes and mash. She hoped he'd toned it down, as much for his sake as for the amount of leftover food. To give him credit though, as soon as she'd told him that he could use the excess potatoes and vegetables to make bubble and squeak, he'd done exactly that and it had been delicious.

Meena was ravenous after skipping lunch yet again, but she wanted to have a quick shower and change into her comfy clothes before she sat down to eat. As she'd already called in to see her mum on the way home from work, Meena had no intention of going out again this evening, and now all she wanted to do was to settle down on the couch and watch something mindless on the TV.

'I'm just going to have a quick shower,' she said, sticking her head around the kitchen door and seeing Oscar wearing one of her pinnies.

He was standing at the stove with a spatula in his hand and his hips were swaying back and forth as he stirred the gravy.

'Hi, love,' he replied, giving her a smile. 'It'll be ready in five minutes.'

'I'll be quick,' Meena promised, dashing upstairs, and true to her word she was back down in record time to find Oscar in the middle of dishing up.

'Do you need a hand?' she asked, old habits dying hard as she itched to wipe up a spill of meat juices that glistened on the worktop.

'You sit down,' he told her. 'It's all in hand. If you want to do something, you can open the wine.'

'We're having wine?' It was a weekday, they rarely drank on weekdays unless they were going out, and she once again wondered what the occasion was.

'I've got news,' he said. 'I've been accepted as a volunteer.'

'That's wonderful!' she exclaimed. 'Who for, and what will you be doing?'

'Didn't I say?' He put a plate in front of her. 'Be careful, it's hot,' he cautioned.

Meena bent her head and sniffed appreciatively. It smelled divine, and it looked it too.

'*Pawprints on Your Heart,*' he said. He looked absolutely thrilled at the prospect.

She was confused. 'Isn't that an animal charity?'

He nodded, his hands enveloped in a tea towel as he carried his own plate to the table.

'Dogs,' he said. 'It's a shelter for abandoned and unwanted dogs, and they always need people to clean out the kennels and walk the mutts. I suspect I might be picking up a lot of poop, too.'

'Dogs,' Meena repeated blankly. 'Since when have you been interested in dogs?'

Oscar looked a little sheepish. 'I've always wanted a dog,' he said. 'I suggested getting one years ago, but you said no. And you were right,' he added hastily. 'What with both of us working and Anton in school, there would have been nobody home to take care of it, and that's not fair on the dog.'

Meena remembered him suggesting it once, and she also recalled that she hadn't taken what was fair on the dog into account when she'd knocked the idea on the head. She had been more concerned with pet hairs left everywhere, muddy paw prints, slobber, and chewed shoes, and that was just the start of it. She'd not wanted the mess an animal would create, and neither had she wanted to walk it every day; because she knew without a shadow of a doubt that the task *would* have fallen to her, no matter how much Oscar had promised to look after it.

Meena listened incredulously as her husband told her all about his visit, describing the dogs and sharing their stories, and suddenly she felt overwhelmed. This was a whole side of Oscar that she hadn't witnessed before. The only thing to have evoked this much passion in the past had been spreadsheets, hitting targets, and turnover figures. Oh yes, and golf. None of which she'd paid a great deal of attention to, and she'd only listened with half an ear.

But this felt different. She got the impression that although he'd only spent a couple of hours there he was already invested, and she had a feeling he would pour his heart and soul into it, the same way he had done with his job and with his golf.

Suddenly she wondered if she would be left behind again, as her husband raced off with this newfound interest firmly between his teeth, and she was abruptly glad that she hadn't resigned from anything yet.

Her thoughts whirling, she shrugged off Oscar's suggestion that they watch a box set together and she retreated to her workroom, saying that she needed an hour or so to herself to decompress after the pressures of the day. It was true, she *did* need some time alone – time to wonder if this new enthusiasm would change the status quo of their marriage yet again, and how she would fit into the new rhythm. Would it be like before Oscar had retired, when he was out of the house all day and sometimes in the evening too, and she would be left to get on without him?

Her mother's words flashed into her mind once more: Meena and Oscar *were* like two ships passing in the night, that they had been more like lodgers than husband and wife. It had taken his retirement and a week spent exclusively in each other's company for her to realise that they simply couldn't go back to the way they had been before.

The question was, what were they going to do about it?

CHAPTER 21

The Annual General Meeting of the school's governing body was this evening, but as Meena sorted through a hundred or so repeat prescriptions that were awaiting collection by various patients, she didn't think she could face it. Dana, who was in the surgery today for one of the "keeping-in-touch" days that everyone on maternity leave was expected to work, patted Meena on the shoulder as she walked into the office.

She took one look at Meena's face and said, 'You look like I feel – fed up.'

Meena smiled tiredly up at her. 'I think we are both shattered,' she said, 'but you've got a good reason. I've been meaning to catch up with you all day – how is your gorgeous little daughter?'

'Waking up every couple of hours for a feed. I was hoping she'd be sleeping through the night by now.' Dana perched her bottom on the edge of Meena's desk. 'My maternity leave won't last forever. How am I going to find the strength to leave her when the time comes for me to return to work? Being in the surgery today has brought it home to me that I'm going to miss so much. It's not been a full day yet and I'm already wondering if she's pining for me. What if she's refused to take the bottle? Did Corinne remember to wind her properly? Did she sing her favourite song to get her off to sleep?'

'Corinne is your mother-in-law, isn't she?'

Dana nodded, her eyes glistening with unshed tears. 'I can't leave her,' she wailed. 'I *can't.*'

'Then don't,' Meena replied. 'They're little for such a short amount of time, that you need to savour every moment. If you can find a way to manage financially, you shouldn't come back.'

Dana gave her a watery smile. 'I might just do that,' she said. 'Enough about me: why do you look as though you could sleep for a week?'

Meena shrugged. 'You'd think with Oscar doing all the cleaning, shopping, cooking and laundry that I'd have more time on my hands, but if anything I seem to have *less*. It would help if I could get a good night's sleep, but I'm waking up at all hours and then I can't get back off.'

Dana tilted her head to the side. 'Are you still suffering from hot flushes?'

'Hell, yes! And mood swings – although if I'm honest, the swings tend to be from grumpy to grumpier, instead of from happy to sad. Everything annoys me.'

'Oscar?'

'Especially Oscar. He has started volunteering in an animal sanctuary and that's all he can talk about.'

'I thought you wanted him to take up a hobby, or something?'

'I did!' she cried. 'But… oh, I don't know. He seems to have settled into retirement and is happier than he's been in years.'

'That's a good thing, isn't it? You'd hate him to be miserable,' Dana said.

'Yes, I would,' Meena agreed. But how could she admit that she was envious? For some reason she'd gone from loving her job, her hobbies, her acting, and all the other things she was involved in, to feeling indifferent at best and dislike at worst. And she couldn't understand why.

'I could prescribe something?' Dana suggested. 'Have you thought about HRT?'

Meena wrinkled her nose. She knew she was going through the menopause and had been for a couple of years, and she was aware that some of her irritability and discontent was down to her hormones.

'I don't want to take anything if I can help it,' she said. Not that she was against HRT, but it was like any other drug – she'd have to come off it at some point, so she thought she may as well get this menopause business over and done with as soon as possible. Besides, she had a horrid suspicion that HRT wouldn't help with the way she was feeling. That was all down to Oscar having retired and her not being able to deal with it.

Meena felt awful for being such a miserable old bag.

***

The dog's name was Lulu and she was a shivering, cowering, malnourished scrap when Oscar first met her. She had been at the shelter for nearly two weeks, and he'd been introduced to her on the very first day that he'd become an official volunteer.

She was terrified of everyone, Oscar included, and seeing her so fearful and miserable had done something to his insides. No dog should feel like that, and although it wasn't a conscious decision on his part, he found himself wanting to help her learn to trust and love again. He wanted to show her that humans could be kind and caring, so over the two weeks since he'd been coming to the shelter, he'd spent increasing amounts of time with her when his work for the day was done.

He remembered the first time he'd set eyes on her. Lulu wasn't the prettiest dog he had ever seen, but Graeme (the bloke who Oscar had been shadowing) had informed him that when she'd arrived her fur had been so matted and long that she'd had to be shaved almost to the skin, which was mostly grey with some white patches. Graeme said she was believed to be a border collie possibly crossed with a poodle, but they weren't entirely certain.

Someone must have loved her once, because she had been micro-chipped and spayed, (although the former owners couldn't be traced) but how she had fallen on hard times no one knew. A member of the public had found her wandering the streets and had taken her to the nearest vet, who'd checked her over and had then brought her to the shelter.

Oscar had asked if he could sit with her for a while and Yvonne had been more than happy. So, after giving him a couple of pointers on how to work with a nervous or scared dog, Oscar had opened her kennel door.

On seeing him, Lulu had retreated to the furthest corner and had turned her head away, refusing to look at him. Her shorn tail had been between her legs, and she had been trembling violently.

Oscar had no idea what had happened to her to make her so fearful and mistrustful, and he remembered thinking that he wanted to get his hands on those responsible and—

As if sensing his simmering anger, Lulu had whimpered and he had taken a deep breath and let it out slowly, trying to let any negative emotions out with it.

'I'm sorry, poppet,' he'd told her. 'You're safe now.' And he had sat in her kennel for ages, speaking to her in a soft monotonous voice, giving her the chance to get used to him.

Eventually her trembling had abated, and Oscar saw her begin to unfurl. She still hadn't looked directly at him, but she'd kept darting glances at him out of the corner of her eye.

By the time his legs were cramping from being in the same position and his back was in bits, he'd felt he was making progress. Slowly, oh so slowly, he'd risen to his feet. As he'd done so, he'd fully expected the dog to regress, and she had to a certain extent, but she hadn't trembled as badly as she had done when he'd first entered her kennel, and he had been convinced he was making progress.

Over the course of the next two weeks Oscar made sure he sat with her for an hour or so every day, letting her get used to his scent and the sound of his voice, and gradually she'd started coming out of her shell.

She was now at the point where she'd actively look for him, although she did still tend to back off when he went inside her kennel and he was careful to respect her boundaries. She'd approach him when she was ready, and he had to take it at her pace. He was convinced that one day soon she would let him pet her, and that was what he was currently aiming for. But it was one small step at a time.

Oscar took three dogs out for three walks, cleaned and disinfected a kennel whose lucky occupant had left this morning for its forever home, did a poop-scoop round of each pen, and sat in on a meet-and-greet, where a prospective new owner met a potential adoptee. Like the other volunteers, Oscar was part of the shelter's rota and he adhered to it diligently, often arriving early and staying later than he needed to, and today was no exception.

Despite having spent the biggest part of the day at the shelter, he was reluctant to go home. He wanted to sit with Lulu for a while.

The dog's black button nose was poking through the mesh of the kennel door when he entered the block she was housed in, and he called out to her as he approached so she knew it was him.

As he grew closer, he could see her tail wagging and she was clearly pleased to see him even though she backed away nervously.

'Hello, sweetie.' He crooned his customary greeting to her as he stepped inside, then he sank to the floor and rested his back against the door.

The dog's tail continued to wag but she held it low, almost brushing the floor. Yvonne had told him it meant she was apprehensive and nervous. He'd learnt that a wagging tail didn't necessarily mean a dog was happy. It could mean a lot of things, and in Lulu's case it probably meant "I want to trust you, but I'm scared you'll hurt me".

A lump came to his throat as he watched her battle with her fear. She so desperately wanted to make friends, but she was scared, and all he wanted to do was to scoop her up and shower her with love.

Instead, he sat motionless, holding his hand out to her, and waited for her to find the courage to approach him. It might not be today, but it would happen eventually – he was convinced of it.

Lulu whimpered and looked away, jiggling from paw to paw, then she paced back and forth at the far end of the pen.

Oscar didn't move a single muscle, despite his arm aching.

Lulu whimpered again, then lay down facing him. She was in a sphinx position and was panting. Oscar had been told that panting might be another sign of her nervousness, but she didn't appear to be unduly distressed (if she had been, he would have retreated and tried again next time) so he stayed where he was, biting his lip.

He almost gasped when she wriggled a centimetre closer, her stomach on the concrete floor, her nose almost on her paws. Her eyes were fixed firmly on him, and he looked away, aware that dogs often interpreted a direct stare as aggression or dominance. He'd learnt such a lot in the brief time he'd been at the kennels, and today he was putting all his newfound knowledge to use.

Another wriggle. Then another.

Closer and closer she came, and Oscar continued to sit motionless, trying to appear as unthreatening as possible, knowing that any movement could startle her and send her scuttling backwards.

Out of the corner of his eye he studied her, noticing how often she licked her lips nervously, how her fur was starting to grow back, the way her nose twitched as she sniffed him.

As he waited and waited, she inched closer, her muzzle a centimetre from his outstretched hand. He could feel her breath tickling his fingers, and for a second he wondered if she had used up all her courage for one day, but then her tongue flicked out and she licked him.

Oscar held his breath, amazement and relief flooding through him. He'd done it! He'd persuaded her to come to him of her own accord, and he was so choked up with emotion he felt like crying.

Slowly, a fraction of a time, he lowered his trembling arm, letting it rest on the floor next to her outstretched paws. She sniffed at it again, and when she rose into a crouch Oscar assumed she was done for today and that she was about to slink away and retreat to a safer distance.

But she didn't. Instead she crawled up to him, clambered warily into his lap, curled up and let out such a huge sigh that Oscar had to bite back a sob.

Lulu, who had been terrified of her own shadow when he'd first met her, trusted him.

It was the most wonderful feeling in the world, second only to when he'd held his newborn son for the first time.

And Oscar knew without doubt that he'd found his vocation, his place in this new world of his, and a deep contentment filled his heart.

***

'You look awful,' were the first words out of Anita's mouth when Meena walked into her living room.

'Thanks, Mum. I don't need it pointing out.'

'You've got bags under your eyes. You should get more sleep.'

'Easier said than done.'

She felt a flush begin, and she caught hold of the neckline of her blouse and wafted the material. She could put up with the physical symptoms of her fluctuating hormones (just about) but constantly waking up in the middle of the night and not being able to drop back off to sleep was getting to her. And then there was the brain fog…

'You're lucky,' her mum said. 'I started the menopause when I was in my late forties. At least you've had a few more years before the rot set in.'

'The menopause is hardly "the rot".' Meena gritted her teeth and tried to ignore the burning sensation sweeping up her neck and into her face. 'It's a natural part of growing older.'

'It's the start of old age,' Anita retorted.

'Nonsense! You're only as old as you feel.'

'By the look of you, you must feel about eighty,' her mother shot back. 'You're doing too much.'

'I'm doing what I've always done,' Meena replied.

'And that's the problem, right there. You're not getting any younger, you know.'

'I'm aware of that,' Meena said. She was gritting her teeth again, but for a different reason. 'Did Nora clean your oven?' she asked, changing the subject.

'Yes, but I don't know why she bothered. She only did it last month and I hardly use it.'

'It still needed doing,' Meena said. She had no idea what her mum had put in it the last time she'd used it, but whatever it was had been caked to a burnt crisp on the floor of the oven, and some of it had been welded onto the wire shelves.

Meena opened the door to check, peered inside, then closed it again, satisfied that Nora had done a good job.

'I'll grab your washing out of the basket,' she said, 'and pop a load on.' She'd take it with her when she left and she'd dry it in the tumble dryer at home.

Meena went up to her mother's bedroom, tutting as she picked up a pair of shoes on the way.

'You can leave those there,' Anita called. 'I'll need them tomorrow.'

Meena shook her head. There was no way she was leaving a pair of shoes in the hall for her mum to trip over. She'd put them in the wardrobe where they belonged; but as she opened the closet door, her face fell.

Clothes had been shoved in on top of the shoes in a crumpled, tangled heap, and most of the hangers were empty. A few stray garments littered the bed, and the coverlet was scrunched up.

She heard the whirr of the stairlift as she straightened the cover and smoothed it, and she waited for her mum to appear. 'Did Nora not see this?' she asked.

Anita looked blank. 'Why would Nora see it? She wasn't here.'

'I thought she came this morning? You said she'd cleaned the oven.'

'She did. But when she'd gone, I went looking for that cardigan I used to wear. You remember – the one with cherries for buttons?'

'It's in the ottoman in my old room,' Meena said. 'You haven't worn it in years. Why do you want it now?'

'I've been invited to an afternoon tea at Anton's old school. They want the youngsters to have more contact with us oldies. You're always up at that school – I'm surprised you don't know about it.' Anita sounded indignant, as if she believed Meena hadn't mentioned it on purpose because she didn't want her mother to go.

'I haven't been to a meeting this academic year,' she said. 'This is the first I've heard of it.' She inhaled deeply. 'I'll put a load in the machine, then let's get this lot hung up,' she said.

'Why bother?' her mum retorted. 'It's only me that'll see it, and I don't care if it's a mess.'

And that, Meena thought sadly, was the problem. Her mother *didn't* care.

Meena was beginning to wish she didn't, either.

***

'Hello? Anyone home? Oscar?' Silence echoed back as Meena hung up her coat, and her heart sank.

She'd become used to Oscar being at home when she got in from work, the house filled with the sound of the radio he liked to listen to and the smell of cooking drifting through the air. But this evening the house was silent and aroma free, apart from the plug-in air freshener in the hall.

The kitchen was spotless, she was pleased to see – although she'd got used to that, too. Since those first few weeks when Oscar hadn't known the rough side of a sponge from the squidgy side, she'd had to go behind him less and less, and these days the house was as clean and as tidy as it had been when she'd been the one doing the chores.

Disconsolately, she assumed he was probably fishing, and she wondered what he was planning for dinner and whether she should get a head start on it.

Opening the fridge, she saw a casserole dish sitting on the middle shelf, so she took it out and popped it in the oven. A pan of cleaned potatoes was on the hob, along with another saucepan containing broccoli. She ignored them for the time being, not knowing when he'd be home, and decided to wait until he came in. They wouldn't take long to cook.

Feeling restless and with nothing on the agenda for this evening, she picked up her phone and called Anton.

'Got time for a chat?' she asked.

'It'll have to be quick – I've got to fetch Robin from football practice and Grace is at a party with Immie. Why they had to hold it on a school night, beats me. Immie will be late to bed as it is, without all the E-numbers and sugar making her hyper. Are you OK?'

'I'm fine.'

'Is there anything in particular you want to chat about?'

'Not really, I was at a loose end, so I thought I'd see how my son was.'

'*You at a loose end?* Words fail me. Haven't you got a society to go to, or a meeting to attend? What about a cake to bake?' He was teasing her, but his words hit home.

'I'll let you get on,' she said. 'I'm sure you're busy.'

'Not as busy as you,' he replied, chuckling.

Meena put the phone down and stared into space.

Was that what he thought? That she was always on the go?

A couple of months ago she had been happy to be busy. But not now. She was sick and tired of rushing around, of always having to be somewhere or do something.

She'd hoped that now Oscar had started volunteering and had something to occupy him that everything would return to the way it had been before he'd been given the push – with the added bonus of her not having to put the vacuum around or disinfect the loo.

But it hadn't. Or, it *had*, in that she was coming home to an empty house; but instead of it not bothering her, it bothered her very much indeed.

Meena gazed around at her pristine sitting room. Oscar had even plumped up the cushions and made a little dent in the tops of them, just the way she'd always done.

He didn't need her, did he? He was perfectly capable of managing on his own.

No, not *managing* – he was *thriving*.

It made her feel superfluous, useless, not needed.

And the governing body didn't appear to need her, either – she'd not heard from either the chair or the headteacher, apart from a generic email with the minutes of the last meeting which was routinely sent out to everyone on the board. They didn't seem to have missed her at all.

And neither had the WI – she hadn't attended a meeting or a coffee morning, or anything else for weeks, and no one had been in touch to ask if she was OK.

No one cared.

Tears filled her eyes and she sniffed loudly. All that time, all that work, dedication and effort – and for what?

She'd have been better off staying at home with her knitting and waiting for Oscar to come home. At least they wouldn't have been like ships passing in the night, as her mother had put it.

Was it too late to make a fresh start, or had her reluctance to give up her hobbies and interests meant that Oscar was now fully immersed in hobbies and interests of his own and she was back to trying to keep herself amused?

She didn't blame him for wanting to find things to do, especially during the day when she was at work. It must have been lonely for him, she realised.

She heaved a sigh and made a decision. Determined to strike whilst the iron was hot, she sent an email to the chair and the headteacher tendering her resignation forthwith, and she did the same with the WI. Dean and *The First Act* could wait until after Christmas, but she was determined to withdraw from the amateur dramatics group as well. That only left the Knit and Natter club with a claim on her time, and she enjoyed knitting so much she wouldn't give that up.

Feeling as though a weight had been lifted off her shoulders, Meena went to check on the casserole. It felt good to be back in her kitchen again, and she made a promise to herself that she'd do more cooking and give Oscar a break from it now and again.

***

'I would have done that,' Oscar said, coming home to find Meena sticking a fork into the casserole to check if the chunks of beef were done. 'Sorry I'm late.'

'Emergency?'

Oscar winced. He'd been late once before because he'd stayed behind to help settle a dog into its new quarters, but cuddling Lulu for an hour couldn't be classed as an emergency. He'd also been reluctant to come home for a quick bite to eat with his wife, who would then dash out and leave him on his own for the evening.

He knew he was being childish and that he should be able to entertain himself, but *darn it*, he loved being with Meena. He loved *her*. But she didn't seem to have any spare time for him, so he might as well be at the kennels where he was wanted and appreciated, and could do some good, instead of sitting at home doing nothing.

'Thanks for preparing the casserole,' Meena said, when he failed to answer her.

'That's what I'm here for,' he joked, weakly.

'How was your day?' she asked, popping the lid back on and returning the dish to the oven. 'It'll be forty-five minutes yet.'

'That's OK. Um… it was good.' It had been more than good – it had been bloody marvellous. He could still feel Lulu's fluffy fur under his hand, and the doggy smell of her lingered on his clothes. It was a nice smell, not a pungent one, and it made him smile.

He couldn't wait to go back tomorrow and cuddle her again. She seemed to have lost most of her fear of him, and her trust squeezed his heart. As he'd left this evening, Yvonne had been full of praise for what he'd achieved with the little dog, and he'd driven home in a warm glow of happiness.

Gosh, he never would have thought retirement could be so rewarding or fulfilling.

It was just a pity that his wife wasn't a part of it.

CHAPTER 22

Oscar opened a drawer and was about to put the T-shirts he'd ironed inside when he noticed a new shirt that was still in its packet. He stared at it for several seconds.

Meena must have bought it for him not long before he'd been forced to retire, and he hadn't had an opportunity to wear it. It was unlikely he ever would. The same went for all the suits and shirts hanging in his wardrobe. It was about time he got rid of most of them. He would keep one or two in case, and a couple of shirts, but he'd take his day-to-day work suits to the charity shop. Let someone else have some benefit from them. His work clothes these days consisted of scruffy jeans and old boots.

He fetched a roll of bin bags from the cupboard in the utility room and began to sort through his wardrobe, and before long he had two bags filled with neatly folded suits, shirts and ties, and he'd added three pairs of shoes for good measure.

He'd also found a few things such as his golfing clothes that he didn't want to get rid of but neither did he want to keep them in his wardrobe, so he filled another bag and decided he'd pop it up the attic: which reminded him…

Sorting out the attic was supposed to have been the price he paid if Meena had gone for a dip in the sea when they had been in New Quay.

She'd chickened out, but that didn't mean he couldn't sort it out anyway.

He'd make a start now, but he knew he wouldn't finish the task today. For one thing, there was far too much stuff to go through, and for another he was due at the kennels in two hours. He'd have another go at it tomorrow or the next day.

Deciding to start in a far corner, theorising that the oldest stuff and the things that hadn't been touched for years and probably never would be and could probably be thrown away, had been stored there, Oscar got to work. He'd brought the radio up with him and he hummed along as he opened boxes and sifted through their contents.

He hoped Meena would be pleased. She'd been rather down lately and he'd considered suggesting another week away because they'd had such a lovely time in New Quay. But the surgery was so short-staffed at the moment that he didn't think she'd be able to get the time off right now. Maybe he could book something for after Christmas, which would give the surgery enough notice, but the weather could be dicey in January and February so—

Oh, look, Oscar thought fondly as he delved into the next box and withdrew what turned out to be one of Meena's school reports. The box contained a few of them, spanning several years, plus there was a piece of paper with a handprint picture on it, a hand-stitched apron with an embroidered pocket, and a Christmas angel with silver doilies for wings.

And when he delved deeper, he discovered several swimming badges, a certificate for coming first in an egg and spoon race, and three exercise books, the kind that pupils were given in class to do their work in.

A quick trawl through the topmost one revealed page after page of rounded handwriting.

Goodness, Oscar remembered writing in books just like this, and he turned to the first page, memories of his own school days flitting through his mind.

The date was written neatly on the top line, and he worked out that Meena would have been around twelve years old.

He quickly read a few lines, conscious that time was ticking along, but the words didn't make a great deal of sense, so he read them again. Meena appeared to have written a to-do list, so he turned the page and was surprised to see another, and another.

Flicking rapidly through the exercise book, he discovered that every single page contained a similar list.

That was unusual in itself, but the items on the lists were not the kind of things he would expect a twelve-year-old to be concerned with.

Change mums bed, wash the cushin covers, sweep under the hall rug, were examples of some of them, and he might have been forgiven for thinking that these books were Anita's if it wasn't for the fact that the handwriting definitely belonged to Meena. And as far as he could tell, next to every item on every list was a tick.

How odd…

Abruptly, Oscar realised that he'd been rooting around in the attic for far longer than he'd intended and that he had better get a move on if he wasn't going to be late.

Without giving the exercise books another thought, he dropped them back in their box and hurried downstairs.

He had a cute little dog to take on a nice long walk.

***

The days were getting shorter and it would soon be the autumn equinox. In his previous life, pre-retirement, Oscar wouldn't have taken much notice of the changing of the seasons – he had been far too preoccupied with work to notice the subtleties of nature during his daily commute. Even when he'd been on the golf course he'd been more concerned about his swing, his score, and the other players, to notice anything other than the state of the green or whether the groundsmen had mowed the grass short enough. It was only when it became too dark in the evenings for a game, would he realise that winter was fast approaching, or when the fallen leaves became a nuisance because they might obscure a ball.

But since he'd been walking several dogs every day, he noticed far more than he'd ever done. And his canine charges had much to do with his increased observation – he had to have eyes in the back of his head with some of them, Lulu included.

She was out with him today, and when he thought about her (which he frequently did) he couldn't believe the difference in her. Her fur was growing back and she was now a scruffy ball of black and white fuzz. Her confidence had also grown and she had a tendency to stick her nose into anything, and she had filled out and with it her energy levels had soared. There was definitely border collie in her, Yvonne said – Lulu could keep going for miles, and now that she was more or less back to full health and fitness it was hard to wear her out.

God knows Oscar tried, but no matter how far he walked her she always returned with her tail still wagging and a bounce in her paws. Oscar, on the other hand, was knackered. The exercise was doing him good however, and he could see an improvement in his own fitness and stamina, as well as a reduction in his waistline. He looked better than he'd done in years, and he felt it too.

It was a wrench to return Lulu to her pen and Oscar stayed with her for a while petting and fussing her as she sat in his lap. She especially loved having her ears stroked and would tilt her head from side to side, her eyes closed in bliss as his fingers caressed the fluffy fur.

'I've got to go,' Oscar told her eventually, gently pushing her off him and clambering to his feet. 'See you tomorrow.'

He gave her one more parting pat, then headed towards the reception area. Yvonne was behind the desk, sifting through a pile of paperwork.

'I'm off,' Oscar called, waving to her as he walked past, but Yvonne stopped him.

'What time are you due in tomorrow?' she asked.

'Eleven. Why? Do you want me to swap with someone?'

'Can you come in at ten? We're doing an assessment on Lulu to see whether she's ready for her next step.'

Oscar froze. 'What next step?'

'We think she would benefit from being fostered for a while before making her available for adoption. She's still so nervous when she's faced with anything new, and although she is doing well here, we think putting her with a foster carer for a few weeks will give her the best chance of ensuring her adoption will be successful.'

'Adoption?' he repeated.

Yvonne smiled sympathetically, as though she knew how he felt about the dog. 'That *is* why we're here – to try to find forever homes for them.'

Oscar didn't hesitate. 'I'll take her.'

'Foster her?'

'Yes.' He couldn't bear the thought of Lulu being sent to a stranger's house where she didn't know anyone. She'd be so frightened and confused. It could set her back weeks.

'Are you sure? It's quite a commitment.'

'I'm sure.'

Yvonne studied him. 'You two have really bonded, haven't you?'

He swallowed down a lump in his throat and nodded.

'You can't take them all home,' she warned.

Oscar's smile was sad. 'I know and I wish I could, but Lulu is special… How soon can you do the checks?'

'I've already done them.'

'Excuse me?'

'I've seen how you are with the dogs, I know you don't have any other pets, you've told me you've got a secure garden, and I know you've got the time to dedicate to her.'

Oscar needed to sit down. Was he really doing this? 'When can I take her?'

'Today if you want.'

Blimey, talk about short notice! 'I've not got any food or a basket for her—' he began.

'While you're fostering, the shelter provides everything you need,' Yvonne said.

'Let's do it,' he blurted. He'd made his decision and he couldn't wait to get Lulu home. There was no room in the utility for her basket, but he had the perfect spot for it in the kitchen, and she'd have more space to stretch her legs. Meena would probably—

Blast! *Meena*. What would she say? Oscar had a feeling she wouldn't be too pleased. Although, she had only said no to them having a dog when he'd suggested it all those years ago because they were both at work all day.

That situation had changed with his retirement, and she couldn't object on the grounds that she'd have to clean up after it because he did all the cleaning now. Meena would hardly know the dog was there. And it would only be for a few weeks until Yvonne decided that Lulu was ready to be adopted.

Meena would be a bit shocked that he'd brought a dog home, but she'd come round to the idea – who could resist Lulu's cute little face?

***

260

'What the hell is that dog doing in my kitchen?' Meena demanded. The last thing she'd been expecting when she came home from work was to find a dog in her house and Oscar kneeling on the floor, with his arms wrapped around a scruffy black and white mutt.

'This is Lulu,' he said.

'I don't care what its name is, it doesn't belong in my kitchen.'

'She can't sleep in the utility, there's nowhere to put her basket.'

'*Sleep?* Do you mean to tell me she's *staying?*' Meena was incredulous. She didn't like the dog being here for a minute, and certainly not overnight.

'Only for a few weeks.'

'*A few weeks?!*' Meena's voice rose several octaves and her mouth dropped open. 'Is this a joke, because if it is I don't think it's very funny.'

'No joke. I've offered to foster her.'

'You can jolly well unoffer!' she cried, furiously. How dare he do that without consulting her?!

'Stop shouting, you're scaring her.' Oscar's arms tightened around the dog and he pulled her closer.

'Whose fault is that? You should have asked me first.' Meena was livid.

'You might have said no.'

'Yes, I would have. So you thought you'd go behind my back?'

'That wasn't it at all. I didn't think—'

He stopped abruptly, but Meena could guess he'd been about to admit that he hadn't considered her at all. Her feelings hadn't come into it. Oscar wanted to bring this creature home, so that's what he'd done, with no consideration for her feelings whatsoever.

She glared at the dog.

Oscar was holding it tightly and it had its back to her, its nose buried under his armpit. It seemed to be shivering.

'It can't stay here. Take it back,' Meena demanded.

'No.'

'Pardon?'

'She's staying.'

Meena couldn't believe what she was hearing. There was no way she was having a dog in the house. No way.

For a few moments Meena and Oscar glared at each other. They were at a stalemate and neither of them wanted to back down. But she could tell he was serious about this, and she was too tired to butt heads with him any more. If he wanted to look after the damned dog, then he jolly well could. She wanted nothing to do with it. And when he realised the kind of mess a dog made and that he'd be the one cleaning up after it, she reckoned he'd soon change his mind and take it back to the shelter where it belonged.

'Fine, but keep it away from me,' she said.

'I don't think that will be a problem,' Oscar said as he got to his feet, and the dog promptly hid behind his legs.

The creature peeped out at her with frightened eyes and Meena had a brief flash of remorse for scaring it, before she tamped down on the feeling. It was Oscar's fault that the dog was scared – he should never have brought it here in the first place.

***

That went about as well as he'd expected, Oscar thought as he lay in bed listening out for the dog. Lulu had been nervous, anxious, and subdued – all the things Yvonne had warned him about – and Oscar felt dreadful for putting the little animal in this position.

Logically he knew that being fostered was the best thing for her and that every new experience and every change in her circumstances would make her feel this way. He also knew instinctively that he was the perfect person to help her overcome her fears.

If he could wave a magic wand and make her into a more confident dog, he would. But he didn't have a magic wand, so he'd have to do this the hard way, and without Meena's blessing. His wife had made it abundantly clear that she wanted nothing to do with Lulu, and when Oscar had persuaded the little scrap to venture into the living room, Meena had made a point of flouncing upstairs to her workroom.

Although he had been sorely tempted to bring Lulu's basket into their bedroom when he retired to bed, he'd thought better of it; instead he'd padded the dog's basket out with blankets that he'd brought from the shelter so she had familiar smells around her, and he'd also added the jumper he'd been wearing today, for the same reason.

Then he'd gone to bed to lie next to a rigid Meena, feeling her silent anger washing over him and listening for the slightest sounds of distress from the kitchen.

He drifted off to sleep hours later, feeling that his heart was being torn between his perfectly capable and competent wife, and a little dog who needed all the love she could get.

CHAPTER 23

'I can't believe I'm jealous of a dog,' Meena said to Janet. They were having a meal out on their own. Their husbands were supposed to be with them, but Oscar had cried off, pleading that he didn't want to leave the dog on her own so soon after bringing her home.

Meena was pleased he hadn't come – and neither had Dean. Instead, Janet's husband had gone to the clubhouse for a pint and a bite to eat, leaving the two women to enjoy a catch-up. They might see each other twice a week at rehearsals but they were always surrounded by members of the cast, so Meena thought it made a nice change to have a quiet meal together. If nothing else, it gave her a chance to vent her spleen about her husband's inconsiderate and selfish behaviour.

'He's all over it,' Meena complained, then she caught Janet smirking. 'I know,' she sighed. 'I'm pathetic, aren't I? And I don't like myself very much at the moment, especially since Oscar described the state she was in when she first came to the shelter, and how it's taken him weeks to get her

"

to trust him. And here am I begrudging her a home for a few weeks.'

'It was bound to be a shock,' Janet said. 'He should have talked it over with you before he brought her home. I wouldn't be happy if Dean sprung a dog on me, and I *like* dogs.'

'I don't *dislike* them,' Meena said. 'I just don't want one in my house.'

'What breed is she?'

'Oscar reckons she's a sheep dog crossed with a poodle, but no one knows.'

'How old?'

'Why all the questions – are you thinking of adopting her?'

'We'd like to have a dog one day, but not yet. We want to retire first so we can give it all the attention it needs.'

Great. Meena felt as though everyone was looking forward to retiring except her.

'I've got ages to go yet before I can consider giving up work,' she said.

'Is that what you want to do, give up work?' Janet asked, as their meals were placed on the table.

'No.' Meena shook out her serviette and gazed at her food. She'd ordered a curry and it smelled divine. 'Perhaps.' She took a breath. 'I don't know.' She played with her fork. 'I used to love my job. I used to love my life. But Oscar had to retire, and everything has gone to pot since.'

'Is it honestly because Oscar retired?' Janet asked.

Meena hesitated, using the excuse of eating a mouthful of food to buy her some thinking time.

'Not entirely,' she admitted. 'I had a kind of revelation the other day. It was something Anton said about me always being busy.'

'You are!'

'I got the impression he meant *too* busy.'

'Ah.'

'He's got a point.' Meena closed her eyes briefly then opened them again. 'All those societies and groups, the meetings and the organisations I've been involved in over the years… And for what? I hadn't been to a governors' meeting all term, and no one even noticed.'

'I'm sure they did,' Janet said.

Meena shook her head. 'I don't think so, and when I emailed to tell them I was resigning all I got was a stock reply thanking me for my contribution to the school.'

'You're better off out of there, then!' Janet declared. 'You don't want to stay on the board if you're not appreciated.'

'I didn't resign because of that,' Meena explained. 'I resigned because I realise I have to be there for the people I love, the people who love me and want me in their lives.'

Janet didn't say anything, but she didn't need to – her expression spoke volumes.

'You've been trying to tell me this for ages, haven't you?' Meena asked.

'Sort of,' Janet said. She reached out to squeeze Meena's hand. The gesture brought tears to her eyes.

'I think I've left it too late,' she admitted. 'Oscar has a new interest now, and how can I compete with soulful brown eyes and unconditional devotion?'

***

'Did you have a good time with Janet last night?' Oscar asked as his wife tottered into the kitchen. She didn't look too well, and he thanked God it was a Saturday and she wasn't on the rota to work this morning.

She slumped into a chair and rested her head in her hands. 'Tea?' she muttered hoarsely.

Oscar poured her a cup, then sat back down, Lulu at his feet. 'Too much to drink?'

'I wish. I was awake for ages in the night. Went for a wee and couldn't get back off.' She lifted her head and looked at him. 'You weren't in when I came home. Where were you?'

'I took Lulu for a walk around the block to stretch her legs,' he said. He'd noticed when he'd returned that Meena had arrived home, and he'd poked his head around the bedroom door to say goodnight and to tell her that he was planning on staying up for an hour or two because there was a film he wanted to watch (he didn't – he wanted to sit with Lulu for a while) but Meena had already fallen asleep.

'Speaking of which, do you fancy going for a stroll in an hour or two?' he asked. 'It'll blow the cobwebs away. Maybe we could take a walk around the lake and drop into the café for a coffee and a slice of cake on the way home? Or have you got plans?' She usually did, so it was silly of him to think she'd want to come for a walk, especially since she didn't care much for the dog.

But she surprised him and said she would.

268

'If you throw her a stick she'll fetch it,' Oscar said to Meena an hour or so later as they strolled through the woods a short drive from their house.

There were plenty of walks nearby they could have gone on, but Lulu wasn't too keen on cars and Oscar was anxious to show her that car rides could lead to fun things, and the little dog was definitely having fun. She was scampering from tree to tree, her daft loobrush of a tail waving jauntily in the air, and she was sniffing madly.

It was only when she remembered that Meena was on this walk too, that Lulu withdrew slightly and became more hesitant.

'She doesn't like me,' Meena had said when Oscar had first loaded Lulu into the car and strapped her in, and the dog had cringed when she'd realised Meena was getting in as well.

'She doesn't know you,' Oscar said, but he felt that Meena might have a point. Lulu didn't appear to like his wife, and he couldn't blame her – dogs could tell if someone didn't like them. 'Give her time to get used to you.'

Meena sent him a sideways look. 'Is there any point? You said she'll only be with us for a couple of weeks.'

Oscar swallowed. Yes, he had said that, but he wasn't sure he meant it.

He wanted Lulu's forever home to be with him. And Meena, of course.

'Throw the stick,' he urged again. 'She needs to get used to being around different people and in different situations.' He handed Meena a stick and she took it gingerly between her thumb and forefinger.

'Ew, it's covered in dirt.' She threw it away, and Lulu bolted after it.

'I didn't throw it for her to fetch,' Meena said.

'Lulu didn't know that. Look, she's brought it back to you.' That wasn't strictly true – Lulu had brought the stick back to him, not Meena, but it was a start.

***

'Oh, dear, the poor thing. I hope Immie feels better soon,' Meena said the following morning.

Grace had phoned to say that Immie had chickenpox and they suspected Robin was coming down with it too, so they wouldn't be able to come for Sunday lunch after all. Meena eyed the piece of pork that Oscar was about to take out of its packaging and put in the oven.

'Hang on,' she told Grace, putting her hand over the phone. 'Oscar? Anton and Grace aren't coming because Immie has chickenpox. Can you put the pork in the freezer? We'll have something else for lunch.' She removed her hand. 'Sorry about that: I was just telling Oscar you won't be coming. He was going to cook a leg of pork.'

'Give Immie my love,' Oscar called from the other side of the room. 'Calamine lotion is what Meena used to dab on Anton when he had chickenpox. It stops the spots itching.' He came to stand beside her. 'Can't we have the pork for lunch anyway?' he asked. 'I promised Lulu some.'

'Who's Lulu?' Grace asked, catching Oscar's comment.

Meena widened her eyes at Oscar, pulled a face and made go-away motions. 'A dog. Oscar is fostering it for a few days,' she said to her daughter-in-law.

Meena had been worried about the dog around the children and she'd made Oscar promise to keep it shut in the utility room while they were here. Oscar hadn't been happy, but Meena wasn't prepared to take any chances, and she suddenly entertained a flash of hope that the dog would have gone back to the shelter by the time they next visited.

Grace cried, 'Oh, how wonderful! The children love dogs. They'll be gutted to have missed it. What sort is it?'

'A scruffy sort.'

'Boy or girl?'

Why did everyone want to know about the dog? 'Girl. Black and white, about two years old. Timid.' There, that should cover it.

'I bet she's adorable. You must take some photos and send them to me. Let's hope she's still with you by the time the spots have started scabbing over. The children would love to see her.'

Let's not, Meena thought. Although she was getting used to having a little black and white creature slinking about the house, the sooner it was gone, the happier she'd be.

'I bet you're spoiling her rotten,' Grace said.

'Hmm.'

'I'd better go, Immie is calling for me.'

'Give her a kiss from me, and Robin too,' Meena said. 'I'll phone you tomorrow to see how they are feeling.'

Meena puffed out her cheeks as she ended the call, disappointment coursing through her. She'd been so looking forward to seeing them.

'It might be a good thing,' Oscar said. 'Having Anton and the kids around might have been a bit much for Lulu. Even if she couldn't see them, she'd hear them. Immie has got a bell on every tooth.'

Meena glared at him. What an insensitive…! Grrr. Fancy putting the damned dog before a visit from their grandchildren!

Where was the dog anyway? She hadn't seen it for ages, and she hoped it hadn't got up to any mischief. Oscar was supposed to be looking after it, but it seemed that he couldn't keep an eye on the dog and prepare lunch at the same time. How did he think she used to manage when Anton was little and she had all the housework to do?

'Pork?' he reminded her.

'You can eat it. I'm not hungry,' she said, turning her back on him as she wiped the draining board.

'You mightn't be hungry now, but you will be by lunchtime,' Oscar pointed out.

'I said I don't want it.'

She felt the weight of Oscar's stare, then she heard him put the pork in the freezer.

'I think I'll go fishing,' he said. 'Lulu might like that.'

Lulu, Lulu, Lulu – is that all her husband could think about? Meena clenched her jaw and clamped her lips shut. If she opened her mouth now, she might say something she'd regret.

As soon as he was gone, taking that blimmin' dog with him, Meena's shoulders slumped. Ever since Oscar had retired the two of them seemed to be at cross-purposes all the time. It was ironic and rather sad that the day after she had made a conscious decision to spend more time with her husband, he'd brought a dog into their lives and that dog was taking up a great deal of his attention.

She could tell he was hoping she'd come around to the idea of having the dog in the house, and she was the first to admit that by fostering a dog in need he was being generous and kind-hearted and providing a valuable service, but she couldn't face a succession of dogs traipsing through the house. She'd put up with it this once because it had been presented to her as a done deal and she'd also wanted to prove to him that she was prepared to give fostering a go, but it had to stop here.

OK, she might have enjoyed the walk yesterday morning, but she didn't need a dog to enjoy a walk. Look at all those lovely walks she and Oscar had taken in New Quay; they hadn't had a dog with them then, had they? She was perfectly happy to go for a long walk every weekend and was looking forward to getting out and about. She'd thoroughly enjoyed scrambling up and down the coastal path, or strolling across the sand, and there was nothing stopping them from going for walks in the woods or exploring the many public rights of way that spread out around their house like threads of a spider's web.

She didn't mind Oscar volunteering at the shelter, but what she objected to was him bringing his "work" home with him.

Not entirely sure what she wanted to do now that she had some unexpected time on her hands, Meena decided to make a cup of tea then perhaps do a spot of sewing.

She flicked the switch on the kettle, and while she waited for the water to boil she went into the utility room to check whether the tumble dryer needed emptying, and that was when she saw the state her gardening shoes were in.

There was a shoe rack near the door where she kept Wellies and other assorted footwear that were only used when working outside. Most of the shoes had been pulled off the rack and lay scattered over the floor. None of them appeared to have been damaged, apart from one single shoe.

Meena bent down to examine it and was dismayed to see that it had been chewed; and not just one or two teeth marks, either. It had been dismembered, the soft inner sole having been bitten through in several places, the toes munched on, and the laces shredded.

With a cry of annoyance, Meena picked it up and carried it outside. She was tempted to keep it as evidence to show Oscar what the dog had done, but she didn't want the soggy thing in the house.

She threw it in the bin, shaking her head as she did so.

Then she turned to go back into the house and stepped in a pile of poo.

'God damn it!' she cried, hopping on one foot, trying to make her way to the doorstep where she could sit down and ease her slipper off.

The smell made her feel sick and she gagged as she used the toe of one foot to ease the offending slipper off.

Right, that was it! Enough was enough – that dog had to go. Now!

***

'No, absolutely not.' Oscar was adamant. 'I said I'd foster her until she's ready for adoption, and I'm not going back on my word.' Meena had pounced on him as soon as he'd walked into the house, and he could tell by one glance at her face that she was furious.

'And you said you'd look after it,' Meena shot back.

'Lulu.'

'Excuse me?' Meena's voice was colder than an iceberg and just as hard.

'Her name is Lulu, not *it*.' He was fed up with her calling the dog "it". Meena mightn't be keen on having Lulu in the house but there was no need to be so nasty about it. And now she was demanding that he take her back to the shelter tonight. Immediately.

'I don't care what she's called,' his wife spat back. 'I want her gone.'

'No.'

'This is not a debate. I can't have her here. I stepped in *poo*, for God's sake. My slippers are ruined.'

'Does it matter in the scheme of things?' he asked. 'I'll buy you a new pair.'

'That's not the point.' Her cheeks were flushed and her eyes were hard. 'You said you were going to clean up after it, but you didn't.'

'I would have if I'd realised she'd done her business in the garden,' he said.

Meena folded her arms. 'I want her gone.'

'She's not going anywhere.'

His wife lifted her chin and stared ceilingwards. 'You think more of that dog than you do of me.'

'The dog needs me. You don't.'

Meena's mouth dropped open. 'You can't really think that?'

Oscar sighed, 'I didn't mean it the way it sounded. She relies on people for everything – food, water, shelter, love… You are perfectly capable of making your own dinner.'

'Love,' Meena repeated. Her voice was flat.

'What about it?'

She drew in a deep breath, her shoulders rising, then let it out slowly. 'Nothing. It doesn't matter,' she said, and left the room.

Oscar watched her go, his gaze on the defeated set of her shoulders, and he wondered whether he was being unreasonable. With an incredibly heavy heart, he guessed that he probably was and that Meena had a point. He'd been stupid to think he could bring a dog home and expect his wife to fall in love with it. No matter how much it hurt to let Lulu go, he'd have to take her back in the morning.

It wasn't fair on Meena, and it wasn't fair on Lulu – the sweet little dog deserved better. And so did his wife.

CHAPTER 24

Meena had come this close (she mentally held up a thumb and forefinger) to giving Oscar an ultimation: the dog or her.

One thing had held her back – she wasn't entirely certain which he'd choose.

After another appalling night's sleep, she'd eventually dropped off into a deep one about an hour and a half before her alarm had gone off, and when she'd gone downstairs neither Oscar nor the dog were anywhere to be seen. The dog's basket and other things were still there, so Meena assumed he had no intention of returning her to the shelter and had taken her out for a walk.

Meena ate a half-hearted breakfast and got ready for work, the silence of the house encasing her like a shroud. She missed Oscar pottering around, she missed him humming along to the radio. Hell, she even missed the click-clack of the dog's paws on the kitchen floor. She'd become used to having someone in the house and for it to now be so still and empty was a shock.

She'd never felt so dismal in all her life, and tears were close to the surface. How she was going to cope today she had no idea. Being constantly complained to by patients and having to sort out problem after problem was difficult enough when she was on top form, but having to go into work when she felt as though her whole world was about to come crashing down around her ears was going to be unbearable.

When she came home this evening, she and Oscar would have to have a serious talk. They couldn't go on like this. They needed to be honest and open, and tell each other what they wanted out of life.

The problem was, Meena didn't know what she wanted – all she knew was that she was unhappy and that something had to change.

She was still churning things over in her mind when she opened up the surgery and ran her hand down the bank of switches to turn the lights on. She'd boil the kettle and have a quick drink before the madness of the day started, because she didn't always have the opportunity to grab one later and she knew she'd be gasping by eleven o'clock.

Her mobile rang just as she was about to fill her mug, and she hurried to retrieve it from her bag, hoping it might be Oscar. But when she picked it up she hesitated; what if it was and he was ringing to tell her he was moving out, that he'd heard her unspoken ultimatum and he'd chosen the dog, not her.

With her heart in her mouth, she looked at the screen and was relieved to see that it was Nora.

'Hi, Nora, what's up?' Meena guessed she might be calling to tell her that she wasn't able to see to her mum today. That happened sometimes, but Nora always made up for it by changing her cleaning day. It wasn't a big deal.

Meena hefted the kettle again and began to pour.

'Meena…?' Nora sounded odd. 'It's your mum. She's had a fall. It happened sometime yesterday evening, after you left. She's conscious but she's been lying on her floor all night. I've phoned for an ambulance.'

Meena closed her eyes, her mouth suddenly dry, opening them again when she felt a splash of hot water on her foot. Carefully she put the kettle down, and automatically reached for a cloth to wipe up the water that had flooded the worktop and was now dripping onto the floor. She'd been lucky she hadn't scalded herself, she thought absently.

'Meena? Are you there? Did you hear what I said?'

Meena snapped back into focus. 'I'm here. How bad is it, do you think?'

Nora lowered her voice and Meena guessed that she didn't want her mother to hear.

'Broken hip, probably. She's in a lot of pain and she's really cold. I've wrapped her in a blanket, but that's as much as I can do.'

'Thanks, Nora. I'm on my way.'

'Don't come to the house,' Nora said hastily just as Meena was about to hang up. 'Go to the hospital. The ambulance has just arrived.'

Her initial shock replaced by a sudden rush of adrenalin, Meena grabbed her bag and coat and shot outside

'Where are you off to?' One of the admin staff caught hold of Meena's arm as she dashed past.

'Hospital. Mum's had a fall.' Thank God the ambulance was there, Meena thought as she drove out of the car park. She had been expecting a long wait for it to arrive, while trying to keep her mother as calm and as comfortable as possible.

Oscar – he needed to know what had happened.

She didn't have time to pull over and ring him – she'd phone him as soon as she arrived.

Meena gulped back a sob; if there was ever a time she needed her husband, this was it.

***

Christmas would be here before long, Oscar thought randomly. But prior to that there was Bonfire Night to endure. He was perched on one of the benches dotted around the lake where he fished, Lulu at his feet, and he wondered whether Lulu would still be at the shelter by then, or whether Yvonne would have found her a new owner. He hoped it was the latter – this sweet little girl deserved someone who'd dote on her.

Even after fostering her for only a few short days, Oscar couldn't imagine being without her. The house would be so still, so quiet. He couldn't believe how quickly he'd become used to her being there, the click of her claws on the tiles, the sight of her in her basket with her brown eyes gazing up at him, the warmth of her little body tucked against his.

He felt her shift against his leg, and her head rested on his knee.

Without conscious thought his hand drifted to her ears and he stroked them absently as he gazed unseeingly into the lake.

The raucous call of a mallard brought him out of his reverie, and he noticed that the sky was getting lighter. He'd left home well before the sun had risen this morning, and before Meena had woken, and he'd been sitting on this bench ever since, letting the peace of the early day steal over him.

He'd brought Lulu out so he could relish these final few hours with her, just him and his dog. Of course, she wasn't *his* dog and he'd undoubtedly take her for a walk tomorrow, but she'd be living back at the shelter then and it wouldn't be the same.

He inhaled slowly, the scent of the lake filling his nose, then suddenly he was overwhelmed with the urge to sink his face into Lulu's fur, so he scooped her up and cuddled her close, sniffing the top of her precious little head.

Lulu squirmed around and licked him on the cheek.

God, he was going to miss her.

'You're going to go to a good home,' he promised her. 'You'll have people who love you, I'll make sure of that. And while you're still at the shelter, you'll see me every day.'

It was going to hurt like hell when she left but it was the best thing for her, and what every dog in the shelter deserved.

It was also a hard lesson to learn, and Oscar wondered whether every volunteer went through what he was going through, rather like a rite of passage before they learnt not to become so attached.

He would have to harden his heart in future if he wanted to avoid this kind of hurt.

And he *was* hurting – more than he would have believed.

Oscar stayed on his bench for another hour, the dog that wasn't his and never would be gazing up at him adoringly, until finally it was time to go and he reluctantly made his way back to the car.

But when he saw his phone sitting in the centre consul and read the message from Meena, all thoughts of taking Lulu back to the shelter this morning fled. Instead, he took the dog home and settled her into her basket with a chew to gnaw on, then he hurried out of the door. His wife needed him and that was the only thing he could think about.

***

The last time Meena and Oscar had held hands had been under very different circumstances; they had been in New Quay having a lovely holiday. Today they were holding hands in one of the relatives' rooms at the hospital, waiting for Anita to come out of theatre. She'd only just been taken down, so it would be a while yet.

Meena sighed shakily, dread threatening to overwhelm her despite the medical staff's assurances that her mum was in capable hands. Meena knew she was, but it didn't stop her from being more frightened than she'd ever been in her life.

'Have you spoken to Anton?' Oscar asked.

'I phoned him earlier to let him know. He wanted to come to the hospital, but I told him to stay in work. He can't do anything here.' She'd promised to let him know the minute she had any news.

'I'm going to have to pop home soon,' Oscar said and Meena blanched.

She didn't want him to go anywhere... just in case. She knew she shouldn't be thinking like that, but her mother was over eighty and there was always a risk with general anaesthetic.

'Why?' she asked.

Oscar swivelled in his seat to face her. 'I'm sorry; I should have taken Lulu to the shelter this morning, but I wanted one last walk with her. I was at the lake when I saw your message, so I took her home and came straight here.'

'That's OK.' Home was closer to the hospital than the rescue centre was.

'She could be eating your kitchen as we speak.'

'It's more your kitchen than mine, these days,' Meena pointed out.

'I'm still going to have to go home. Lulu needs to go out for a wee.'

Meena thought. 'Couldn't you ask Grace if she could do it?'

She saw his quick intake of breath and she knew he realised exactly how worried she was.

'I can,' he said slowly. 'If you don't mind.'

'Only if you think it's safe,' Meena replied. She didn't want to risk the dog biting their daughter-in-law.

'It's safe. Lulu isn't aggressive, not even when she's scared,' he assured her, recognising her concerns. 'I'll ask Grace if she can feed her, too.'

Meena released his hand so he could make the call, and she listened to his side of the conversation.

'Grace?... It's Oscar... No, no news yet. We'll call as soon as we have any. I'm sorry to ask, but it's about the dog. I wondered if you could do me a favour and let her out?... Thanks, that'll be great... If you could feed her, too? The pouches are kept in the utility room, one will be enough... You can, but she'll probably be scared... Of course you can't, but if she's not happy about it, then it might be best if they stay in the living room... Yes, use your judgement. You'll give me a call and let me know she's OK?... Thanks, I appreciate it, and I'm sure Lulu will too... Bye.'

'What was that about Grace using her judgement?' Meena asked as soon as he came off the phone.

'She's happy to let Lulu out, but she'll have to take the children with her. She'll ring with an update later.'

'Right.' Meena frowned; yet one more thing to worry about, as if she hadn't got enough already.

Grace was sensible though, and there wasn't any other choice than to let her get on with it. Meena mightn't be too keen on the animal, but she wouldn't want to cause her any suffering. Anyway, the dog was the least of her worries, so she caught hold of Oscar's hand again, needing to borrow some of his calm strength for herself.

But they still hadn't had any news about Meena's mum by the time Grace phoned to give Oscar an update on the dog.

This time Meena made grabby hands, wanting to speak to Grace directly, so after Oscar had told their daughter-in-law they were still waiting and Grace had assured him that the dog was OK, he gave the phone to Meena.

'How are you bearing up?' Grace asked.

'I'm OK. The waiting is getting to me a bit. You should have seen her, Grace, she looked so old and frail, and her face was sunken and grey. I thought we were going to lose her, but she rallied after she'd been given some pain relief and she'd warmed up a bit.'

'That's good. She had us all worried.'

'She's not out of the woods yet but she's in the best hands,' Meena said. 'How are Immie and Robin? Has he developed any spots?'

'Not yet. Fingers crossed he won't. He seems lively enough, and from the way Immie was running about the garden after the dog, she's feeling much better. They *love* Lulu. You didn't tell me she was so adorable. She's gorgeous! And she had a great time playing with the kids in the garden. I think they wore her out. If you need me to go over again, let me know.'

'Thanks, Grace. I hope Mum will be out of surgery soon and back on the ward. As soon as I've seen for myself that she's OK, we'll head home. I'll keep you posted.'

Meena was thoughtful as she ended the call. It seemed that her fears regarding the dog and her grandchildren were groundless. From the sound of it, Lulu had taken to them straight away.

Maybe if Meena had made more of an effort with Lulu, the dog would have taken to her, too?

She felt a little guilty about that, but with so much on her mind, she pushed the thought aside. She'd have enough on her plate with a mother who had a broken hip without concerning herself with a dog.

***

'She looks so old,' Meena whispered, bending over her mother's bed and smoothing her hair.

Anita hadn't long come out of surgery and had just been brought onto the ward. Nurses flittered around her, checking vitals, writing on charts and generally making sure that the old lady was as comfortable as they could make her, considering what she had been through.

Oscar pulled up a chair and gestured for Meena to sit down, which she did with a grateful smile.

'How did it go?' she asked one of the nurses.

'The procedure was successful,' the nurse reported. 'Her surgeon will be along shortly to speak to you, and after that it's probably a good idea to go home so you can get some rest.'

'I don't need any rest,' Meena began, having second thoughts about going home anytime soon.

Oscar caught hold of her shoulder. 'I think the nurse is tactfully trying to kick us off the ward so your *mum* can get some rest,' he said, and the woman sent him a little smile.

'Mrs Blake? Anita? Open your eyes for me, my lovely.' The nurse turned to Meena. 'She'll be groggy for a while, so don't expect too much. Anita? Your daughter is here to see you. She's been worried about you.'

Anita stirred and her eyes flickered open briefly before closing again, and she mumbled something incomprehensible. The nurse did a final check then moved away, leaving Meena and Oscar alone with Anita.

Meena looked up at him helplessly. 'What do we do now?'

'Take one day at a time,' Oscar replied.

'But—'

'Stop.' He clutched her arm. 'You're tired and upset; you're not going to be able to think straight. Let's wait to see what the doctor says and what your mum's prognosis is, then we can take it from there. We don't have to do anything right now. She's going to be in here for a while, so we've got time to sort things out.'

Meena inhaled shakily and nodded.

She'd rally, Oscar knew; his wife was strong and resourceful, plus she didn't have to face this alone. A broken hip wasn't to be sneezed at and it would take Anita a long time to recover, but recover she would, and Oscar vowed to do everything in his power to help.

Meena squirmed restlessly in her seat, so Oscar wasn't surprised when she stood up and said, 'I'm going to have a chat with that nurse.'

'I'll stay here with your Mum, shall I, in case she wakes?'

Meena smiled gratefully and wandered out of the ward.

Oscar turned his attention back to his mother-in-law, wondering what the future held for her and for them, and when a ringtone sounded, it took him a moment to realise it was Meena's phone. The noise was coming from her bag which was hanging on the back of the chair she had been sitting on, and he took it out, thinking it might be Anton or Grace.

It was neither. The name on the screen was Nora.

Meena had said a lady by the name of Nora had found Anita, and he vaguely remembered her mentioning the woman previously – a neighbour, maybe?

'Hello, this is Meena's phone. I'm her husband.'

'Oh, hello, um, I'm Nora, Anita's cleaner. It was me who found her. How is she?'

'She's had surgery on her hip and is back on the ward,' he said.

'That's a relief! I've been worried sick about her.' Nora hesitated. 'I know this isn't the best time to mention it, but what with Anita having a broken hip I doubt if she'll be back home anytime soon. So, can you ask Meena if she wants me to come in at all? I need to know because I'll have to find another job if not. I hate to ask, but you know how it is.'

Oscar frowned. 'You're Anita's *cleaner*?'

'That's right.'

'I wasn't aware she had one. Have you been doing it long?' Meena hadn't mentioned anything, but maybe his offer to help out with her mother had prompted her into making alternative arrangements.

'About seven or eight years.'

'That long? Um, OK, I'll be sure to pass the message on. And thank you for being there for Anita.'

'Tell her I was asking after her and to get well soon.'

'I will. Bye.'

Oscar was still holding Meena's phone when she came back onto the ward.

'Who was that?' she asked.

'Nora.' He was still trying to work out why Meena hadn't told him about her.

Meena bit her lip. 'Ah.'

'It's not a biggie, but why didn't you tell me Anita had a cleaner?'

'I probably did tell you – you must have forgotten.'

'She's ashamed,' Anita croaked, and Oscar's gaze shot to his mother-in-law.

Meena let out a cry. 'Mum! You're awake. How are you feeling?' She hurried to her side and took hold of her hand.

'Like crap,' Anita murmured.

Meena gave Oscar a look, then turned her attention back to her mother.

'That's only to be expected,' she said. 'You've had a major operation and—'

'It's not because of the operation.' Anita shifted slightly and groaned.

A frown creased Meena's forehead. 'What is it? Are you in pain?'

'No. It's you.'

'*Me?*' Meena shook her head. 'I don't understand.'

'You're ashamed of me. You always have been.' Anita's voice was weak but there was steel in its depths.

Meena gasped. 'That's not true! *Mum*, how could you say such a thing? You're confused—'

'You thought I couldn't tell? All that cleaning…' Anita trailed off, her eyes drifting closed again.

Meena stared at her mum for a long time, then she looked at him. 'She doesn't know what she's saying.'

But Oscar thought Anita knew exactly what she'd been saying and suddenly everything fell into place. 'I've been sorting out the attic,' he said.

His wife blinked, bewilderment flitting across her face.

'I found a pile of exercise books,' he continued.

Meena's puzzled expression was gradually replaced by dismay, as his meaning sank in.

'All those lists,' he said quietly. 'They were yours.' It wasn't a question; he was stating a fact.

Meena slowly released her mother's hand and sat back, her face pale. She nodded.

'You did all those jobs? Why? Were you her carer? Was she ill?'

'No.'

He could barely hear her, and he leant forward, his elbows resting on his knees, and he clasped his hands together. 'Then, why?'

'Because she didn't.' Meena looked at him with a stricken expression. 'She's right,' his wife whispered. 'I *was* ashamed.'

'I don't understand.' What on earth could she have been ashamed about?

'Not here.' She glanced helplessly at her mother. 'Can we go home? I've got something to tell you.'

***

Meena was drained. They say confession is good for the soul but hers felt heavier than ever. She'd told Oscar everything, starting with the mean comments made by Caroline and Wendy's mothers all those years ago.

Oscar hadn't said anything. He'd listened intently and as her sad little story unfolded, she'd watched his growing comprehension.

'I thought you were going to tell me something awful,' he said, after a long silence.

'It was awful, to me.' She pressed her lips together, then said, 'I didn't think you'd understand.' She hadn't expected him to.

'On the contrary, I *do* understand,' he said. 'It explains a lot.'

Meena supposed it did.

Oscar was sitting on the floor, his back against the armchair. The dog was cuddled against him, her head on his thigh, his arm draped over her. Lulu was watching Meena with wary eyes. When Oscar got slowly to his feet, the dog leapt up. 'I'm going out for a walk,' he announced.

Meena blinked back tears. 'Do you hate me?'

His eyebrows shot up. 'Good Lord, no! Whatever gave you that idea?'

'You can't stand to be anywhere near me.'

'I'm taking Lulu around the block before bed. She needs to stretch her legs. You can come with us, if you like?'

Meena didn't hesitate. 'I'll come.'

She could do with some fresh air. She was exhausted but she knew she wouldn't be able to sleep, and after being cooped up in the hospital all day and with the rollercoaster of emotions that she'd been through, a walk would do her good.

She watched Oscar clip the dog's lead onto her collar. He was so gentle with her, so caring as he caressed the fluffy head and stroked the animal under her chin. The dog gazed up at him with adoring eyes, her tail waving from side to side. And when Oscar lifted his head, Meena saw the same adoration reflected in his, and her heart twisted. Her husband used to look at *her* like that, once.

'You love her, don't you?' she said, nodding towards the dog.

'I suppose I do.' He paused. 'But I love you more.'

He was looking into her eyes and the adoring look was still on his face, and suddenly Meena understood that it was for *her*. It had never gone away.

A sob broke free, and another quickly followed. Before she knew it, she was howling and Oscar's arms were around her, holding her tight.

'It'll be all right,' he murmured into her hair. 'It'll be all right.'

And Meena realised without a shadow of a doubt that with Oscar by her side it would be.

CHAPTER 25

Meena carefully eased herself out of bed, not wanting to wake Oscar, and tiptoed downstairs. She'd managed to drop off to sleep for a couple of hours, but had woken at two a.m. and, despite lying there and praying it would happen, she'd been unable to go back to sleep.

After three-quarters of an hour, she'd thrown in the towel and decided to get up.

The dog was curled up in her basket when Meena opened the kitchen door and barely stirred as Meena made a cup of Horlicks in the vain hope that the malty drink would make her sleepy; but Meena was conscious she was being watched. A pair of brown eyes regarded her solemnly, tracking her every move.

'What?' Meena whispered. 'Are you thirsty? Do you want a drink?'

She rinsed the dog's bowl under the tap and filled it with fresh water. Lulu blinked at her.

'You can't have any of this,' Meena told her, stirring her Horlicks and taking it into the living room. She didn't know much about dogs, but she suspected sweetened milky drinks wouldn't be good for them.

She sank into the sofa and sipped slowly, her thoughts whirling. So much had happened yesterday that she couldn't even begin to start processing it.

It was ironic though, to think that the one thing she'd hidden all her life, the one secret she'd dreaded revealing for fear of being ridiculed or judged, had been received with little more than a raised eyebrow. Oscar hadn't given two hoots that her mum was slovenly. It didn't bother him in the slightest. What *had* bothered him was that Meena had been so ashamed of it that she'd spent all her life trying to cover it up.

Had she allowed the unkind and thoughtless remarks of a pair of women who were no better than they should be, affect her whole life? Her obsession with cleaning had definitely damaged her relationship with her mother, and it had come very close to damaging her relationship with her husband.

It was also ironic that once she'd learnt to let Oscar do the chores without constantly peering over his shoulder, she'd been glad to have him take them off her hands.

She couldn't get over the fact that she'd wasted so much time and effort worrying about what other people might think. Her mother hadn't cared and yes, Meena conceded, she could have been more houseproud, but had it really mattered? The important thing was that Meena had been loved, deeply and unconditionally. She'd been clothed and fed, sang to and read to. She'd been allowed to play in the mud and splash in the bath. She'd been cuddled and kissed, praised and guided. But all Meena had seen was dirty dishes and unswept floors.

She must have hurt her mother so much and Meena was most definitely ashamed – of herself, this time.

Oscar deserved an apology, too. She hadn't made life easy for him since he'd retired. Instead of being sympathetic and understanding, she'd jumped on every little thing he'd done wrong, or failed to reach to her exacting standards. And when he'd wanted to start this new chapter in his life by spending more time with the woman he'd married, she'd pushed him away. She'd been so reluctant for things to change, that she'd nearly changed them for good, drastically and irrevocably.

Nothing remained the same forever. Everything changed eventually. It was time Meena did some changing of her own.

With tears trickling down her face, she was only vaguely aware of a little black and white body creeping onto the sofa. But when the dog curled onto her lap, Meena stroked Lulu's head, the rhythmic movement soothing her and calming her sobs. And with a flick of a warm pink tongue on her fingers, the little dog's fate was sealed.

***

The last thing Oscar had expected to see when he staggered downstairs the next morning was to find Meena and Lulu fast asleep on the sofa. Meena was on her side, the dog stretched out full length beside her, Meena's arm draped over her.

Lulu raised her head a little and wagged her tail when she saw him, but otherwise didn't move.

'Good girl,' he whispered to her, but his heart was heavy. He might not have managed to take Lulu back to the shelter yesterday, but he'd make sure to do it today. After Meena's revelation, he appreciated why she had been so against having a dog, and it wasn't fair of him to ask if Lulu could stay. Dogs shed hairs, they had muddy paws, and inquisitive noses which they shoved into some truly nasty places, and they left steaming piles of poop in the garden.

Meena simply wouldn't be able to cope with it. Besides, she'd have enough to do with Anita; his mother-in-law was going to need a lot of looking after, and he hoped Meena would accept his help.

Lulu came padding into the kitchen as he was making a coffee, and she stood by the door, asking to go out.

'I'll see to her,' Meena said. She was tousled and her eyes were heavy, but she had an air of calmness about her that hadn't been there yesterday.

Damn! Coffee granules scattered across the worktop and Oscar hastened to clean them up.

'Leave it,' Meena said, and he glanced at her in surprise.

'It won't take a sec—' he began.

'I want to talk to you.'

She pulled out one of the chairs around the dining room table and sat on it.

Oscar caught his bottom lip between his teeth and gave the spilt coffee another look, before joining her at the table.

'First of all, I want to apologise for being such a cow,' she said, and when Oscar opened his mouth to deny it, she added, 'Don't tell me I haven't, because I know I have.'

He shrugged. She was right, she had; but he'd not been on his best behaviour either, so there was fault on both sides.

He'd save his own apology for later though, when she was more willing to hear it.

'Second, I think we should keep Lulu,' she said.

Oscar froze.

'What did you say?'

'Lulu can stay.'

'Don't say that just because I'd like her to,' he told her. He didn't want Meena to agree to Lulu staying with them as a kind of apology.

'She should stay because it's the right thing for her. And for you,' Meena said.

'But it's not the right thing for you,' he countered. It was a lovely gesture and extremely generous, but if it was going to cause his wife more stress...

'It will be,' she said. 'Lulu and I have made a start.' She cleared her throat. 'There's something else; I'm thinking of giving up work. You're not the only one who can take early retirement.'

Oscar spluttered. 'I thought you loved your job?'

'I did,' she replied slowly, 'but work isn't the be-all and end-all, is it?'

'No,' he said, 'it's not.' He could feel a grin beginning to spread across his face.

'I think we should spend more time together now that you're retired,' Meena added. 'How about we take Lulu out before I go to the hospital?'

'We can start as we mean to go on, and both go to the hospital,' Oscar said. Meena didn't have to deal with anything on her own again.

'Let's not get carried away, eh? We can't do *everything* together,' she said.

'Why not?' he teased, his heart feeling lighter than it had done for ages.

'I'm not going to volunteer at the shelter with you, if that's what you're hoping,' she told him, with a shake of her head.

Oscar's grin widened. 'You might enjoy it! And have you tried lake fishing yet?'

'One thing at a time, Oscar, one thing at a time...'

About the Author

Liz Davies writes feel-good, light-hearted stories with a hefty dose of romance, a smattering of humour, and a great deal of love.

She's married to her best friend, has one grown-up daughter, and when she isn't scribbling away in the notepad she carries with her everywhere (just in case inspiration strikes), you'll find her searching for that perfect pair of shoes. She loves to cook but isn't very good at it, and loves to eat - she's much better at that! Liz also enjoys walking (preferably on the flat), cycling (also on the flat), and lots of sitting around in the garden on warm, sunny days.

She currently lives with her family in Wales, but would ideally love to buy a camper van and travel the world in it.

www.ingramcontent.com/pod-product-compliance
Lightning Source LLC
Chambersburg PA
CBHW061604190726
48288CB00007B/2173